Paper Girls
3

BRIAN K. VAUGHAN writer
CLIFF CHIANG artist
MATT WILSON colors
JARED K. FLETCHER letters

image

Dee Cunniffe - Color Flats
Jared K. Fletcher - Logo + Book Design

PAPER GIRLS, VOLUME 3. First printing. August 2017. Copyright ©
2016 Brian K. Vaughan & Cliff Chiang. All rights reserved. Published by
Image Comics, Inc. Office of publication: 2701 NW Vaughn St., Suite
780, Portland, OR 97210. Originally published in single magazine form
as Paper Girls #11-15. "Paper Girls," its logos, and the likenesses of all
characters herein are trademarks of Brian K. Vaughan & Cliff Chiang,
unless otherwise noted. "Image" and the Image Comics logos are
registered trademarks of Image Comics, Inc. No part of this publication
may be reproduced or transmitted, in any form or by any means (except
for short excerpts for journalistic or review purposes), without the express
written permission of Brian K. Vaughan, Cliff Chiang or Image Comics, Inc.
All names, characters, events, and locales in this publication are entirely
fictional. Any resemblance to actual persons (living or dead), events,
or places, without satiric intent, is coincidental. Printed in the USA. For
information regarding the CPSIA on this printed material call: 203-595-
3636 and provide reference #RICH-750680. For international rights,
contact: foreignlicensing@imagecomics.com. ISBN: 978-1-5343-0223-5.

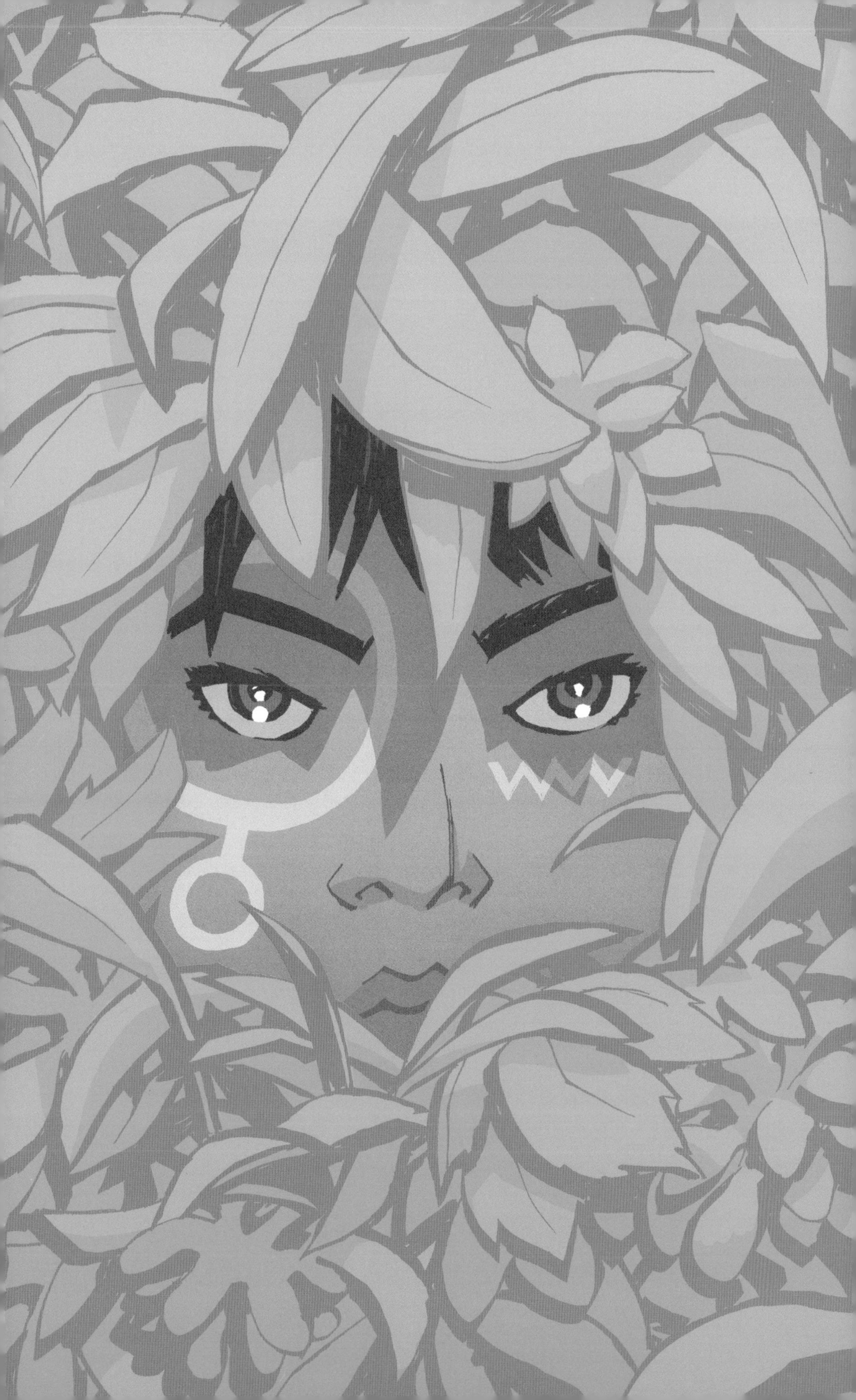

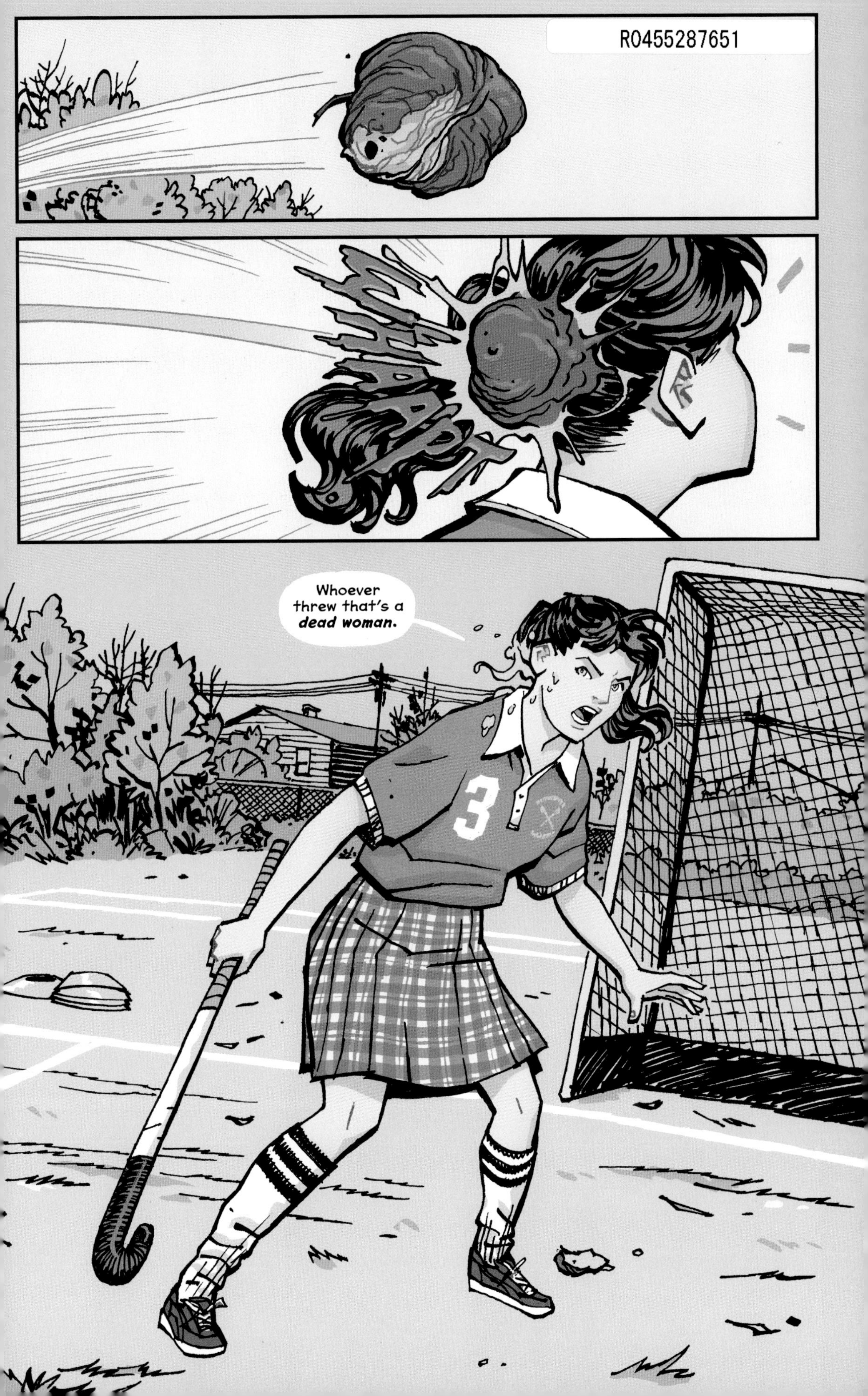
Whoever threw that's a *dead woman.*

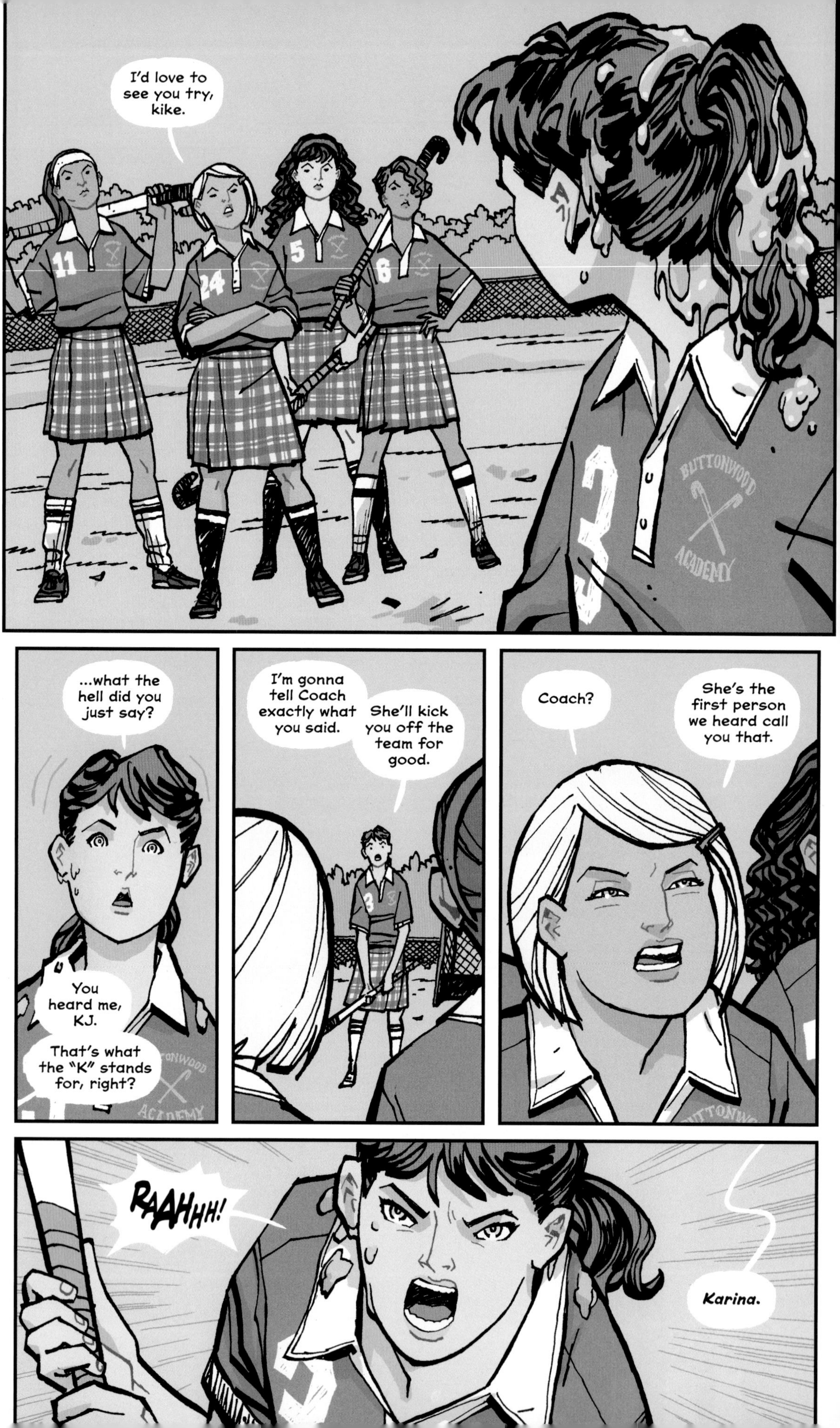
I'd love to see you try, kike.
BUTTONWOOD ACADEMY
...what the hell did you just say?
You heard me, KJ.
That's what the "K" stands for, right?
I'm gonna tell Coach exactly what you said.
She'll kick you off the team for good.
Coach?
She's the first person we heard call you that.
RAAHHH!
Karina.

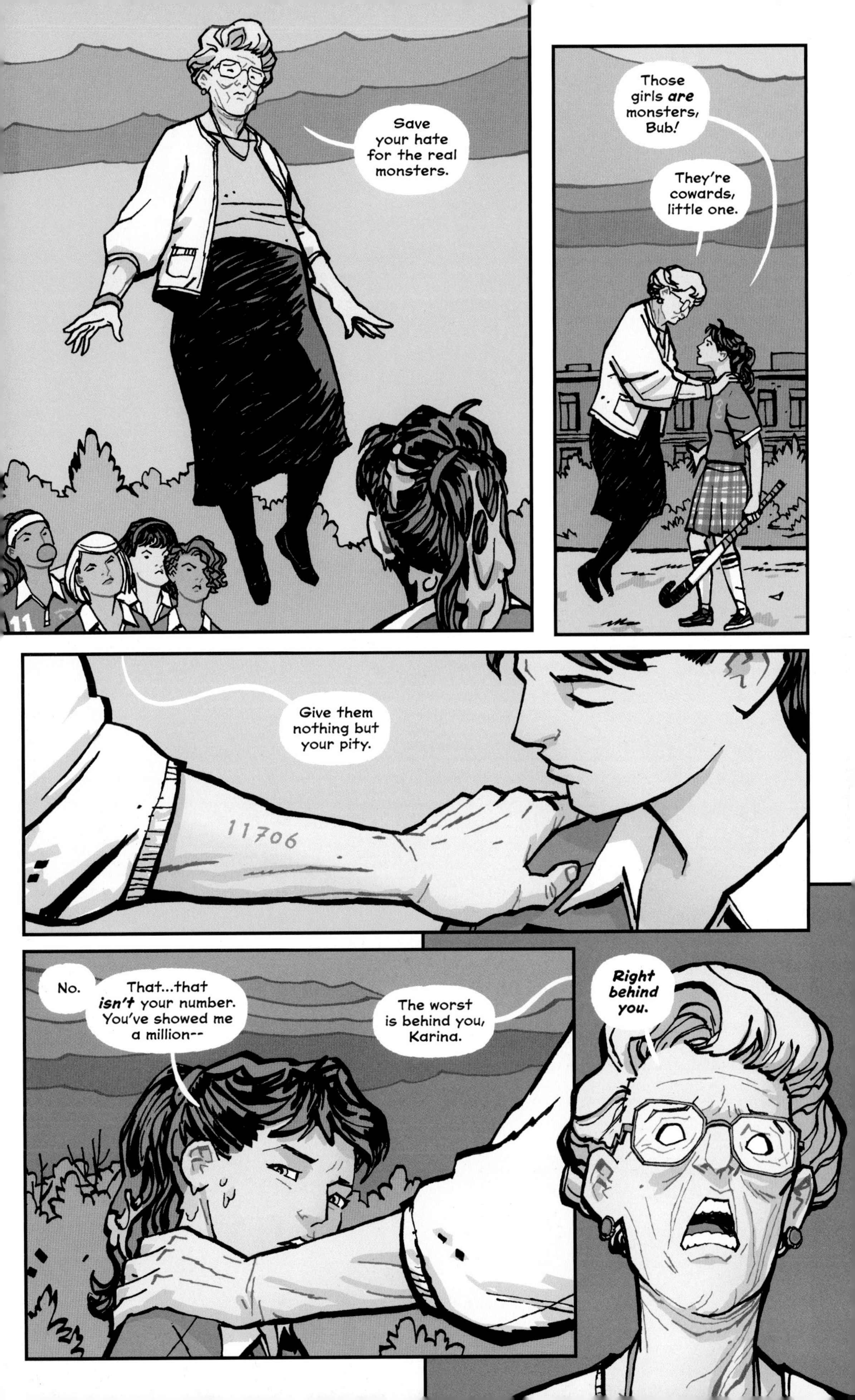
Save your hate for the real monsters.
Those girls are monsters, Bub!
They're cowards, little one.
Give them nothing but your pity.
11706
No.
That...that isn't your number. You've showed me a million--
The worst is behind you, Karina.
Right behind you.

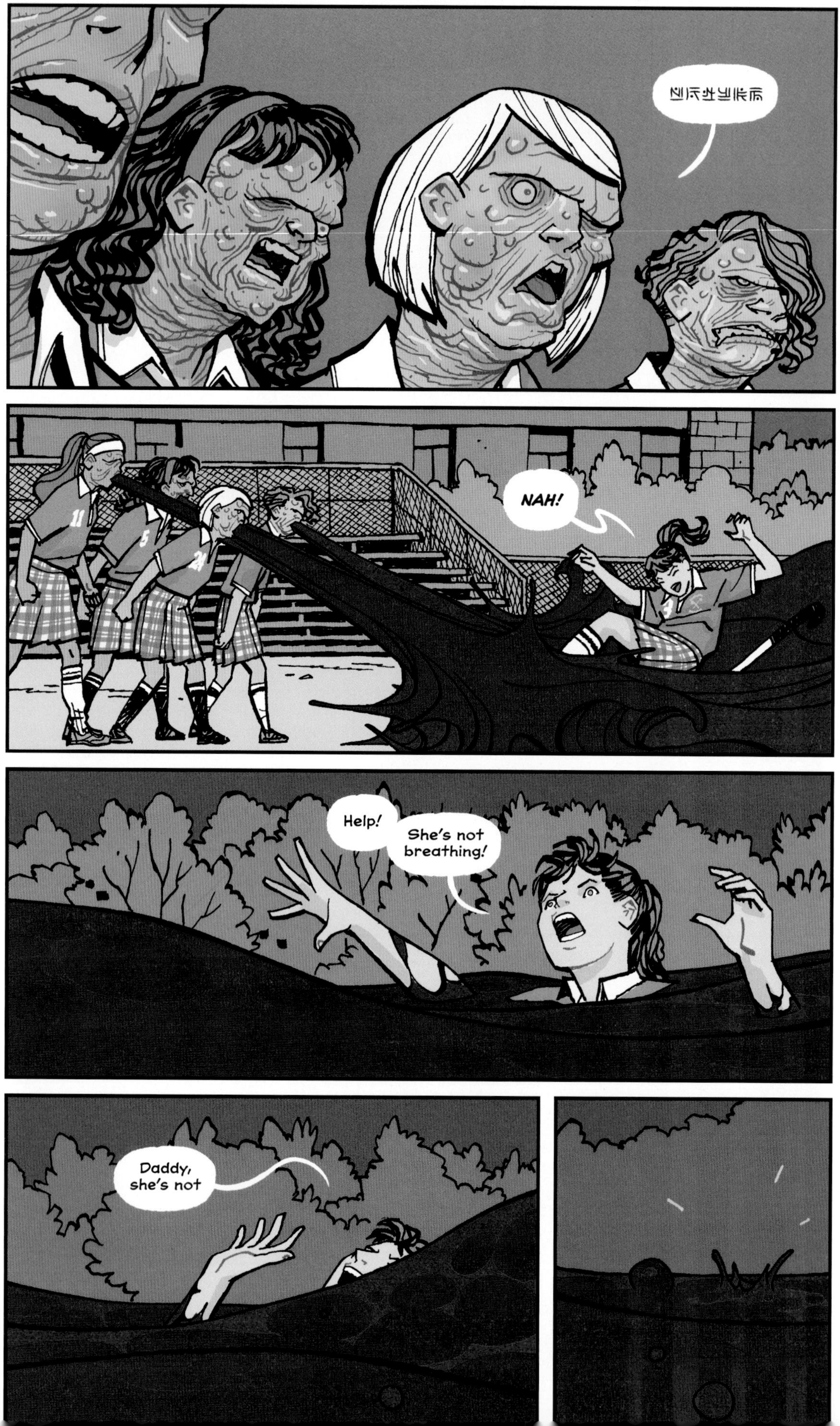
NAH!
Help!
She's not breathing!
Daddy, she's not

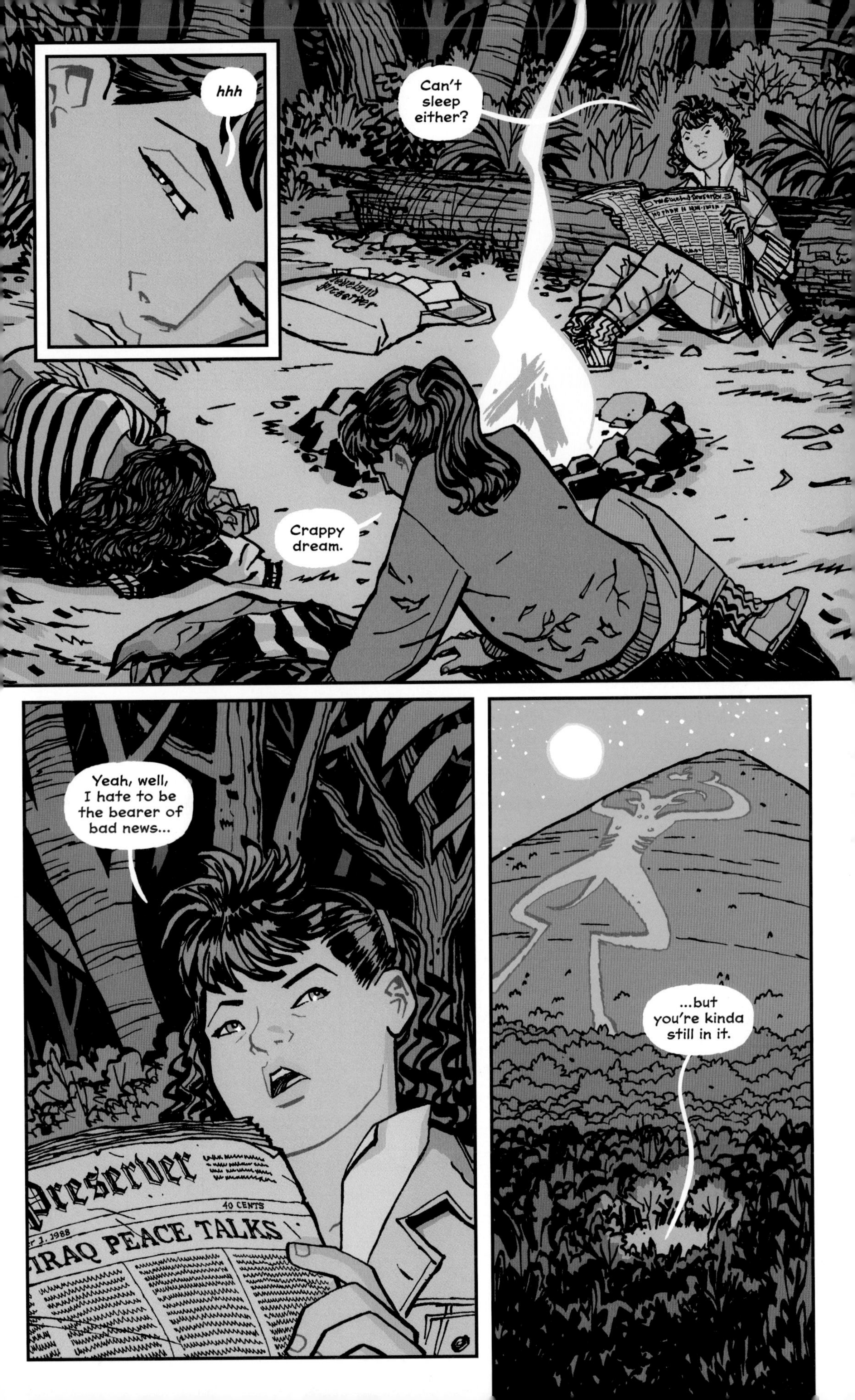
hhh
Can't sleep either?
Crappy dream.
Yeah, well, I hate to be the bearer of bad news...
Preserver
40 CENTS
IRAQ PEACE TALKS
...but you're kinda still in it.

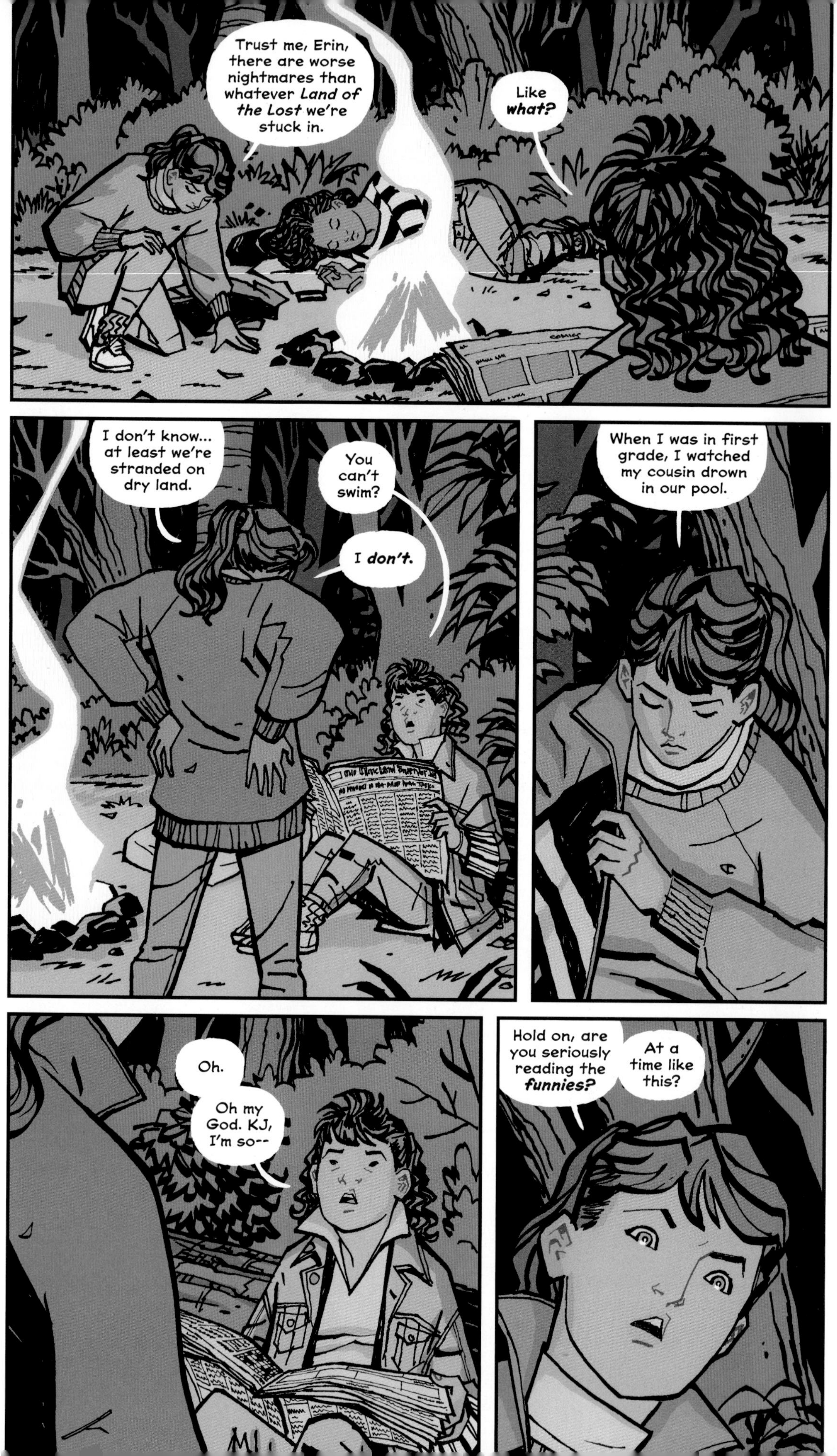

Trust me, Erin, there are worse nightmares than whatever *Land of the Lost* we're stuck in.
Like ***what?***
I don't know... at least we're stranded on dry land.
You can't swim?
I ***don't.***
When I was in first grade, I watched my cousin drown in our pool.
Oh.
Oh my God. KJ, I'm so--
Hold on, are you seriously reading the ***funnies?***
At a time like this?

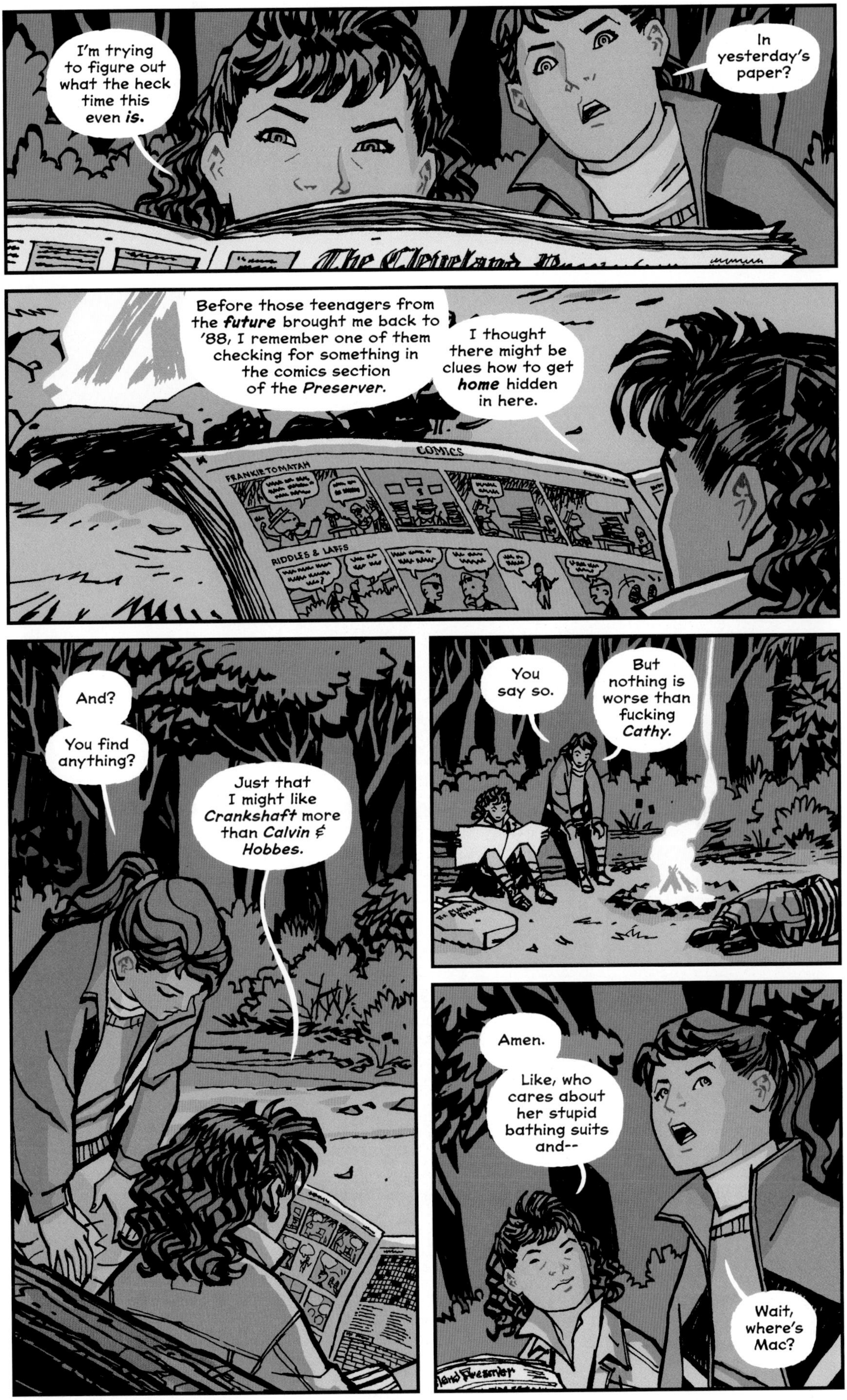

I'm trying to figure out what the heck time this even *is.*
In yesterday's paper?
Before those teenagers from the ***future*** brought me back to '88, I remember one of them checking for something in the comics section of the *Preserver.*
I thought there might be clues how to get ***home*** hidden in here.
COMICS
RIDDLES & LAFFS
And?
You find anything?
Just that I might like *Crankshaft* more than *Calvin & Hobbes.*
You say so.
But nothing is worse than fucking *Cathy.*
Amen.
Like, who cares about her stupid bathing suits and--
Wait, where's Mac?

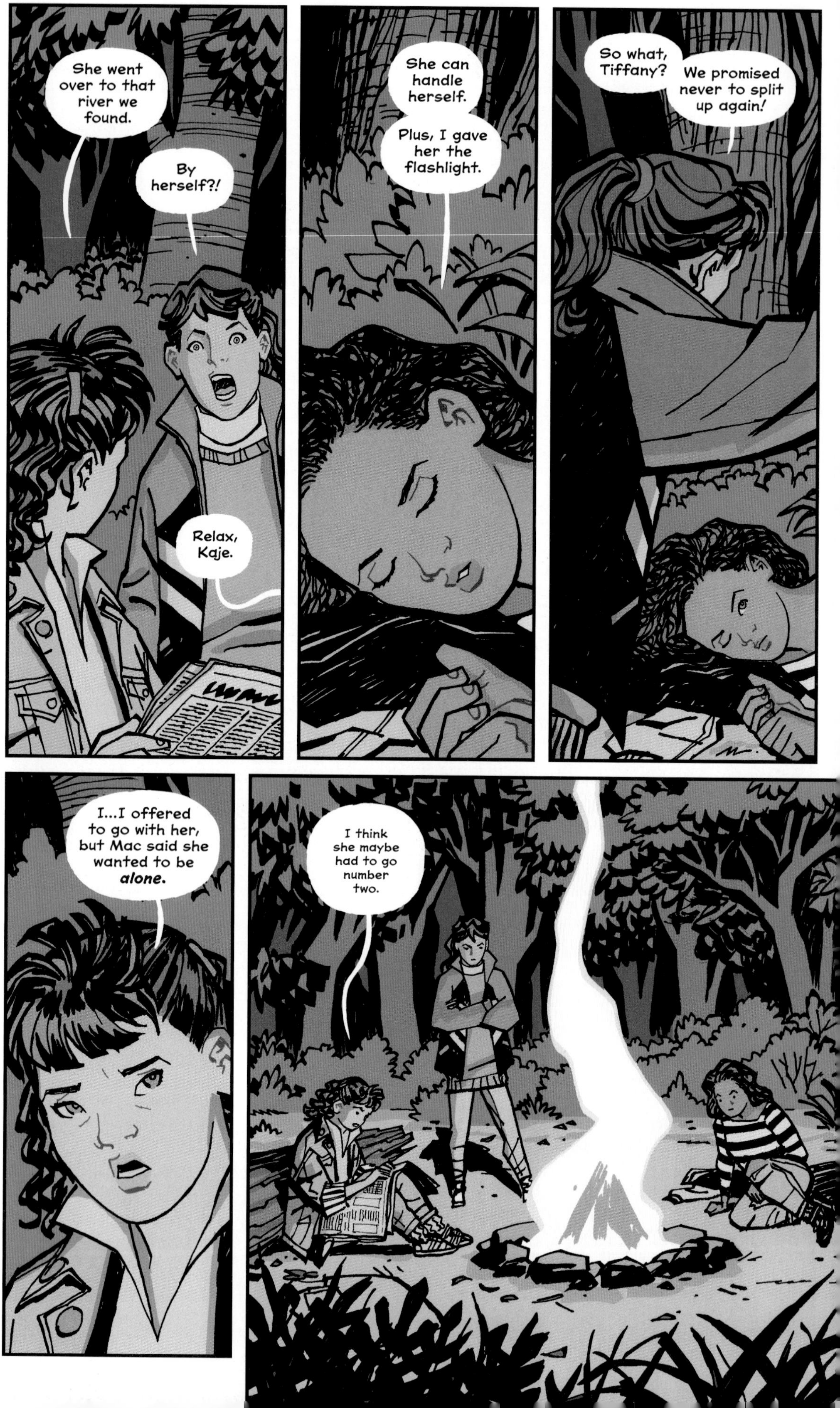

She went over to that river we found.
By herself?!
Relax, Kaje.
She can handle herself.
Plus, I gave her the flashlight.
So what, Tiffany?
We promised never to split up again!
I...I offered to go with her, but Mac said she wanted to be *alone*.
I think she maybe had to go number two.

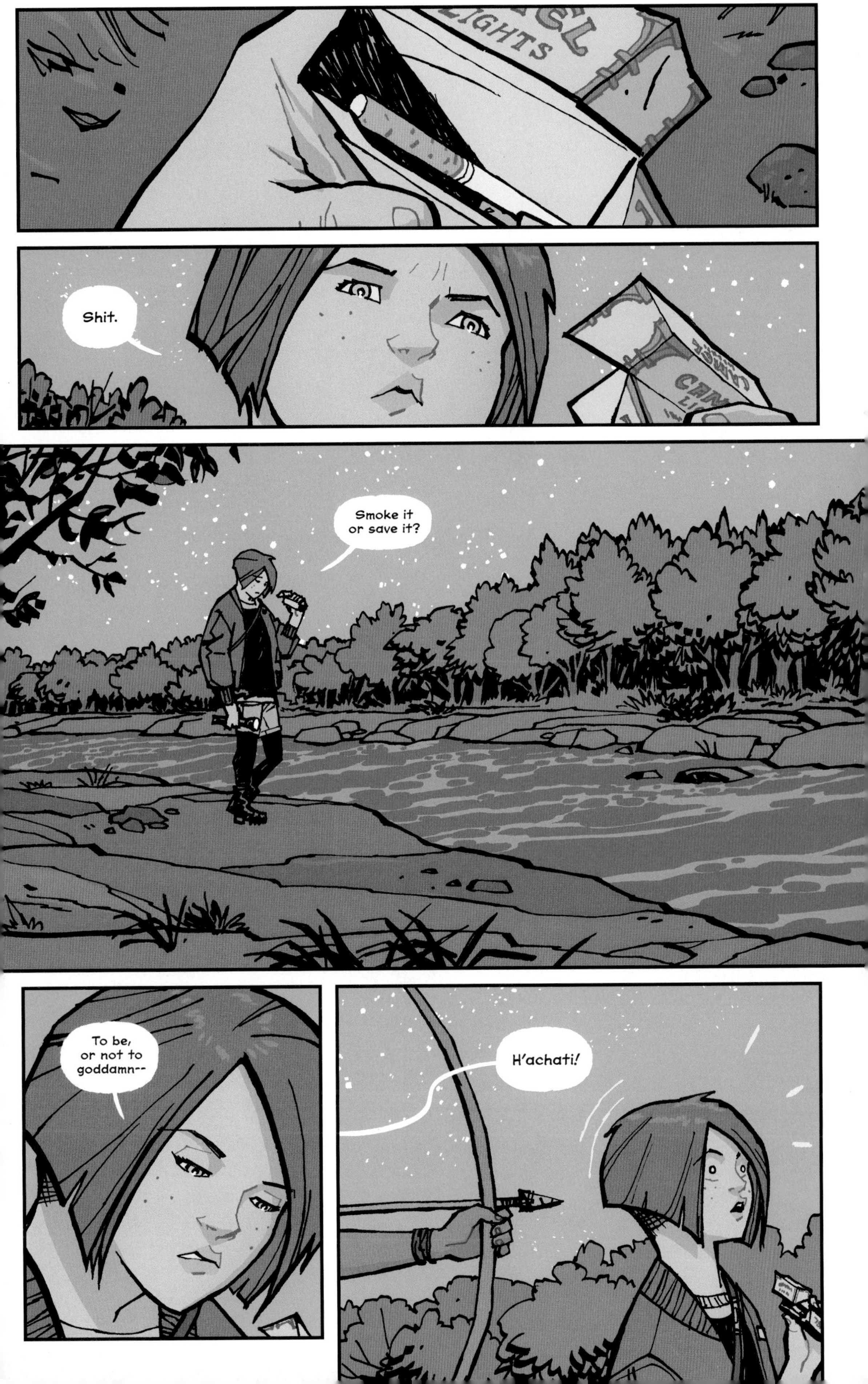
CAMEL LIGHTS
Shit.
Smoke it or save it?
To be, or not to goddamn--
H'achati!

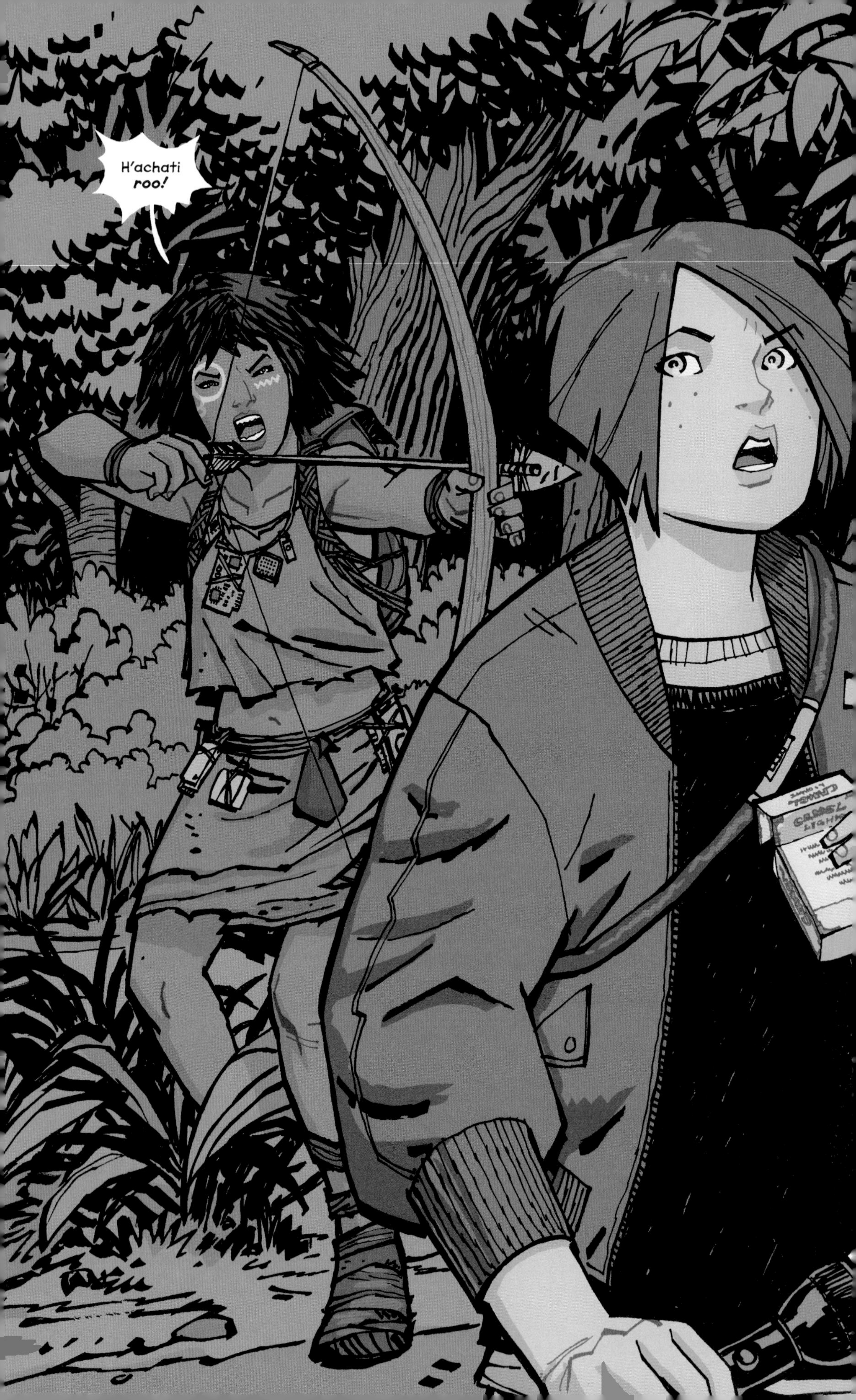
H'achati roo!

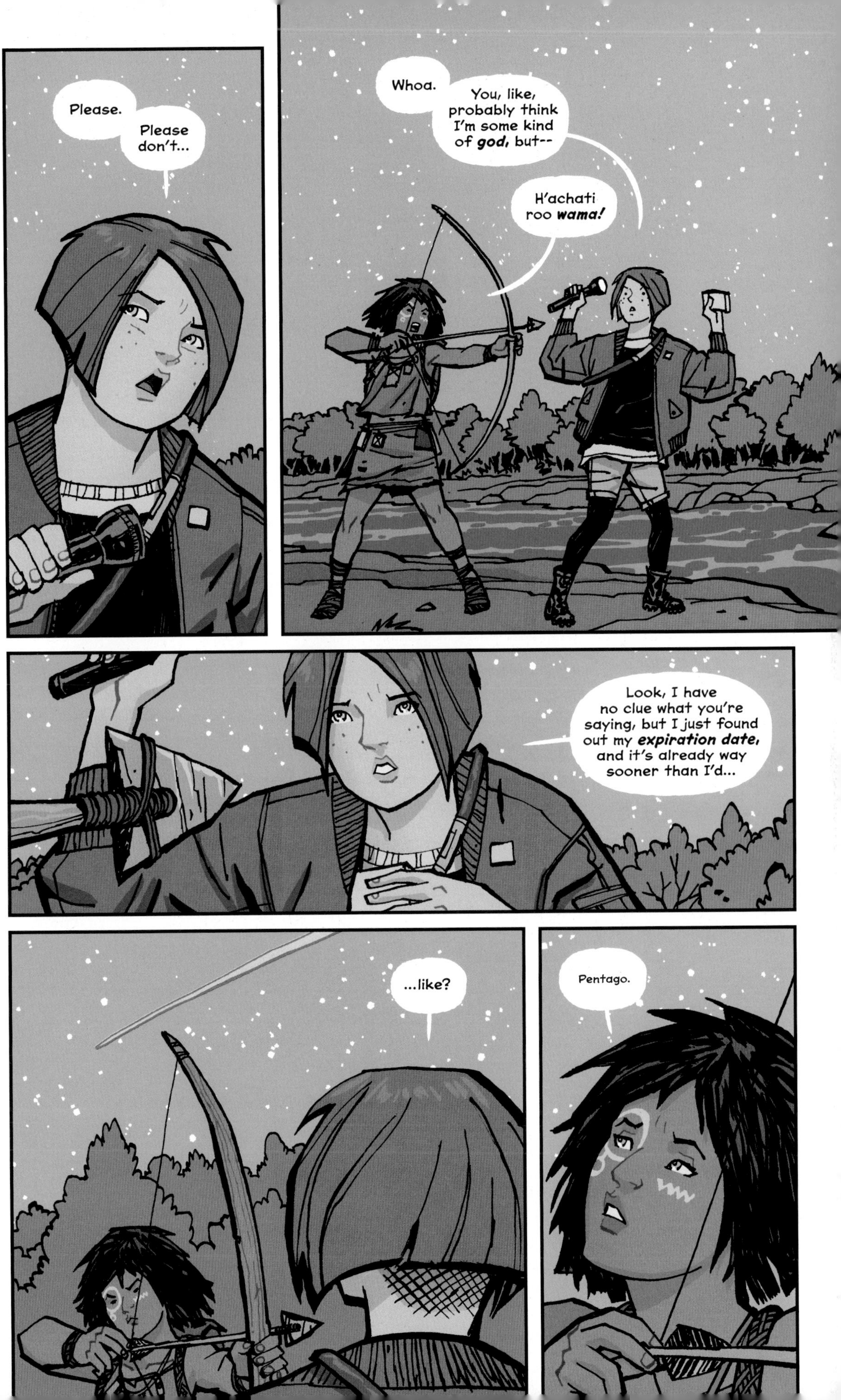
Please.
Please don't...
Whoa.
You, like, probably think I'm some kind of god, but--
H'achati roo wama!
Look, I have no clue what you're saying, but I just found out my expiration date, and it's already way sooner than I'd...
...like?
Pentago.

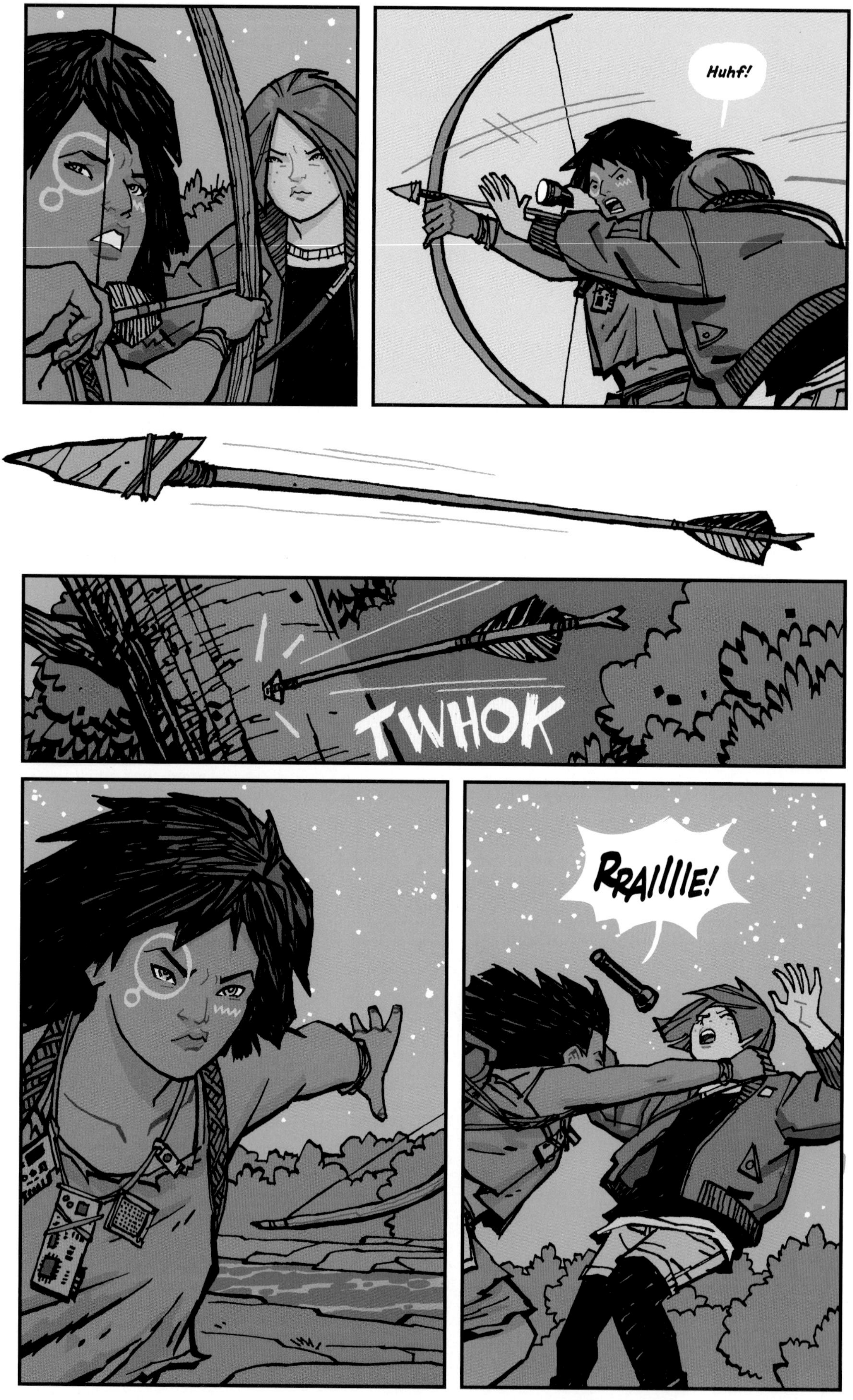
Huhf!
TWHOK
RRAIIIIE!

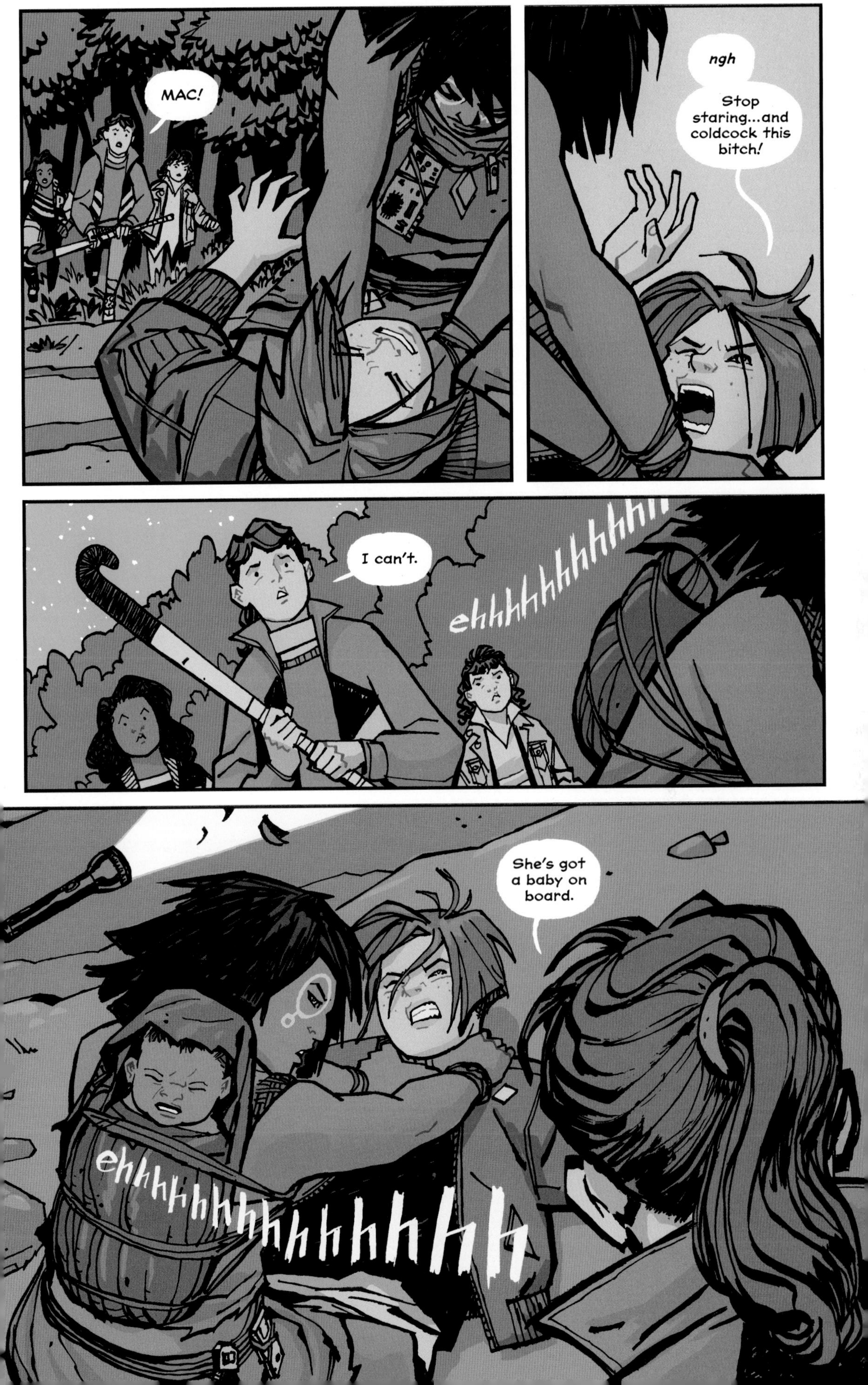
MAC!
ngh
Stop staring...and coldcock this bitch!
I can't.
ehhhhhhhhhhhhhh
She's got a baby on board.
ehhhhhhhhhhhhhhhh

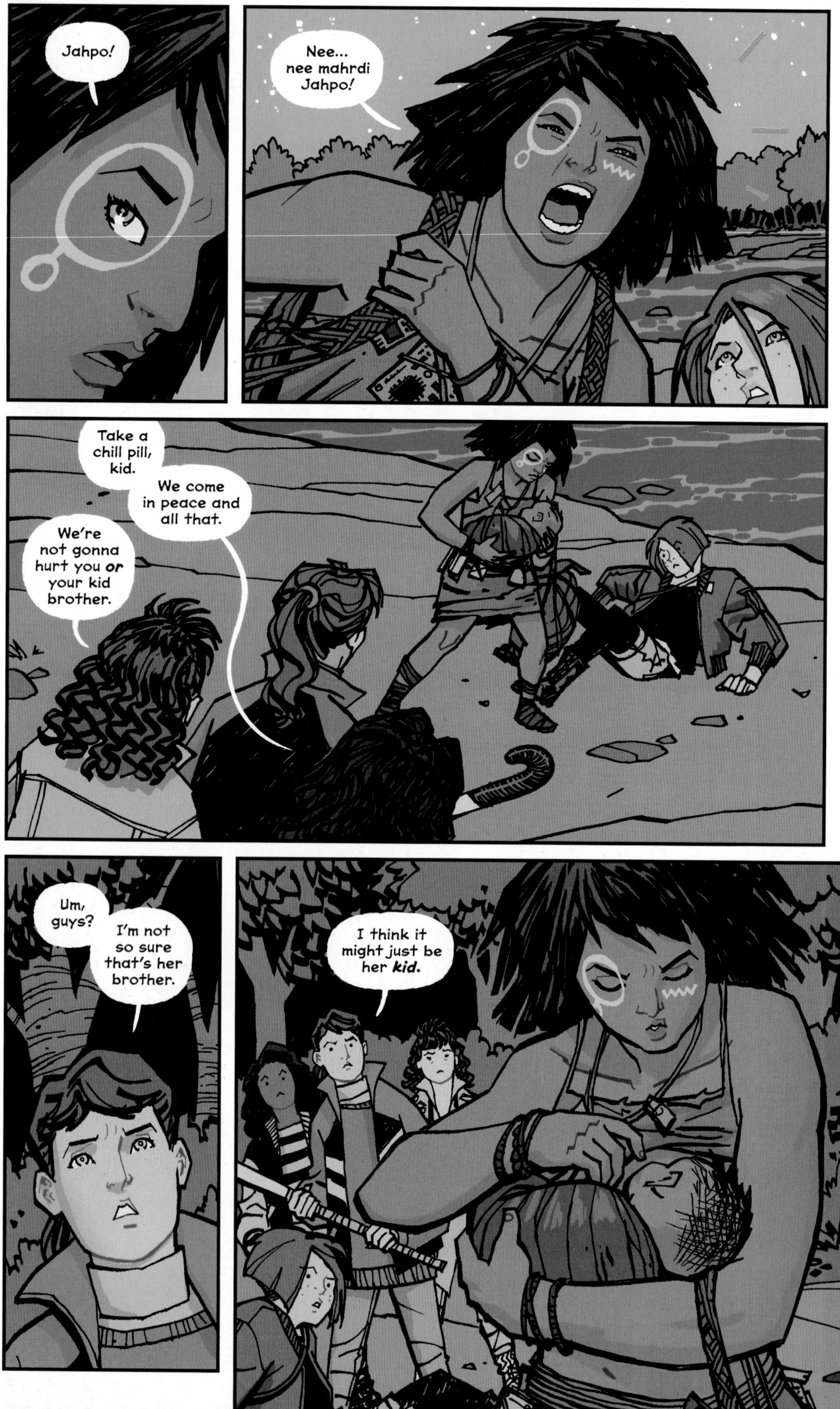
Jahpo!
Nee... nee mahrdi Jahpo!
Take a chill pill, kid.
We come in peace and all that.
We're not gonna hurt you *or* your kid brother.
Um, guys?
I'm not so sure that's her brother.
I think it might just be her *kid.*

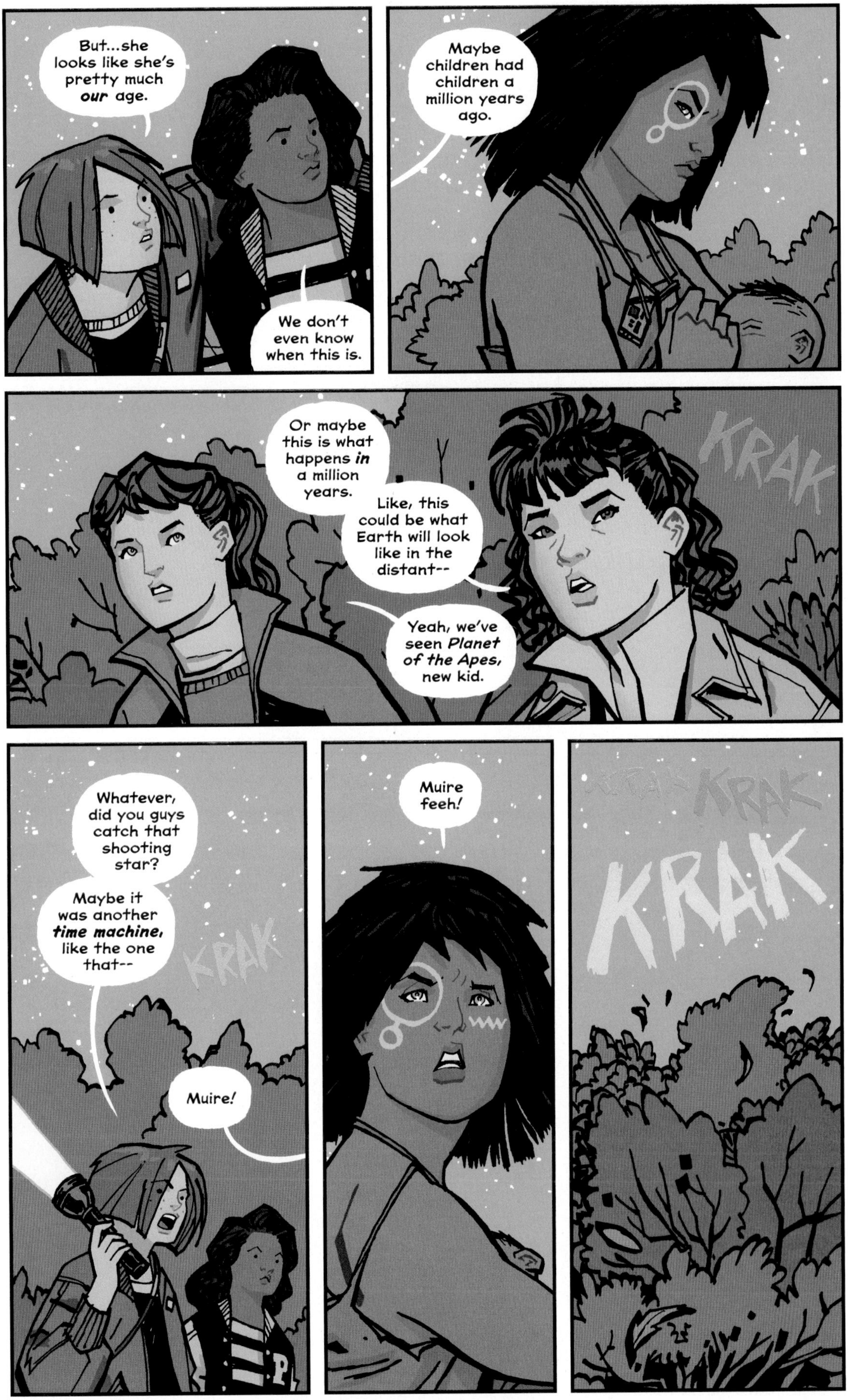

But...she looks like she's pretty much *our* age.
We don't even know when this is.
Maybe children had children a million years ago.
Or maybe this is what happens *in* a million years.
Like, this could be what Earth will look like in the distant--
Yeah, we've seen *Planet of the Apes*, new kid.
KRAK
Whatever, did you guys catch that shooting star?
Maybe it was another ***time machine***, like the one that--
KRAK
Muire!
Muire feeh!
KRAK KRAK
KRAK

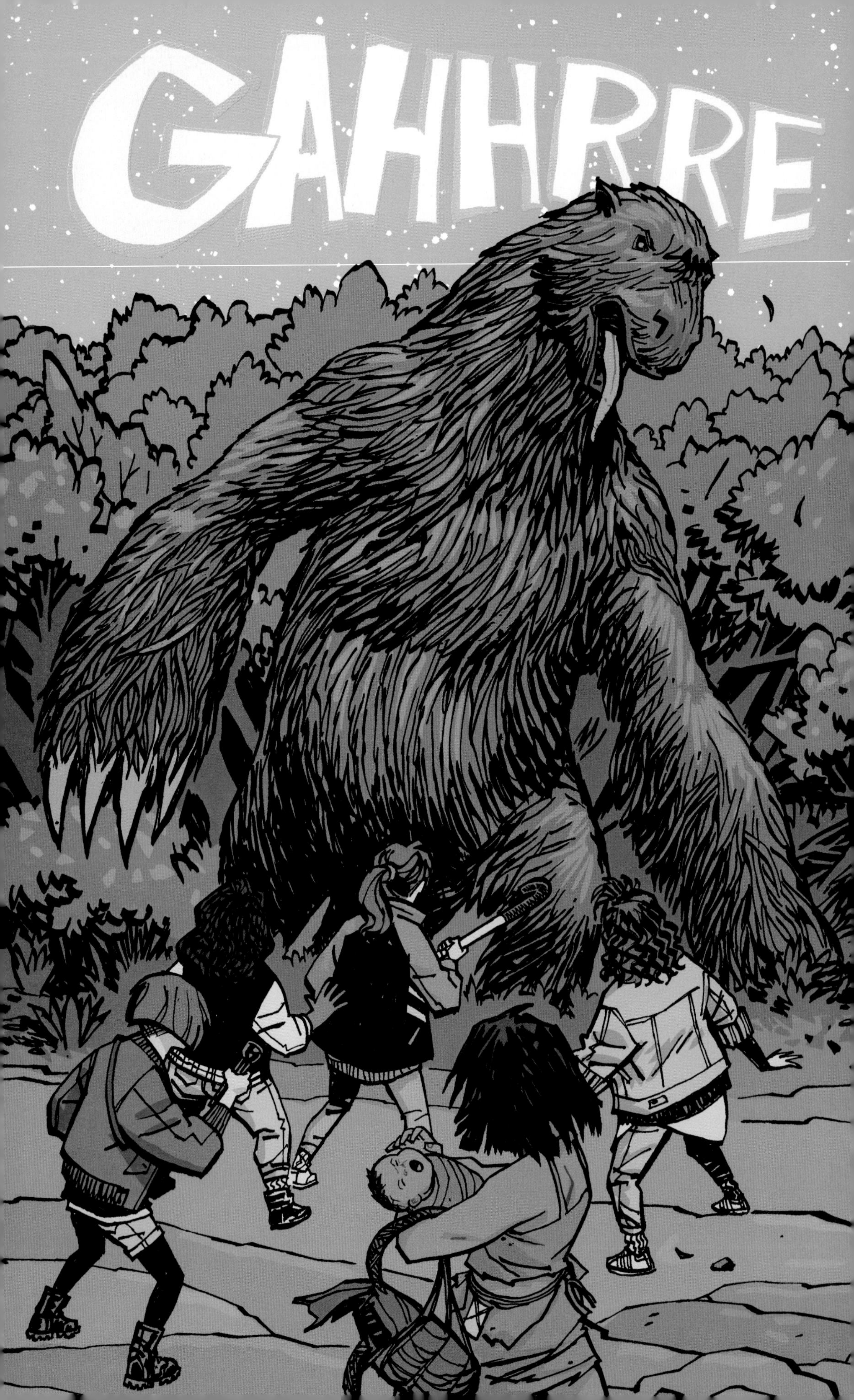
GAHHRRE

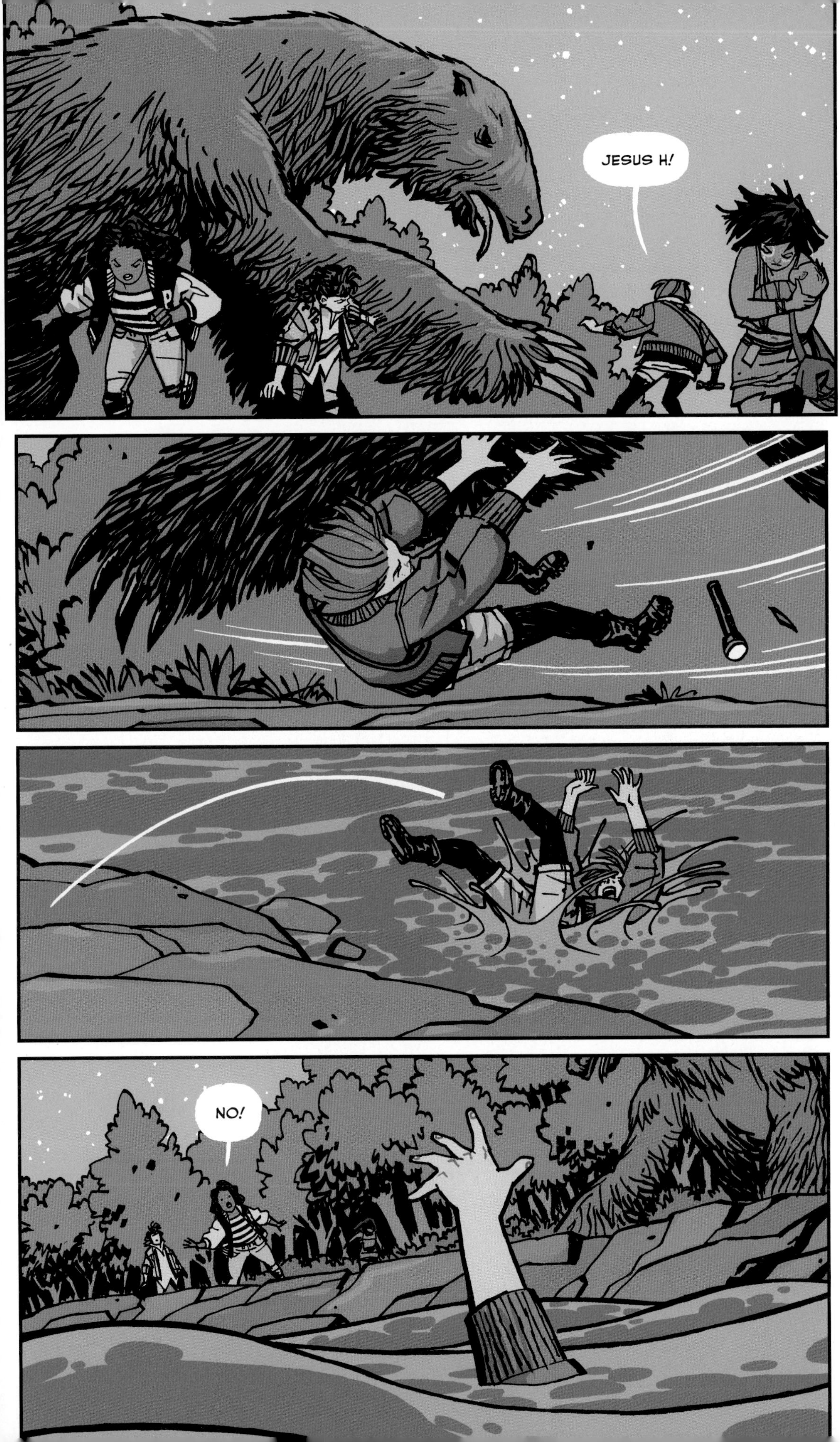
JESUS H!
NO!

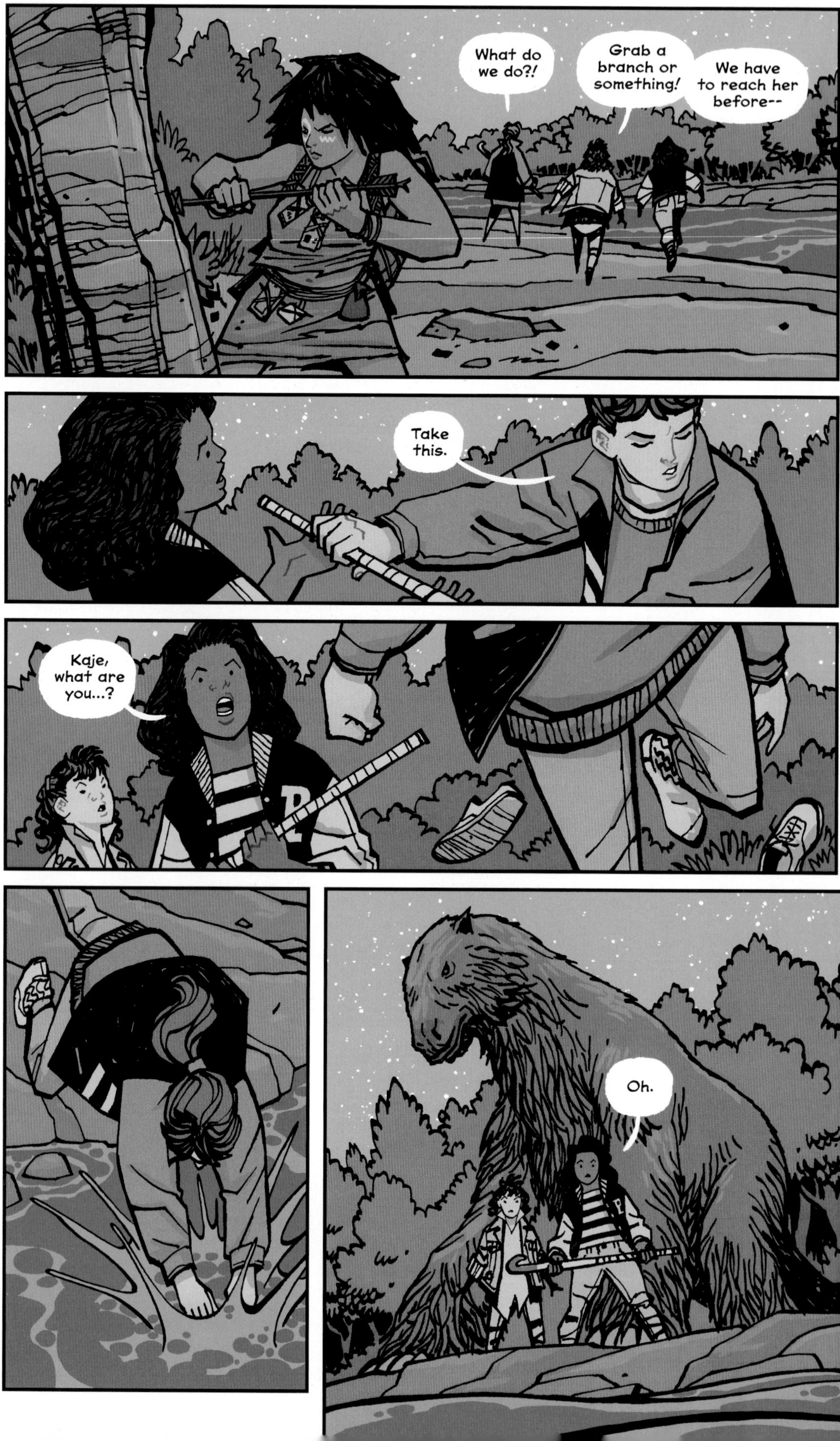
What do we do?!
Grab a branch or something!
We have to reach her before--
Take this.
Kaje, what are you...?
Oh.

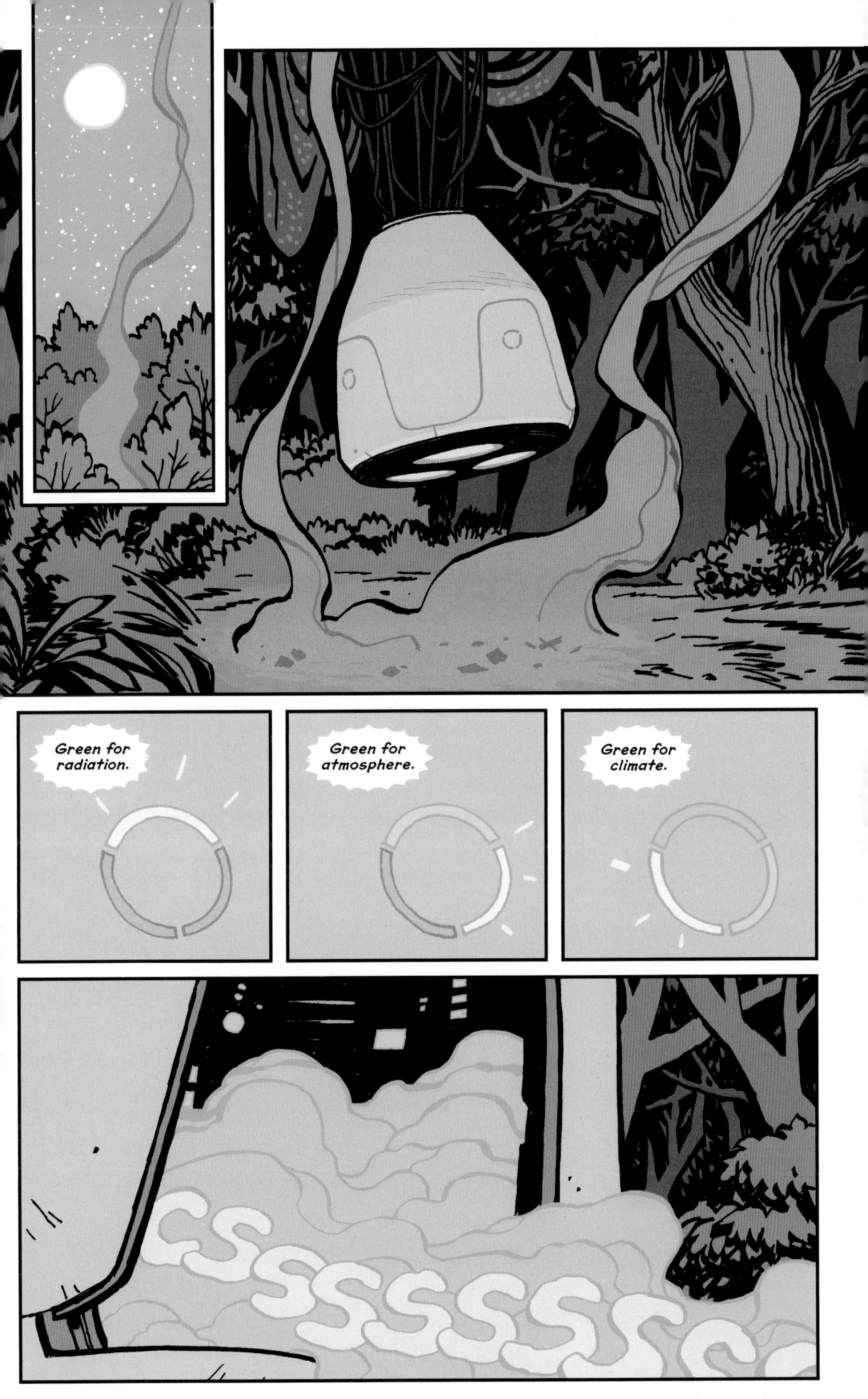
Green for radiation.
Green for atmosphere.
Green for climate.
SSSSSSSSS

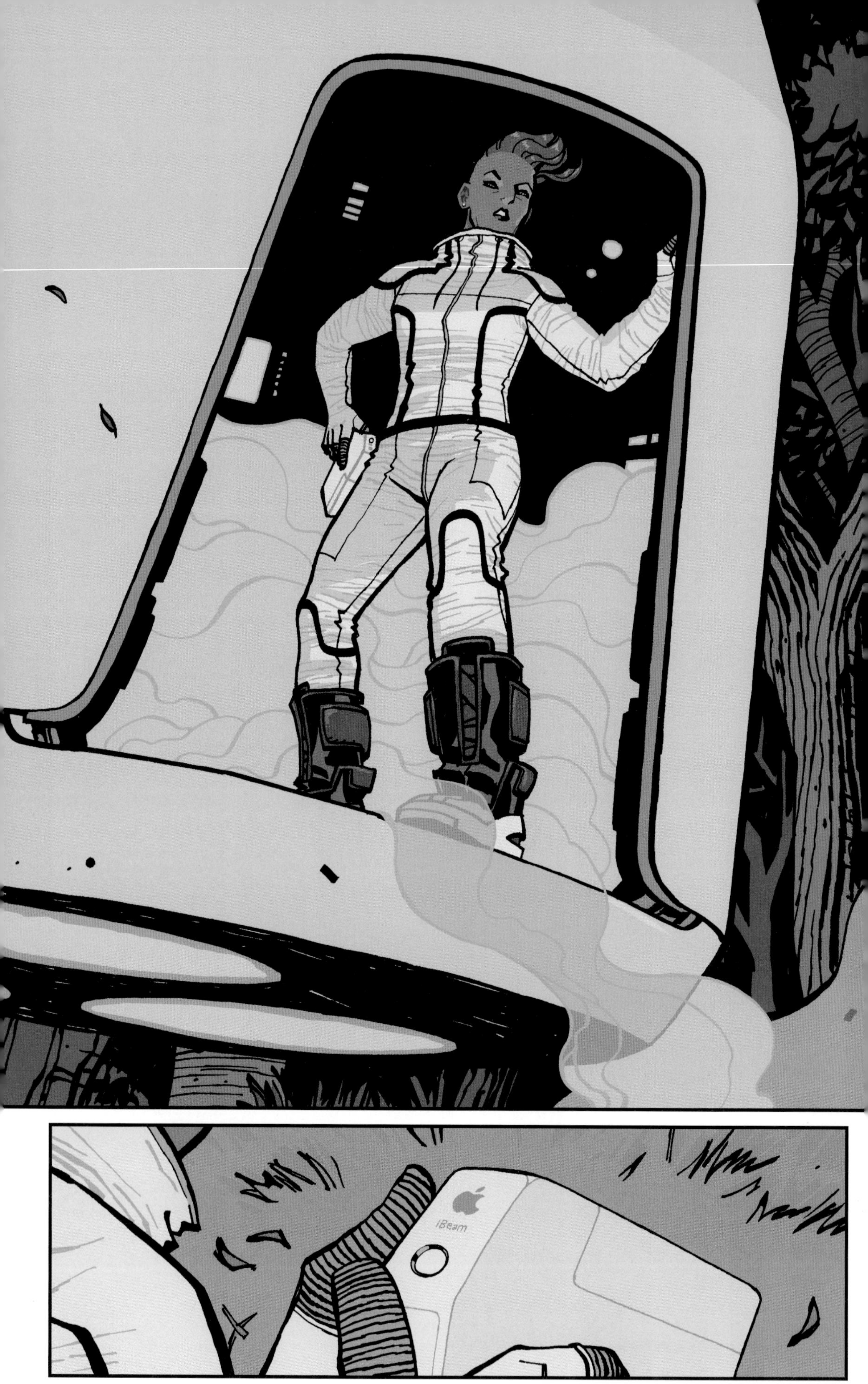
iBeam

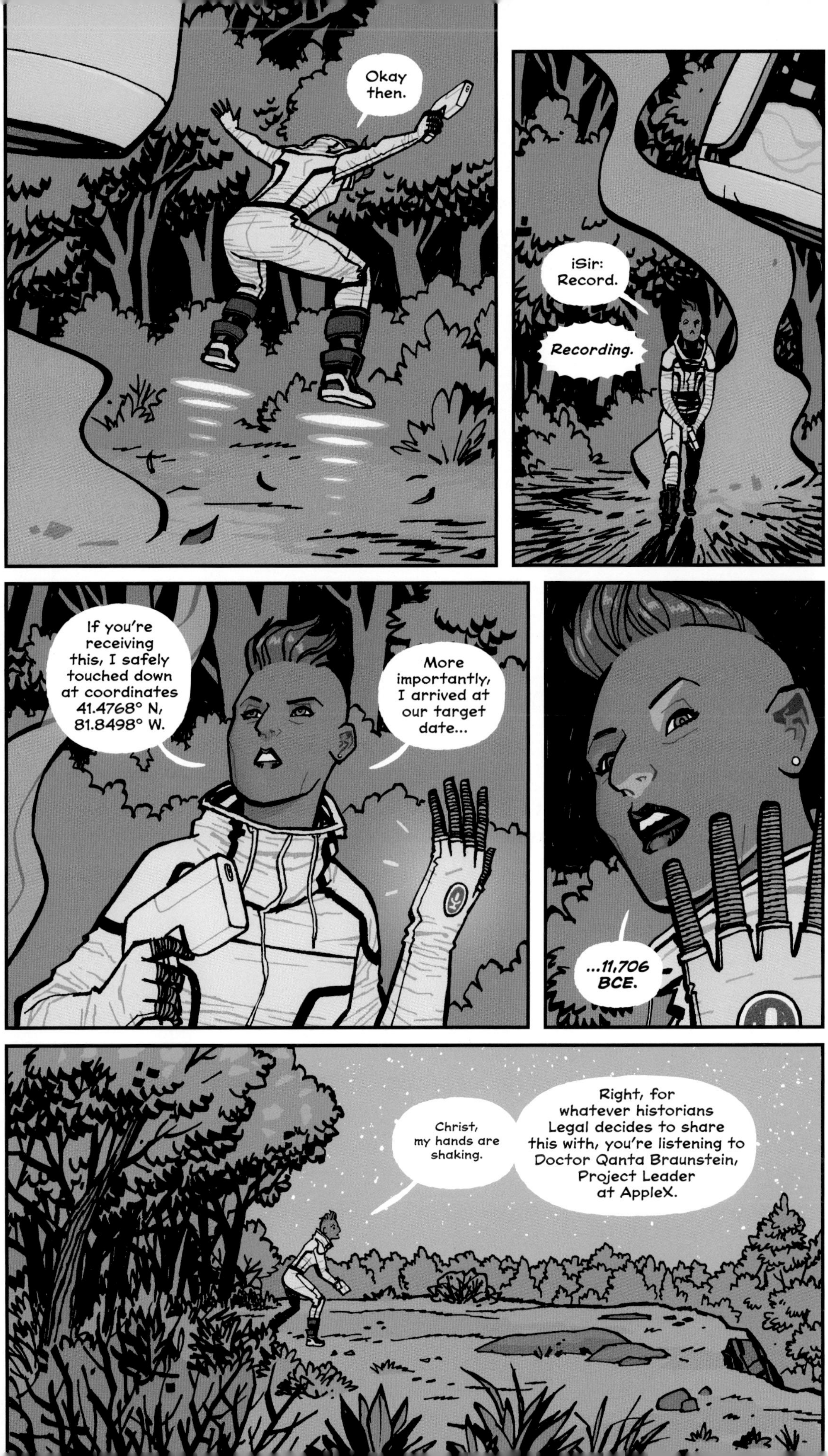
Okay then.
iSir: Record.
Recording.
If you're receiving this, I safely touched down at coordinates 41.4768° N, 81.8498° W.
More importantly, I arrived at our target date...
...11,706 BCE.
Christ, my hands are shaking.
Right, for whatever historians Legal decides to share this with, you're listening to Doctor Qanta Braunstein, Project Leader at AppleX.

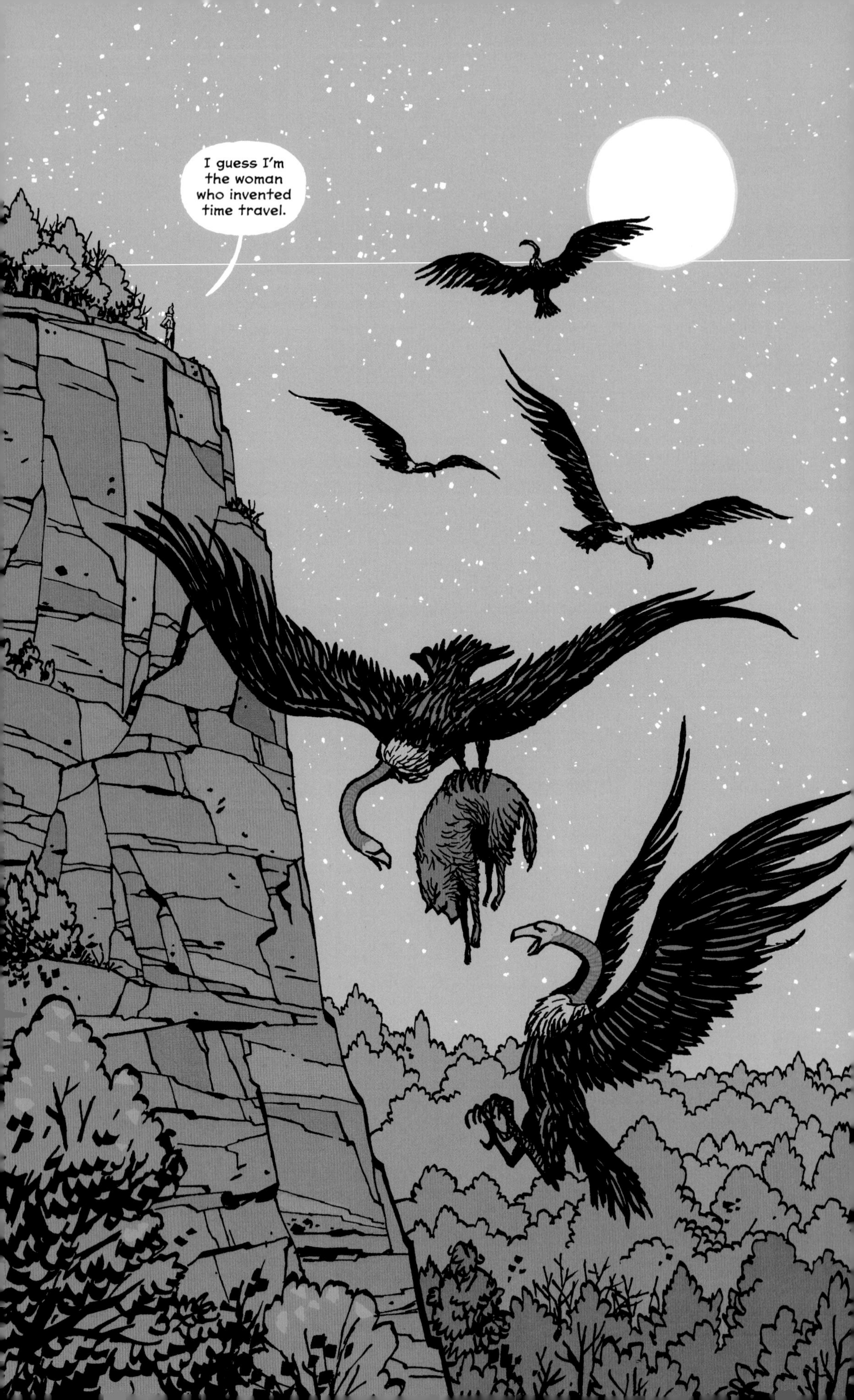

I guess I'm the woman who invented time travel.

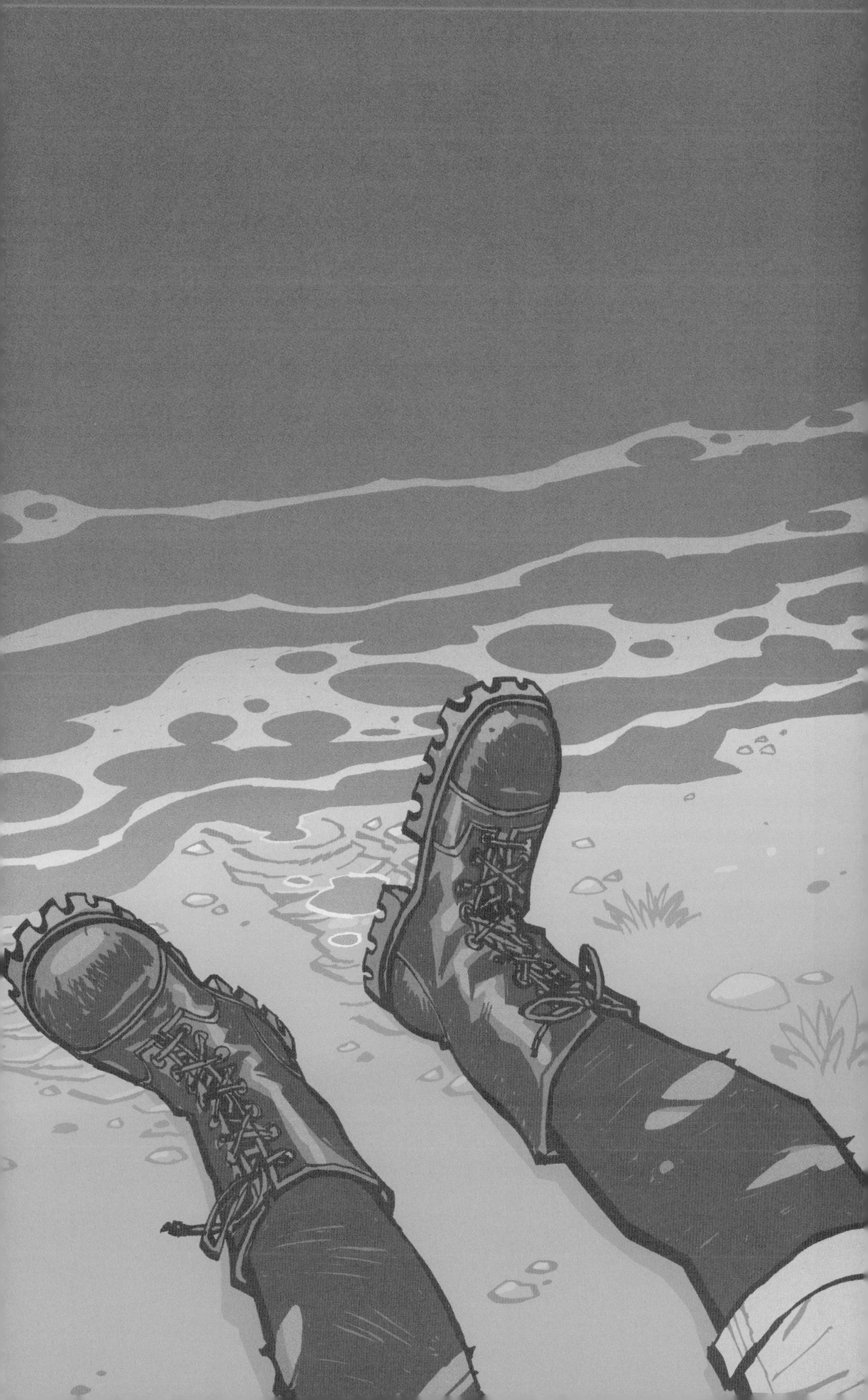

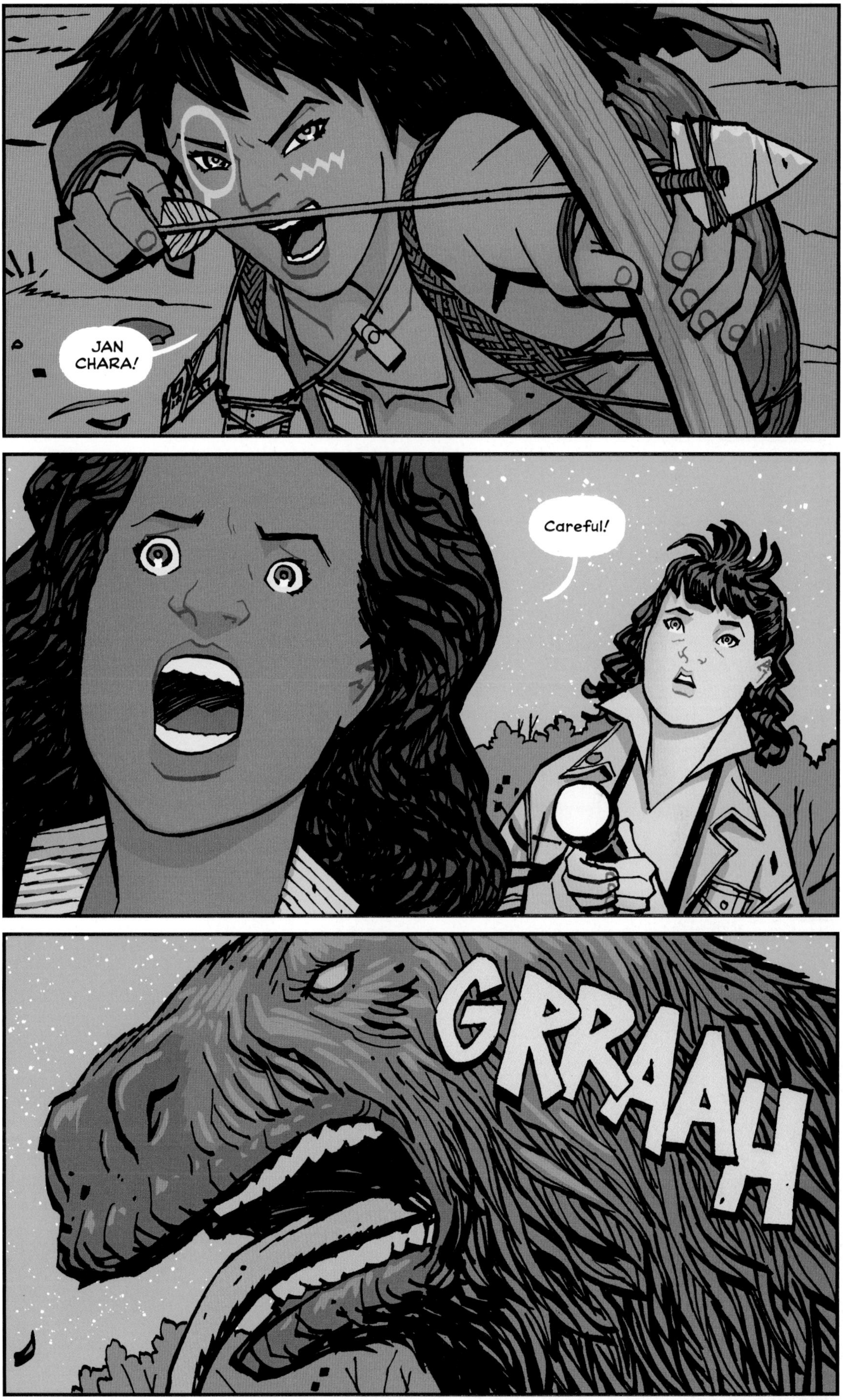
JAN CHARA!
Careful!
GRRAAH

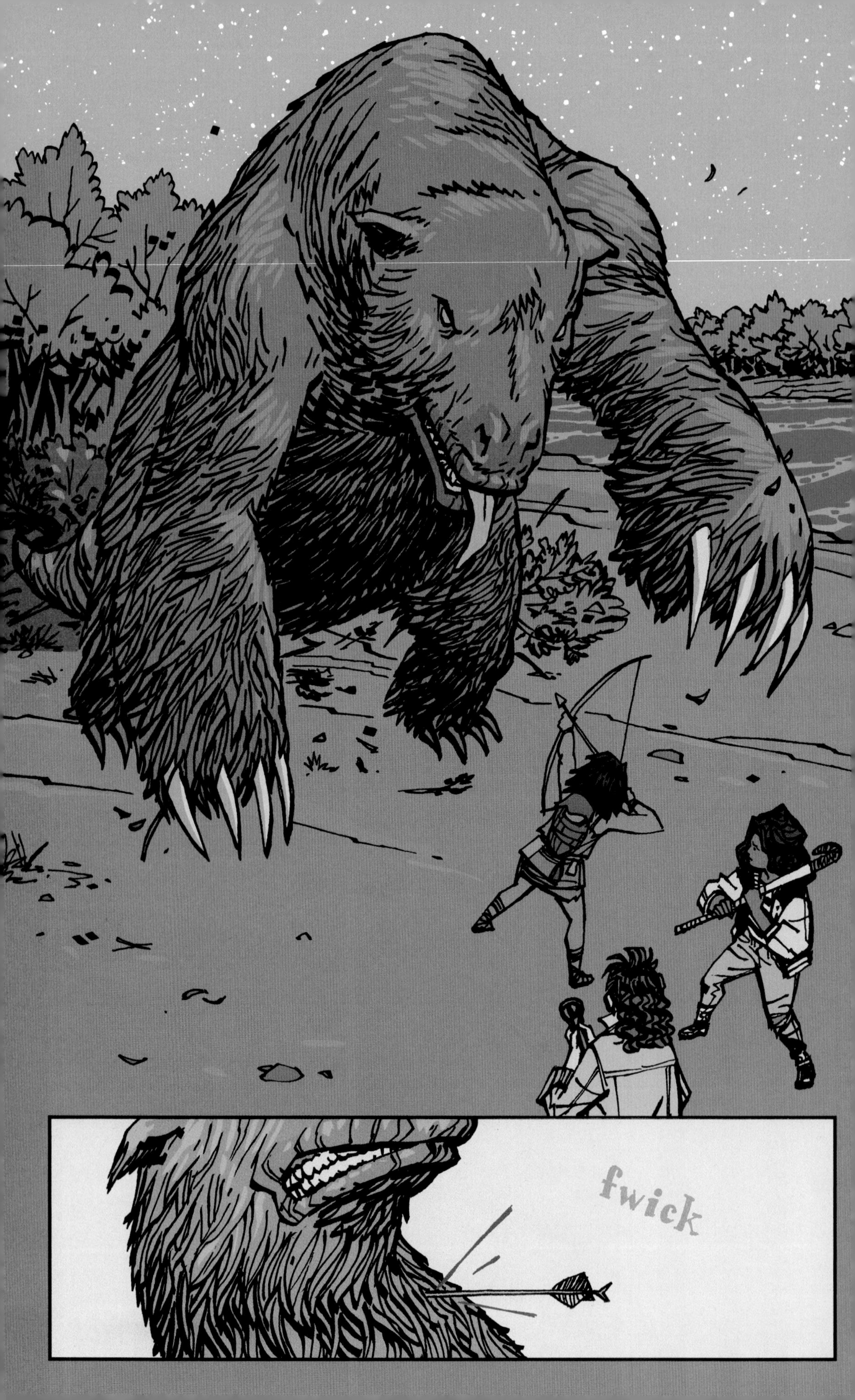
fwick

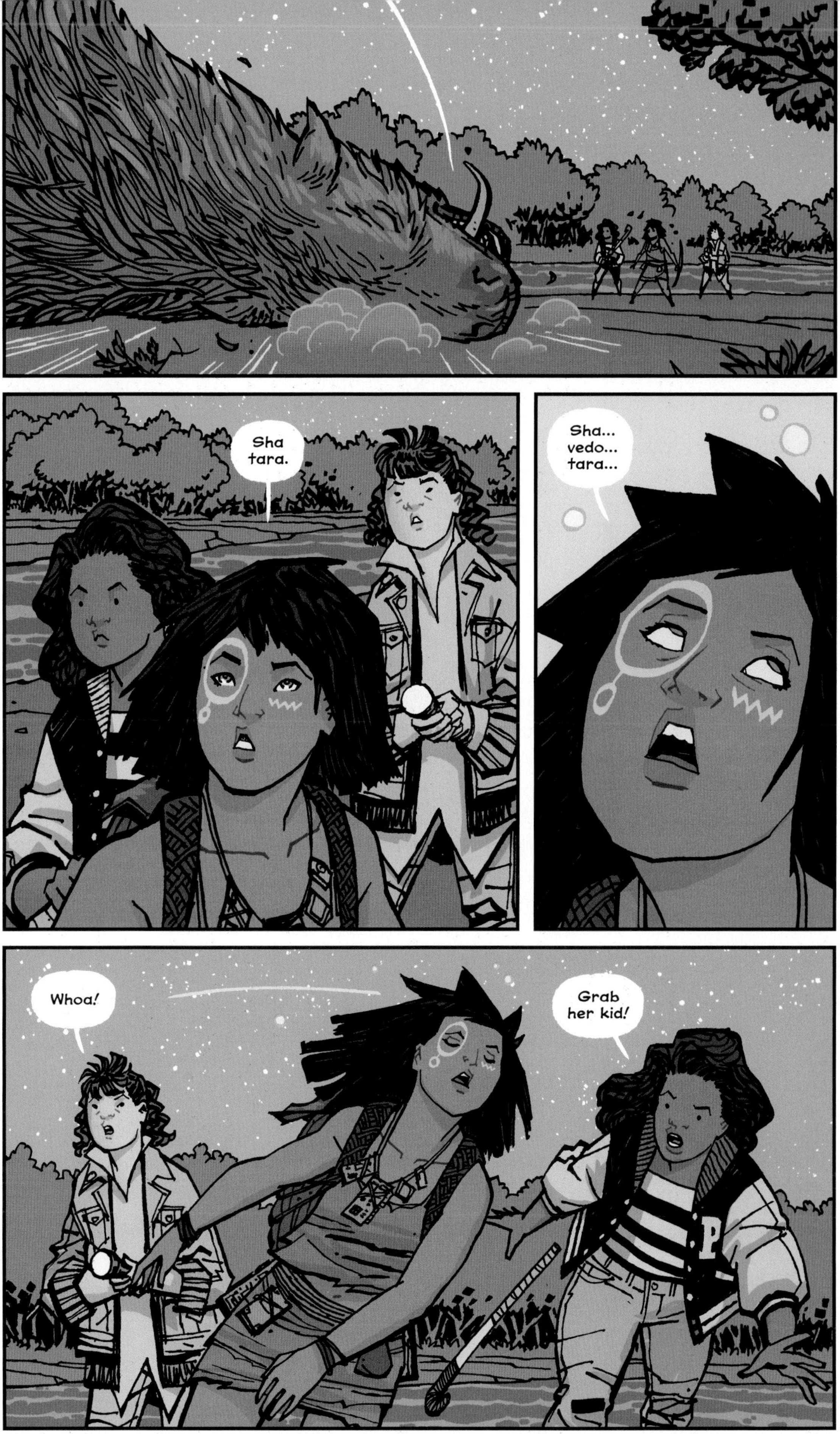
Sha
tara.
Sha...
vedo...
tara...
Whoa!
Grab
her kid!

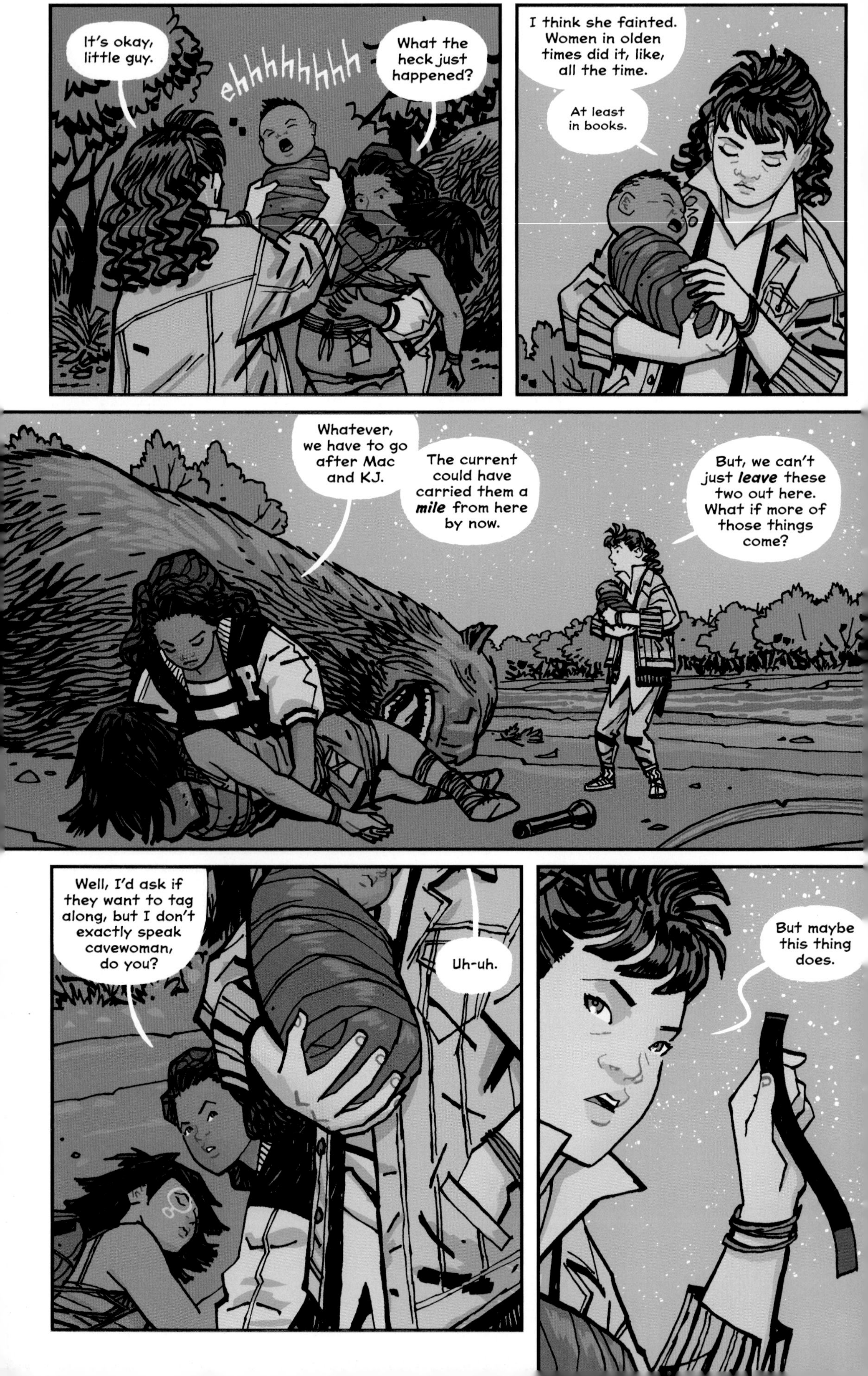
It's okay, little guy.
ehhhhhhhh
What the heck just happened?
I think she fainted. Women in olden times did it, like, all the time.
At least in books.
Whatever, we have to go after Mac and KJ.
The current could have carried them a *mile* from here by now.
But, we can't just *leave* these two out here. What if more of those things come?
Well, I'd ask if they want to tag along, but I don't exactly speak cavewoman, do you?
Uh-uh.
But maybe this thing does.

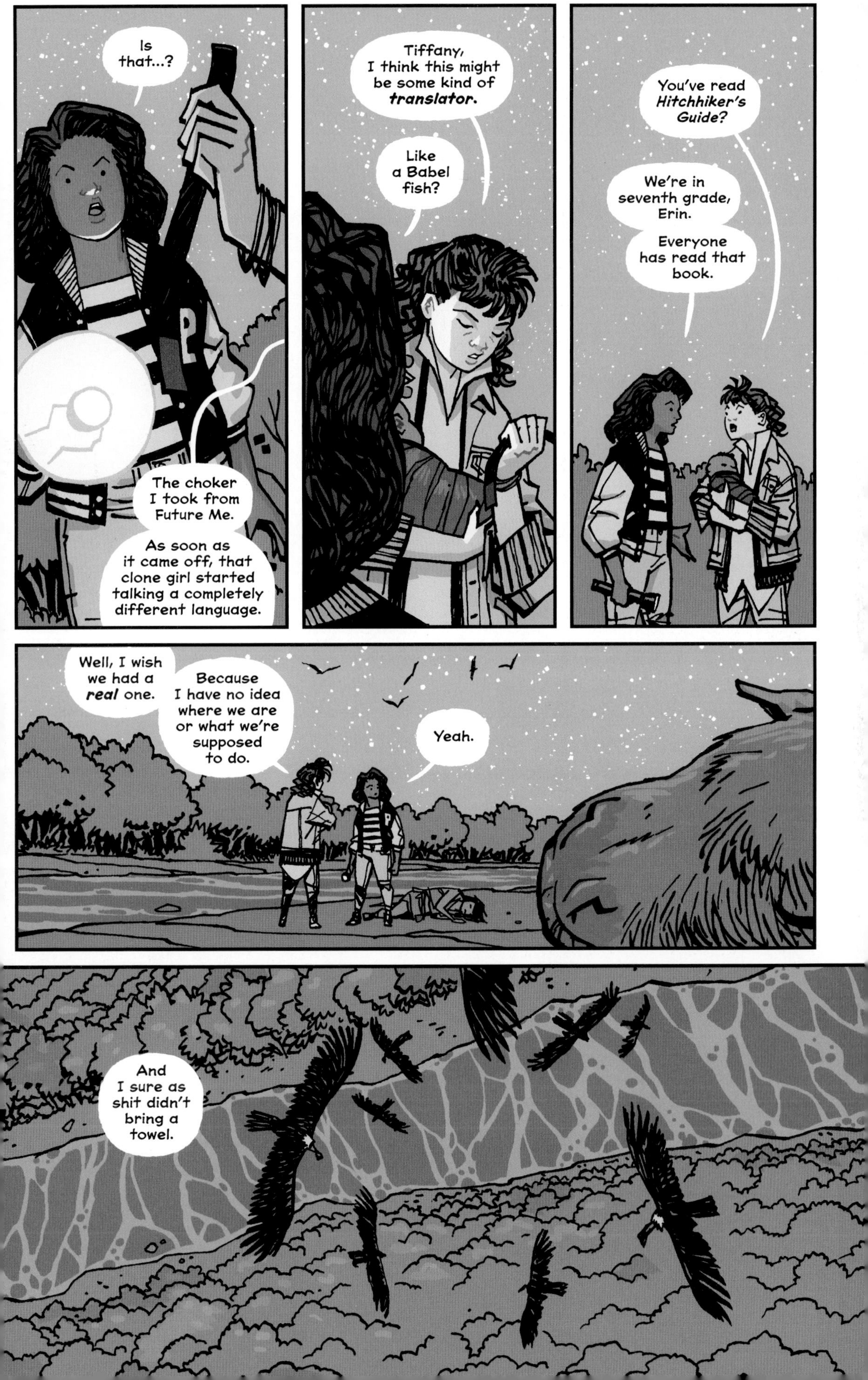
Is that...?
The choker I took from Future Me.
As soon as it came off, that clone girl started talking a completely different language.
Tiffany, I think this might be some kind of **translator.**
Like a Babel fish?
You've read *Hitchhiker's Guide?*
We're in seventh grade, Erin.
Everyone has read that book.
Well, I wish we had a **real** one.
Because I have no idea where we are or what we're supposed to do.
Yeah.
And I sure as shit didn't bring a towel.

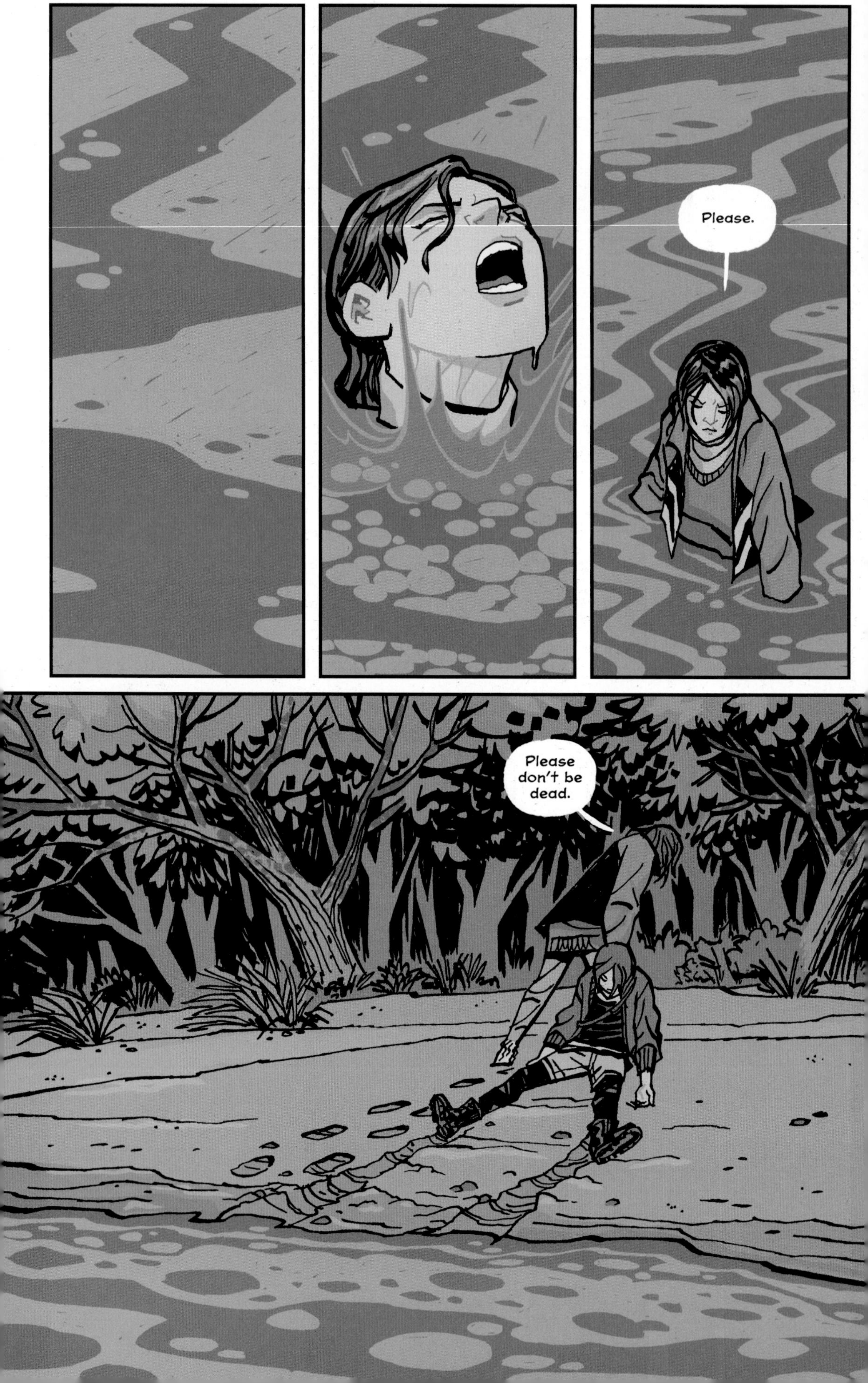
Please.
Please don't be dead.

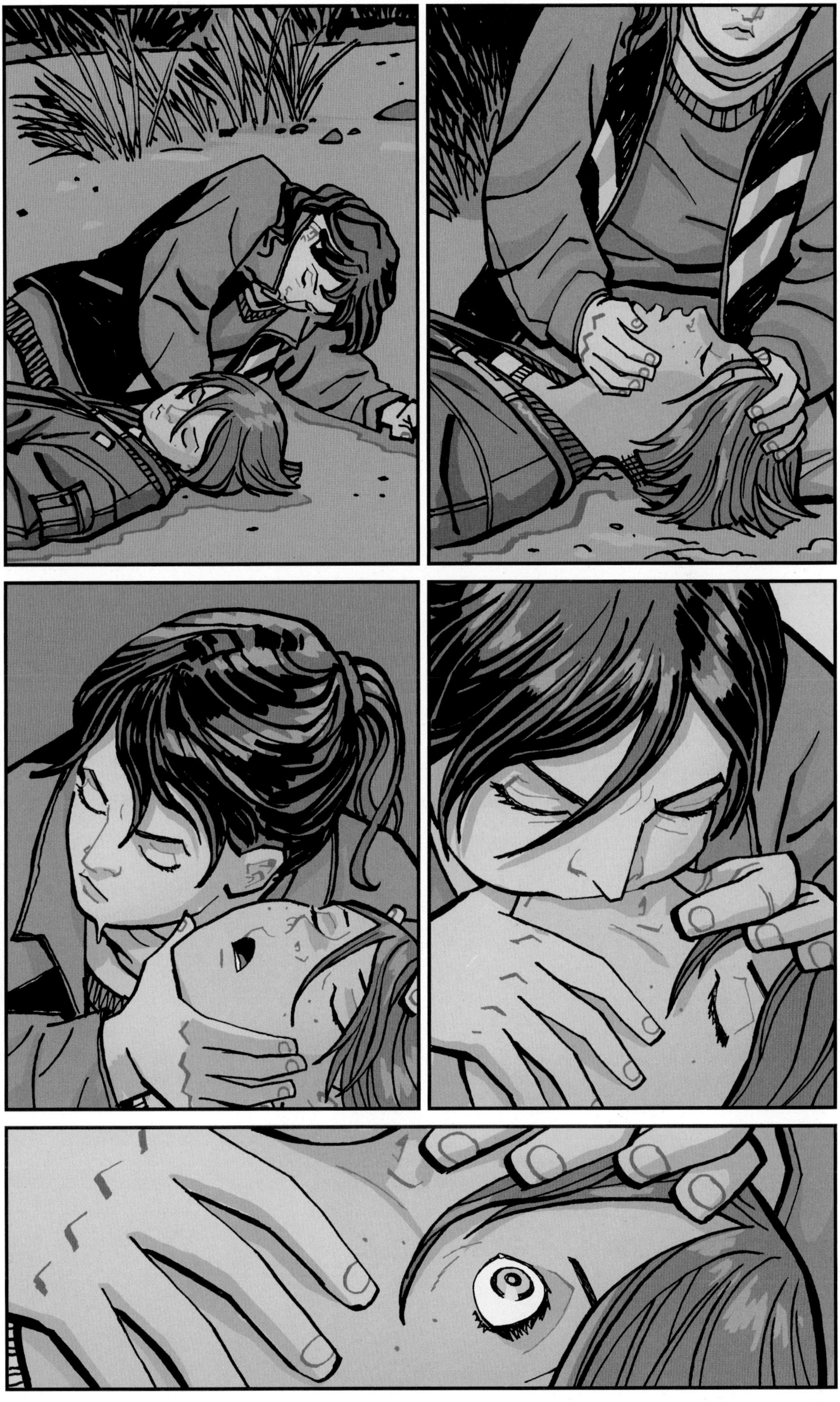

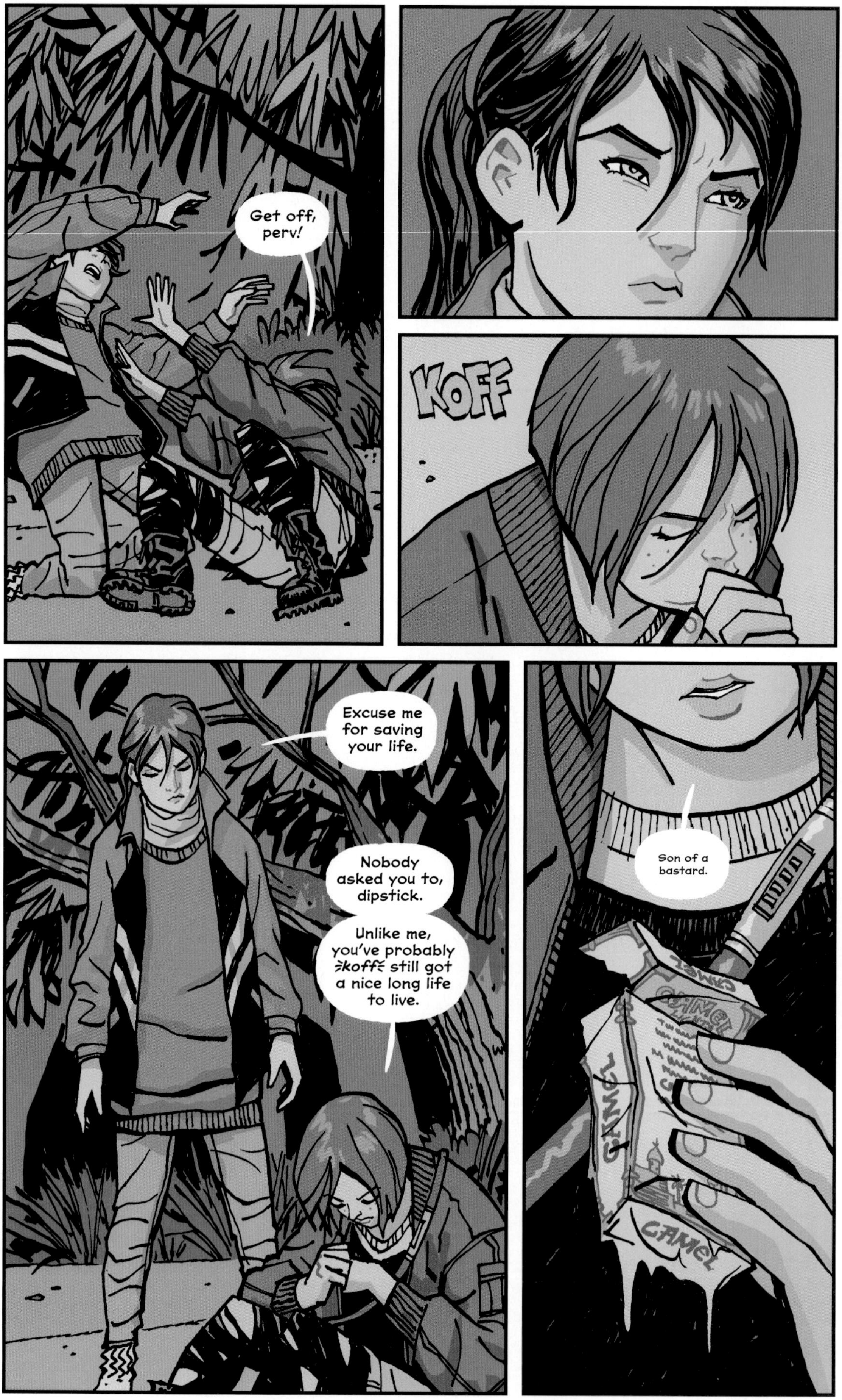
Get off, perv!
KOFF
Excuse me for saving your life.
Nobody asked you to, dipstick.
Unlike me, you've probably *koff* still got a nice long life to live.
Son of a bastard.
CAMEL

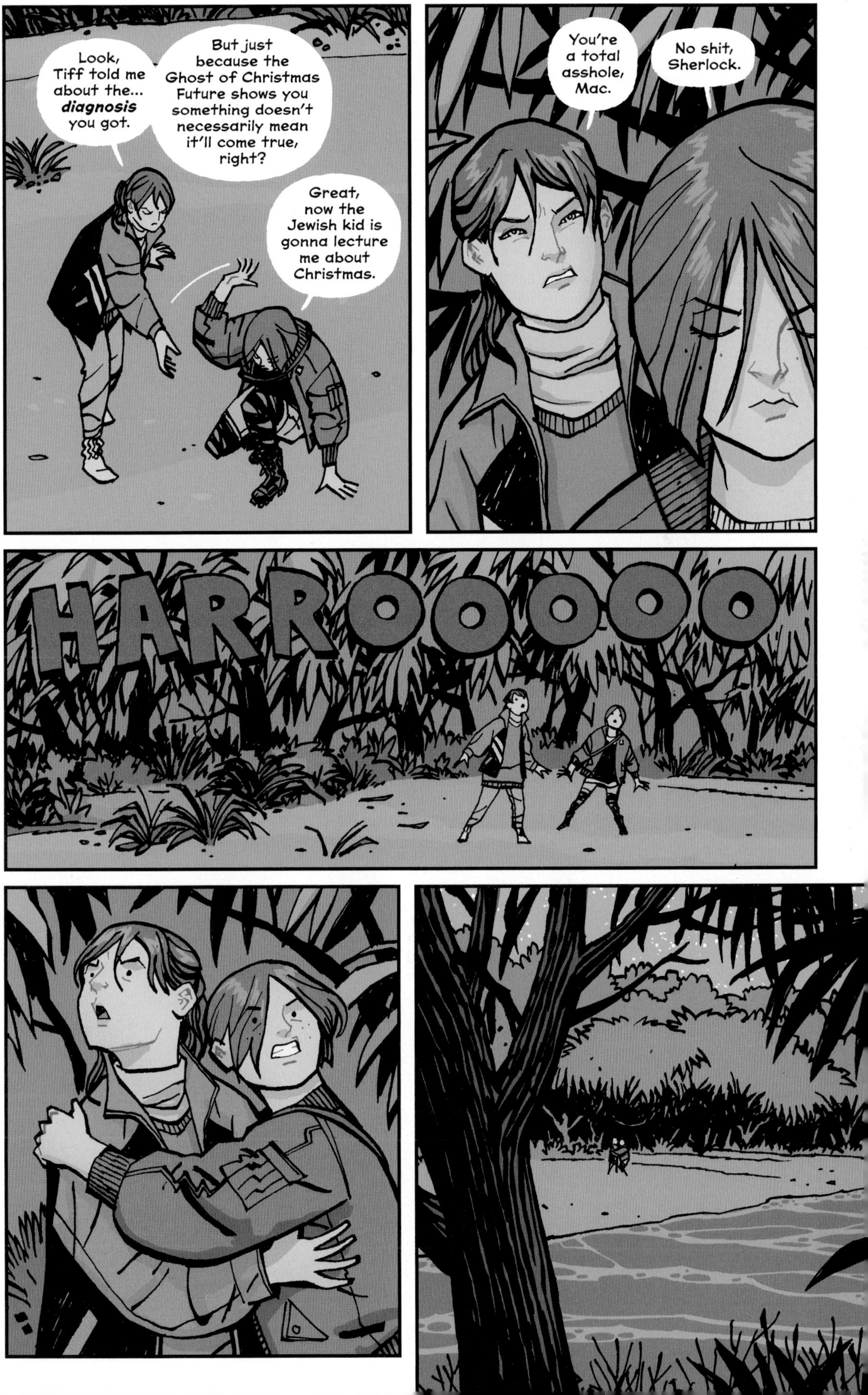
Look, Tiff told me about the... *diagnosis* you got.
But just because the Ghost of Christmas Future shows you something doesn't necessarily mean it'll come true, right?
Great, now the Jewish kid is gonna lecture me about Christmas.
You're a total asshole, Mac.
No shit, Sherlock.
HARROOOOO

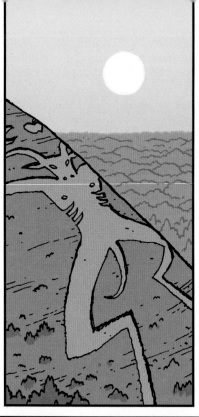

What...?

What the holy fuck?!

It works!

Little *too* well.

Don't kill my baby!

We only came to this place because I...I thought it's what you dream women wanted!

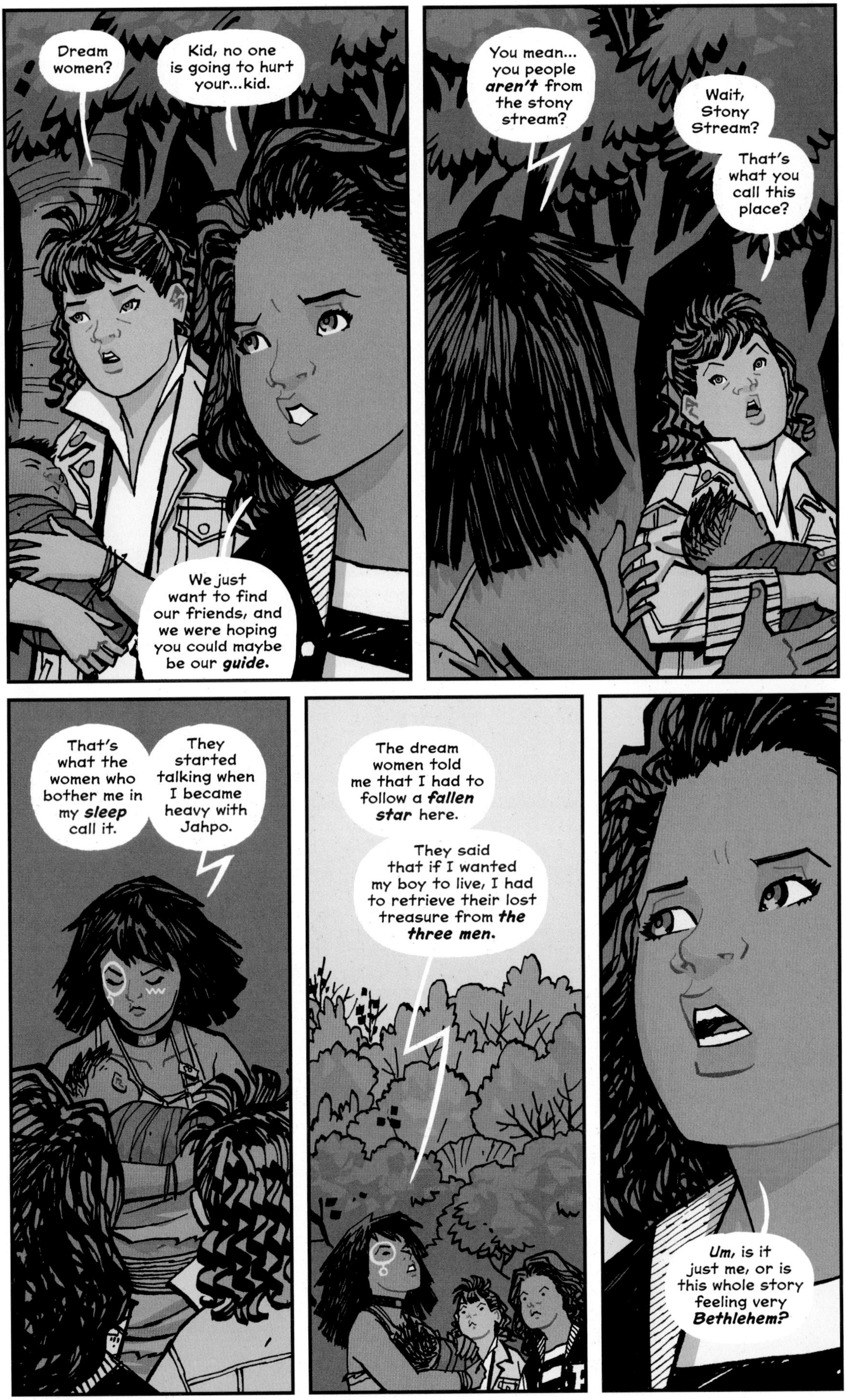

Dream women?
Kid, no one is going to hurt your...kid.
We just want to find our friends, and we were hoping you could maybe be our *guide*.
You mean... you people *aren't* from the stony stream?
Wait, Stony Stream?
That's what you call this place?
That's what the women who bother me in my *sleep* call it.
They started talking when I became heavy with Jahpo.
The dream women told me that I had to follow a *fallen star* here.
They said that if I wanted my boy to live, I had to retrieve their lost treasure from *the three men*.
Um, is it just me, or is this whole story feeling very *Bethlehem?*

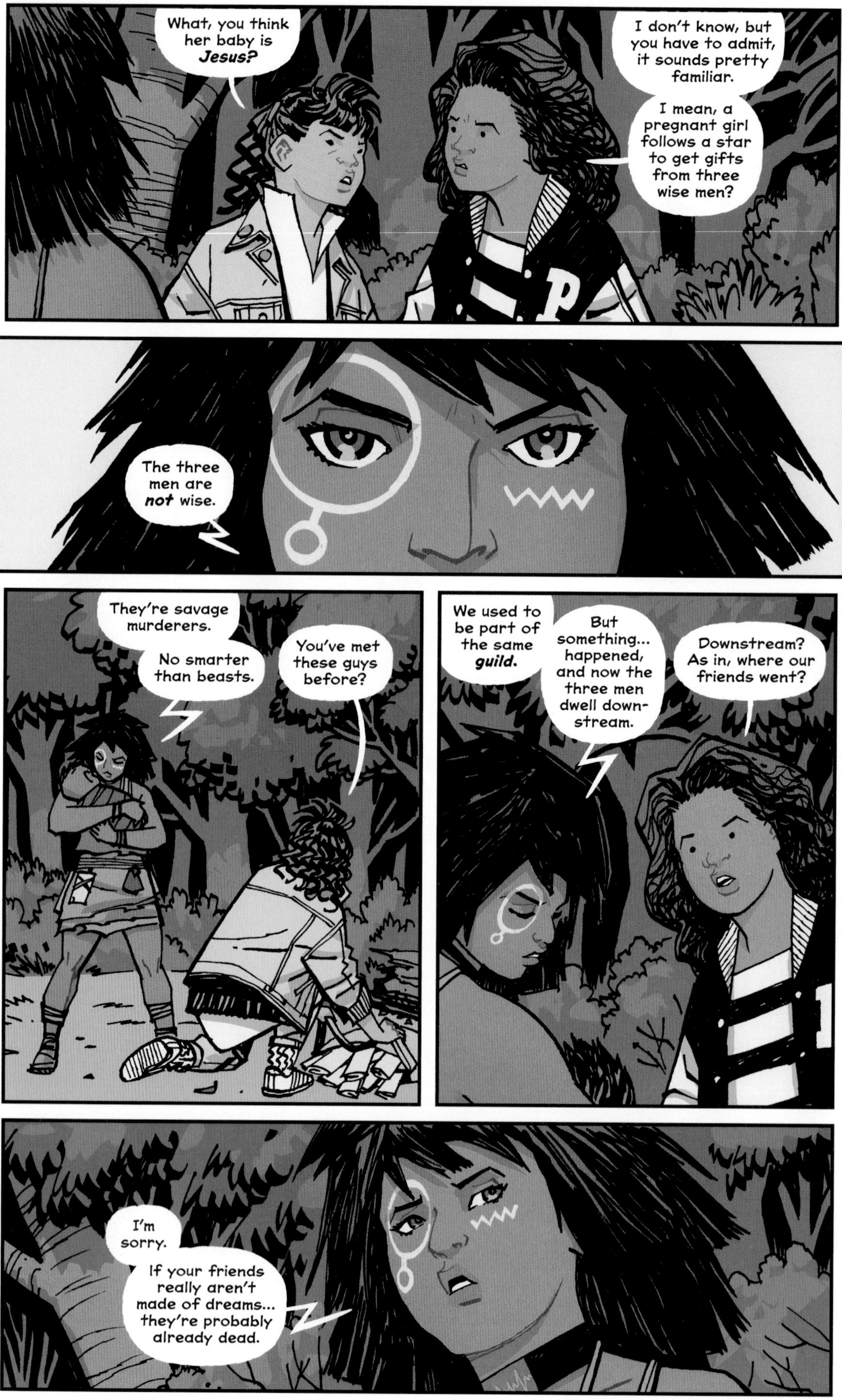
What, you think her baby is *Jesus?*
I don't know, but you have to admit, it sounds pretty familiar.
I mean, a pregnant girl follows a star to get gifts from three wise men?
The three men are *not* wise.
They're savage murderers.
No smarter than beasts.
You've met these guys before?
We used to be part of the same *guild.*
But something... happened, and now the three men dwell down-stream.
Downstream? As in, where our friends went?
I'm sorry.
If your friends really aren't made of dreams... they're probably already dead.

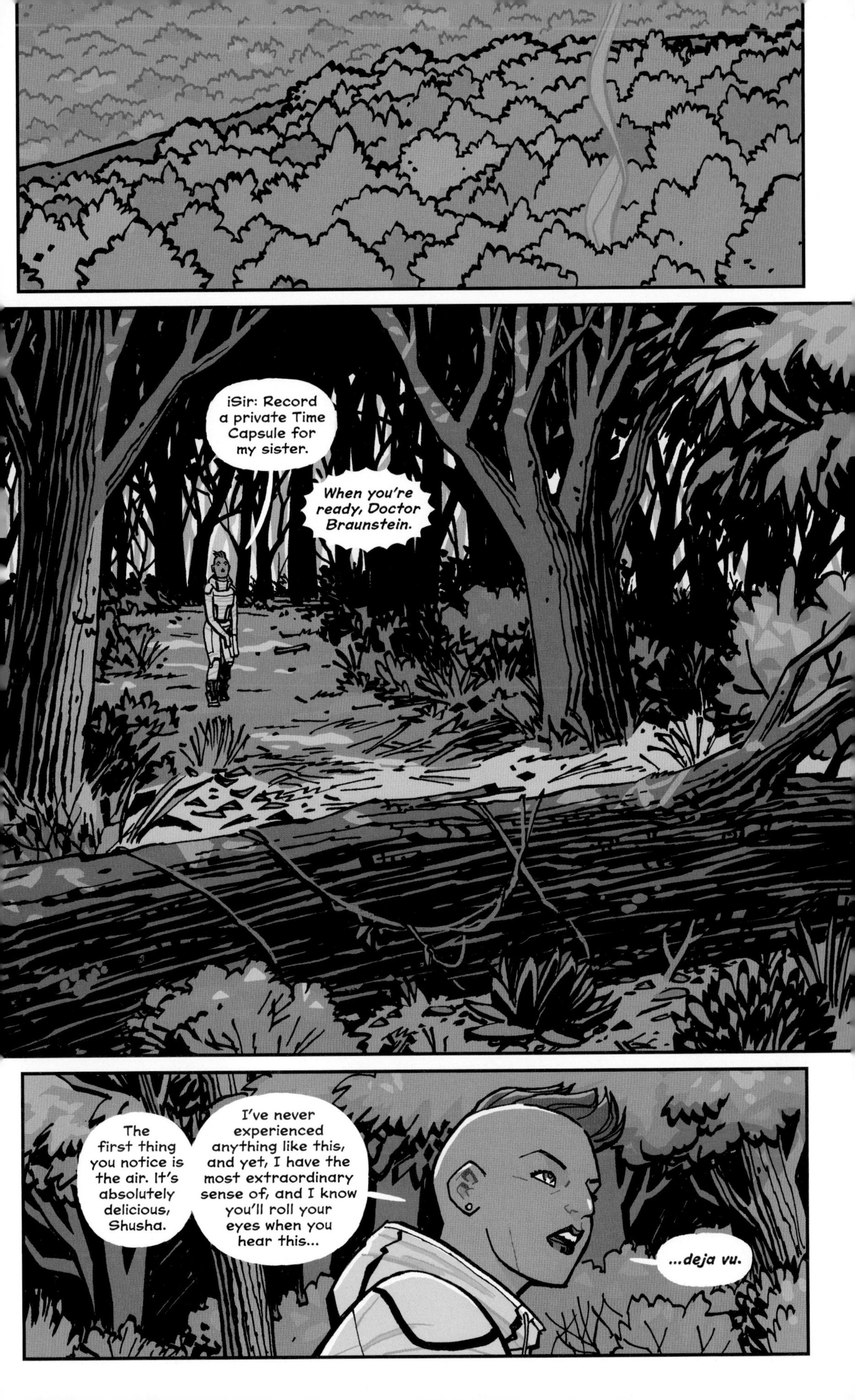
iSir: Record a private Time Capsule for my sister.
When you're ready, Doctor Braunstein.
The first thing you notice is the air. It's absolutely delicious, Shusha.
I've never experienced anything like this, and yet, I have the most extraordinary sense of, and I know you'll roll your eyes when you hear this...
...deja vu.

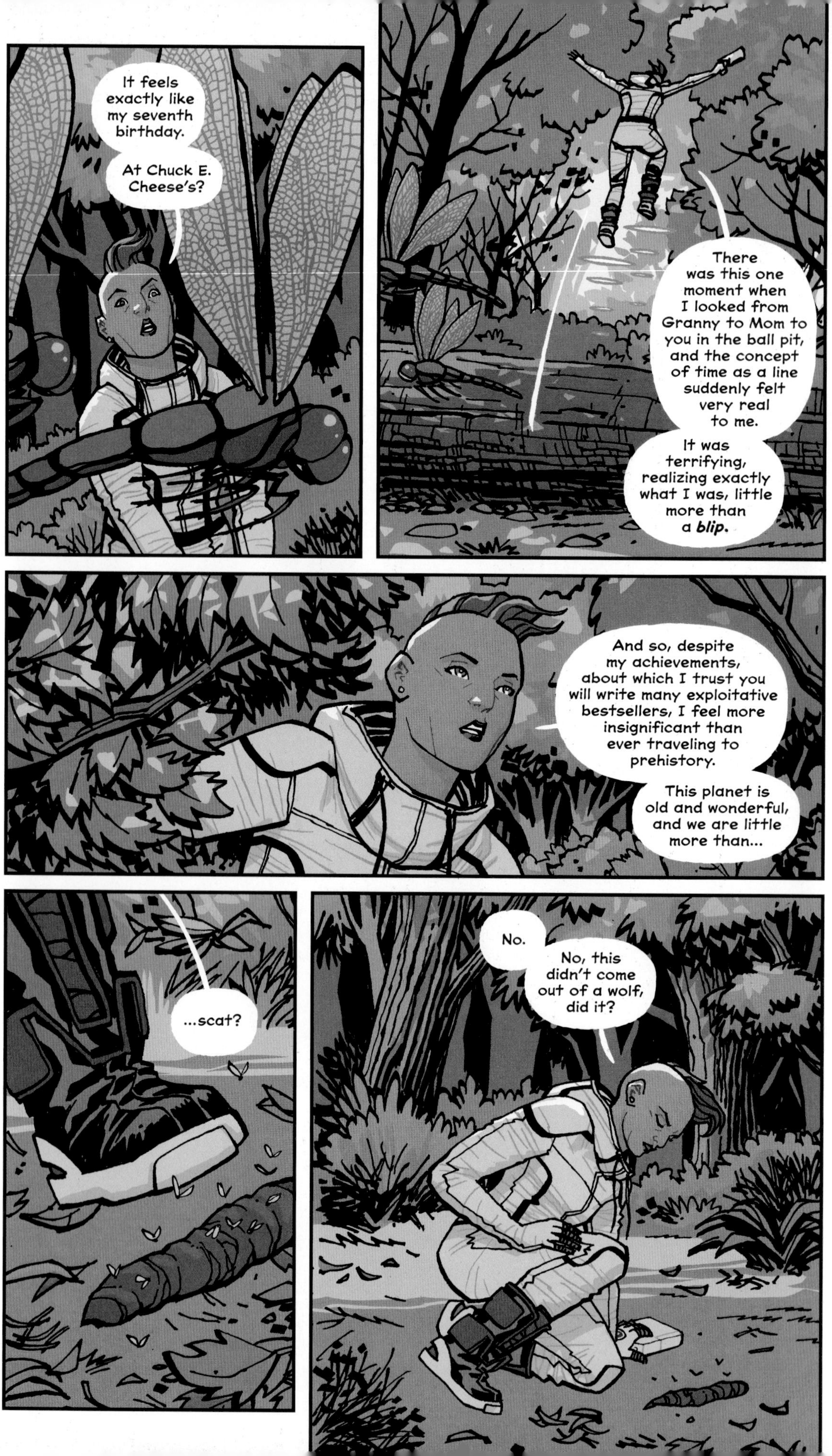
It feels exactly like my seventh birthday.
At Chuck E. Cheese's?
There was this one moment when I looked from Granny to Mom to you in the ball pit, and the concept of time as a line suddenly felt very real to me.
It was terrifying, realizing exactly what I was, little more than a *blip.*
And so, despite my achievements, about which I trust you will write many exploitative bestsellers, I feel more insignificant than ever traveling to prehistory.
This planet is old and wonderful, and we are little more than...
...scat?
No.
No, this didn't come out of a wolf, did it?

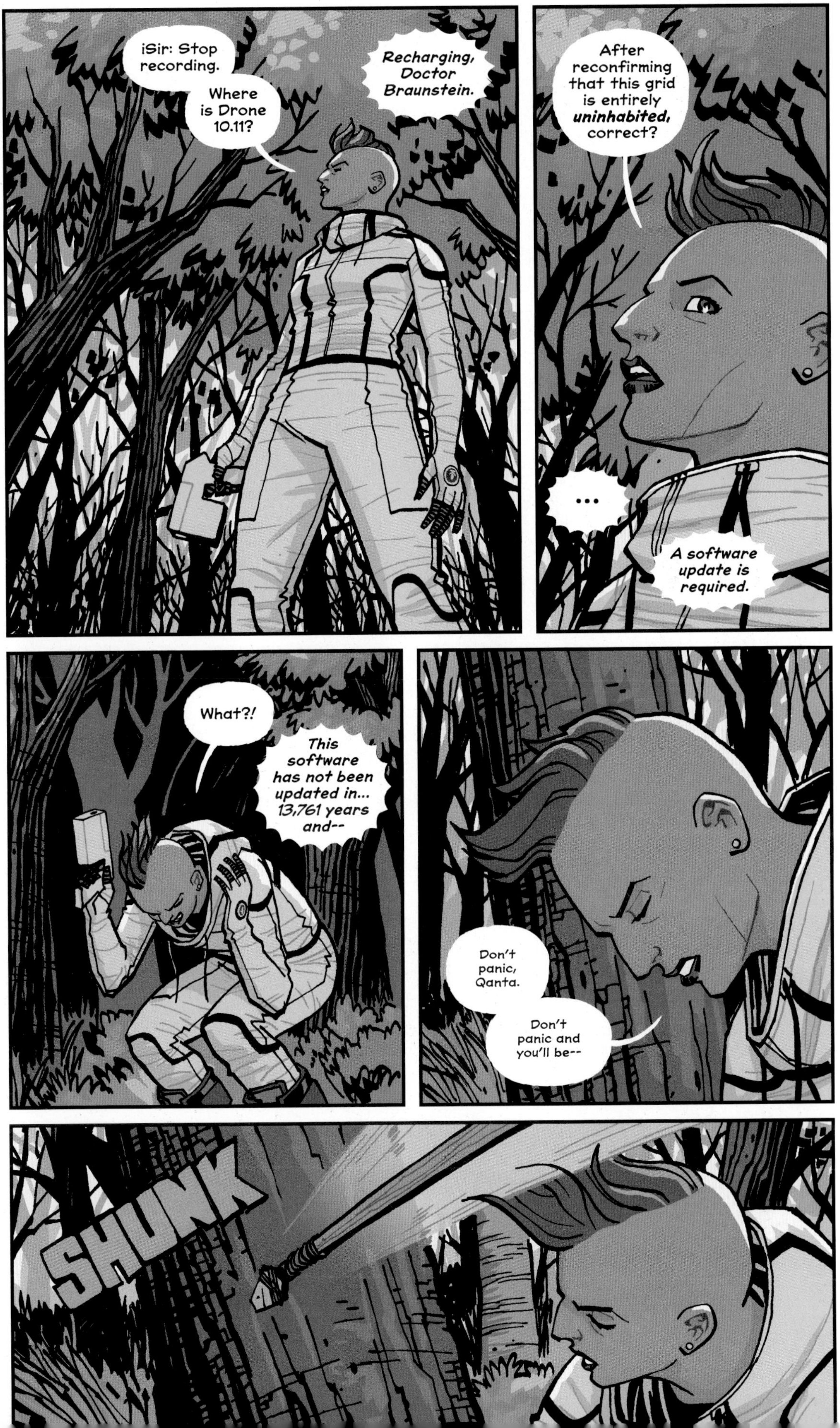
iSir: Stop recording.
Where is Drone 10.11?
Recharging, Doctor Braunstein.
After reconfirming that this grid is entirely uninhabited, correct?
...
A software update is required.
What?!
This software has not been updated in... 13,761 years and--
Don't panic, Qanta.
Don't panic and you'll be--
SHUNK

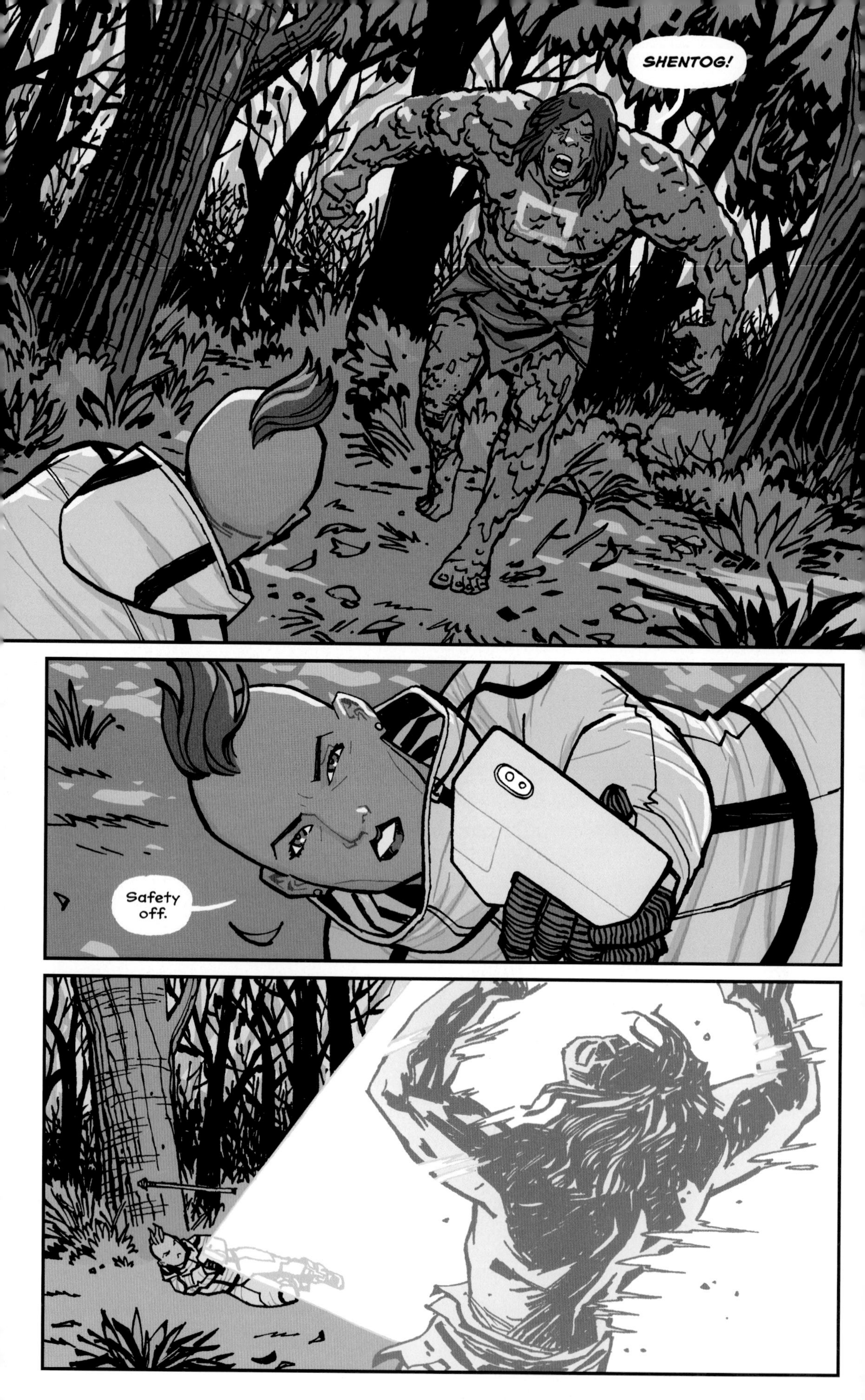
SHENTOG!
Safety off.

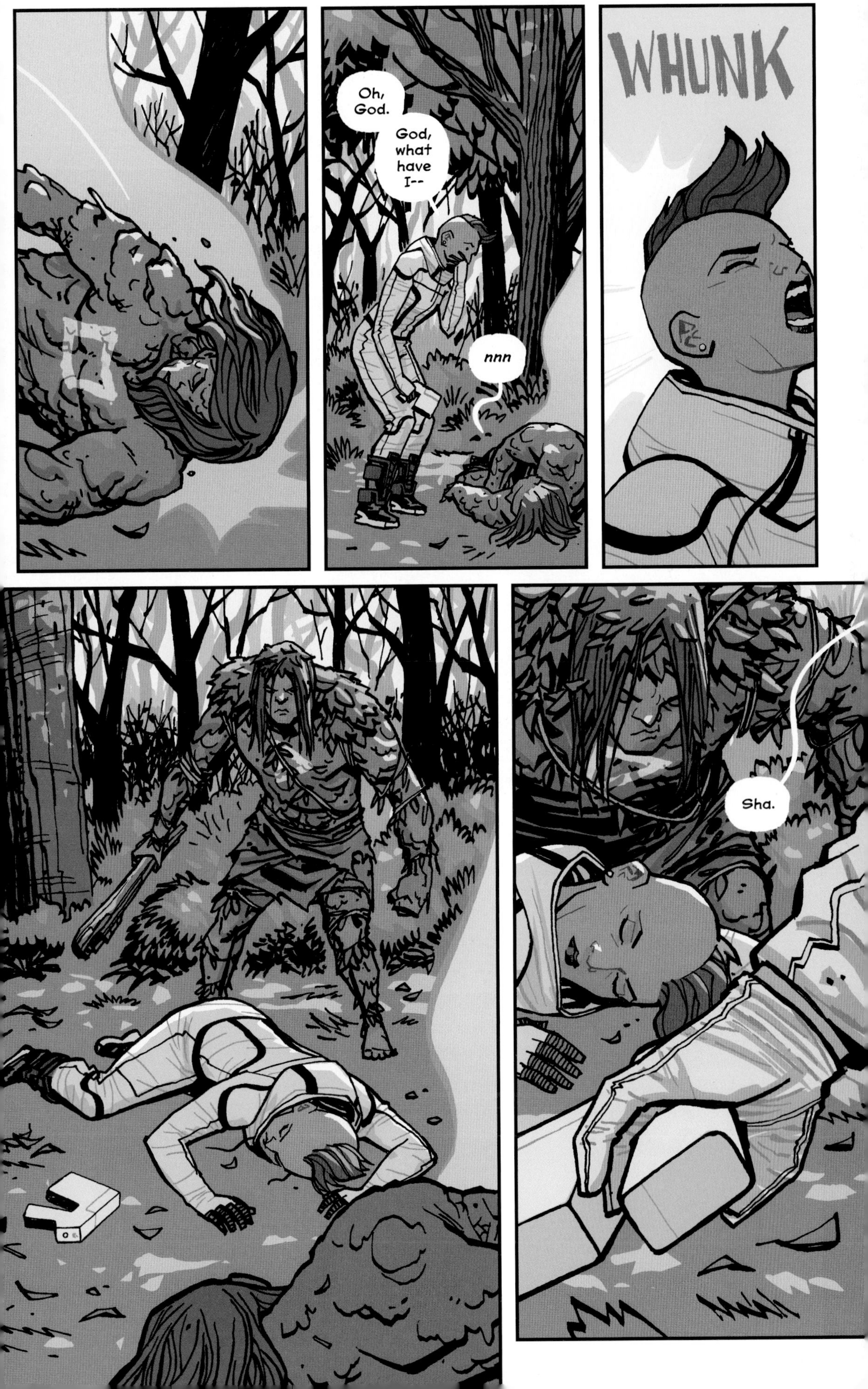
Oh, God.
God, what have I--
nnn
WHUNK
Sha.

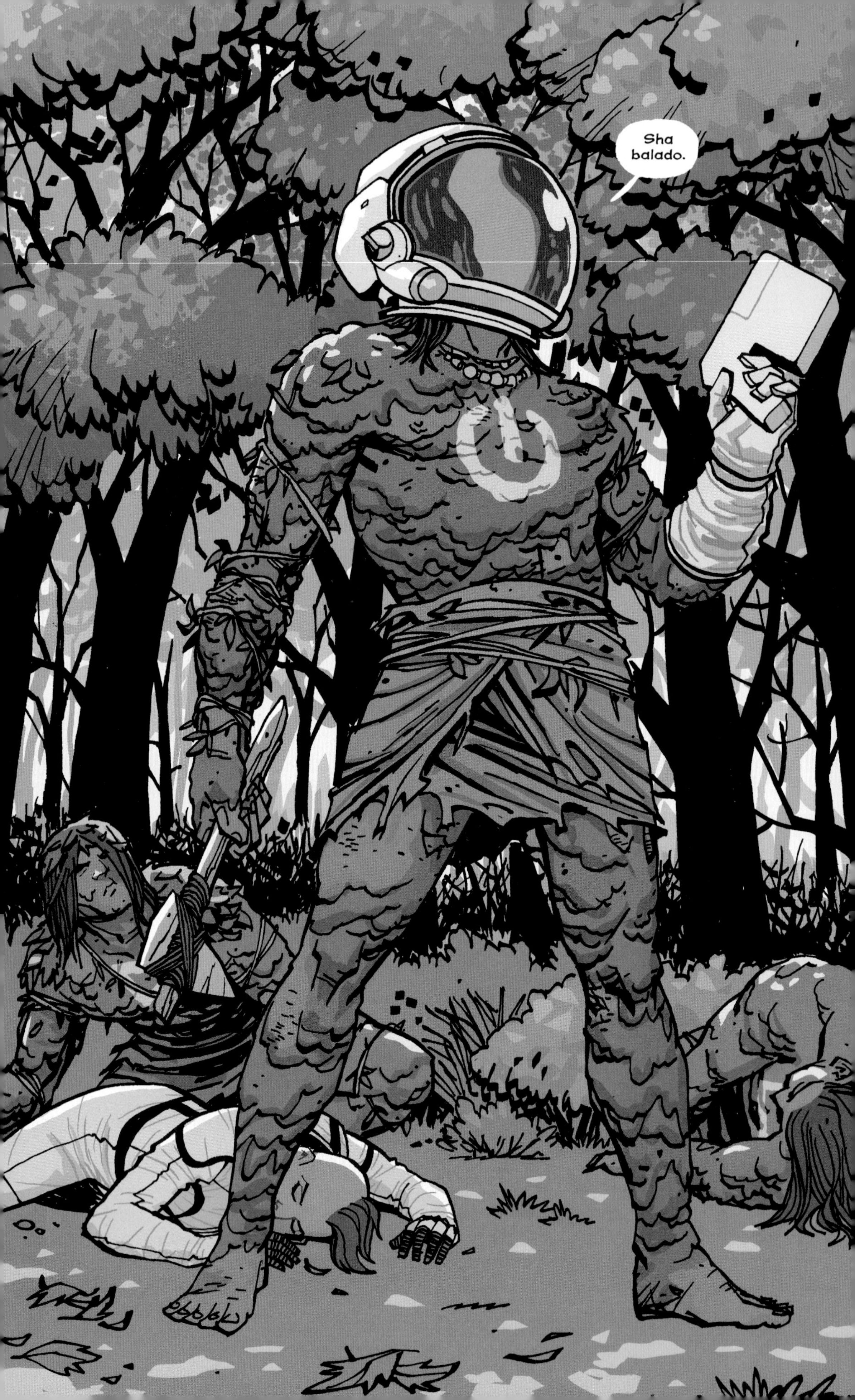
Sha
balado.

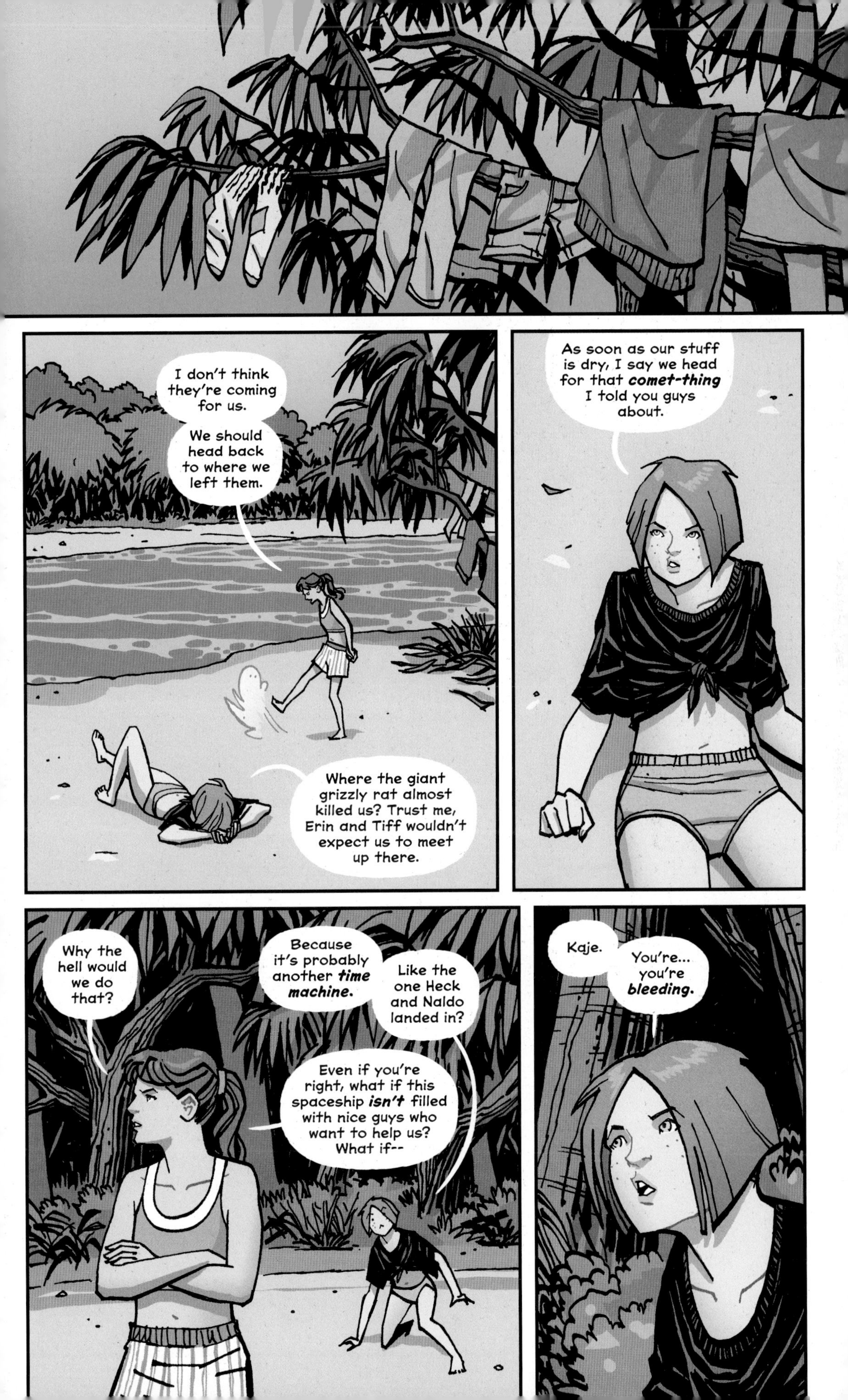
I don't think they're coming for us.
We should head back to where we left them.
Where the giant grizzly rat almost killed us? Trust me, Erin and Tiff wouldn't expect us to meet up there.
As soon as our stuff is dry, I say we head for that comet-thing I told you guys about.
Why the hell would we do that?
Because it's probably another time machine.
Like the one Heck and Naldo landed in?
Even if you're right, what if this spaceship isn't filled with nice guys who want to help us? What if--
Kaje.
You're... you're bleeding.

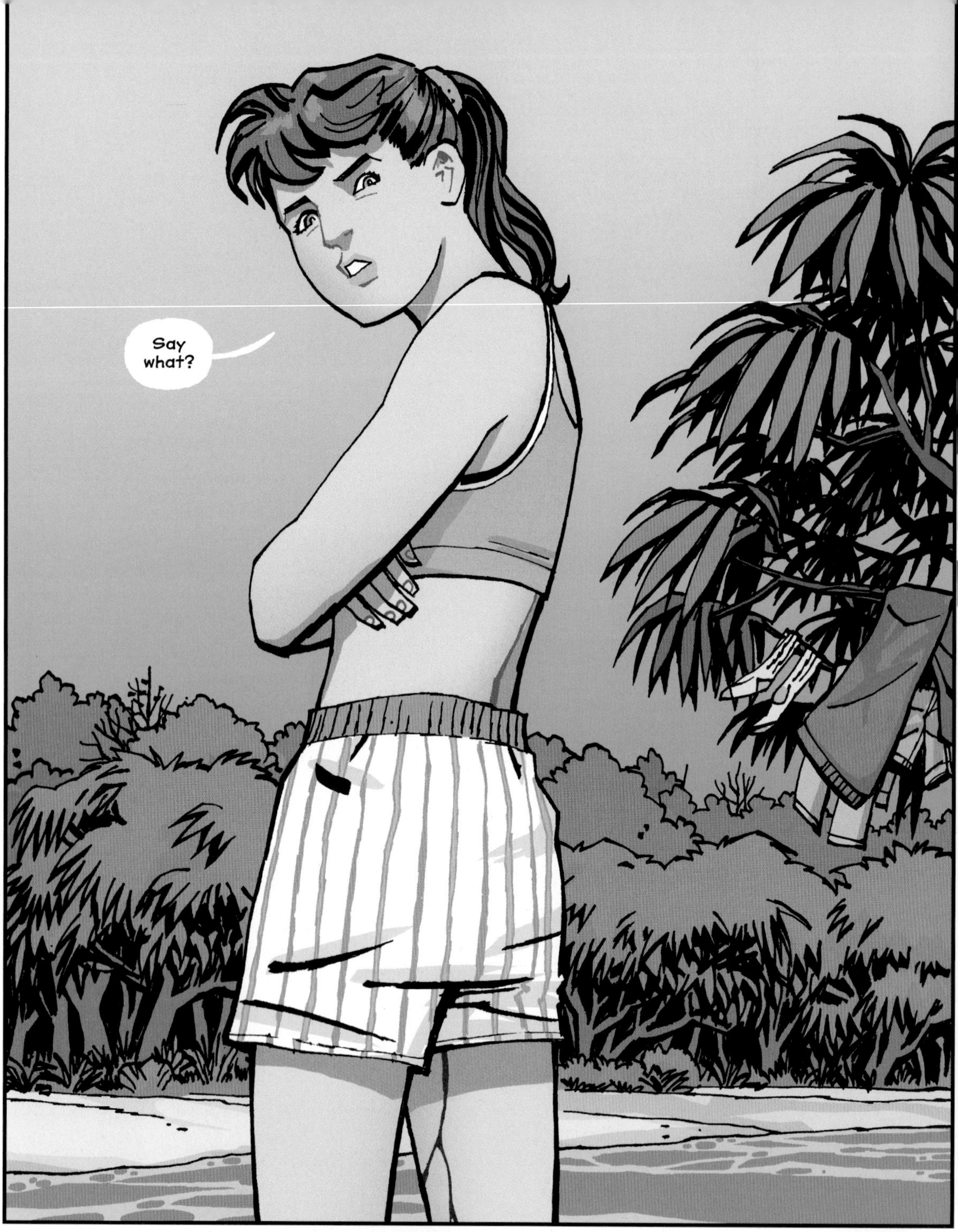
Say what?

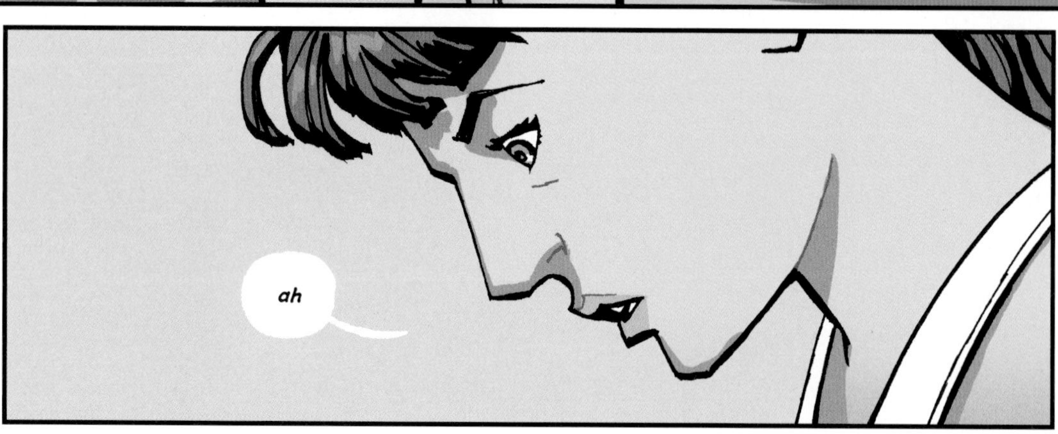
ah

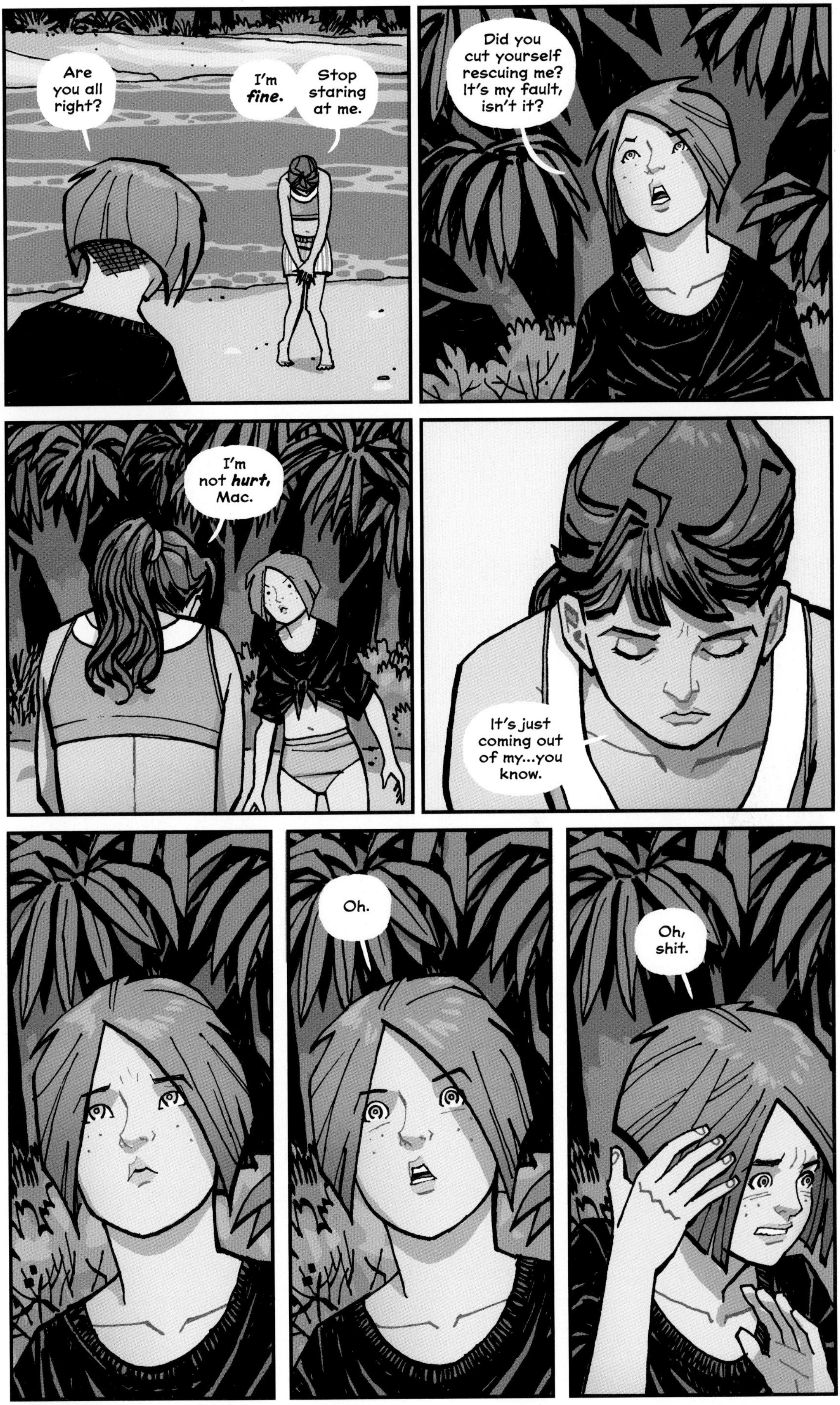

Are you all right?
I'm *fine.*
Stop staring at me.
Did you cut yourself rescuing me? It's my fault, isn't it?
I'm not *hurt,* Mac.
It's just coming out of my...you know.
Oh.
Oh, shit.

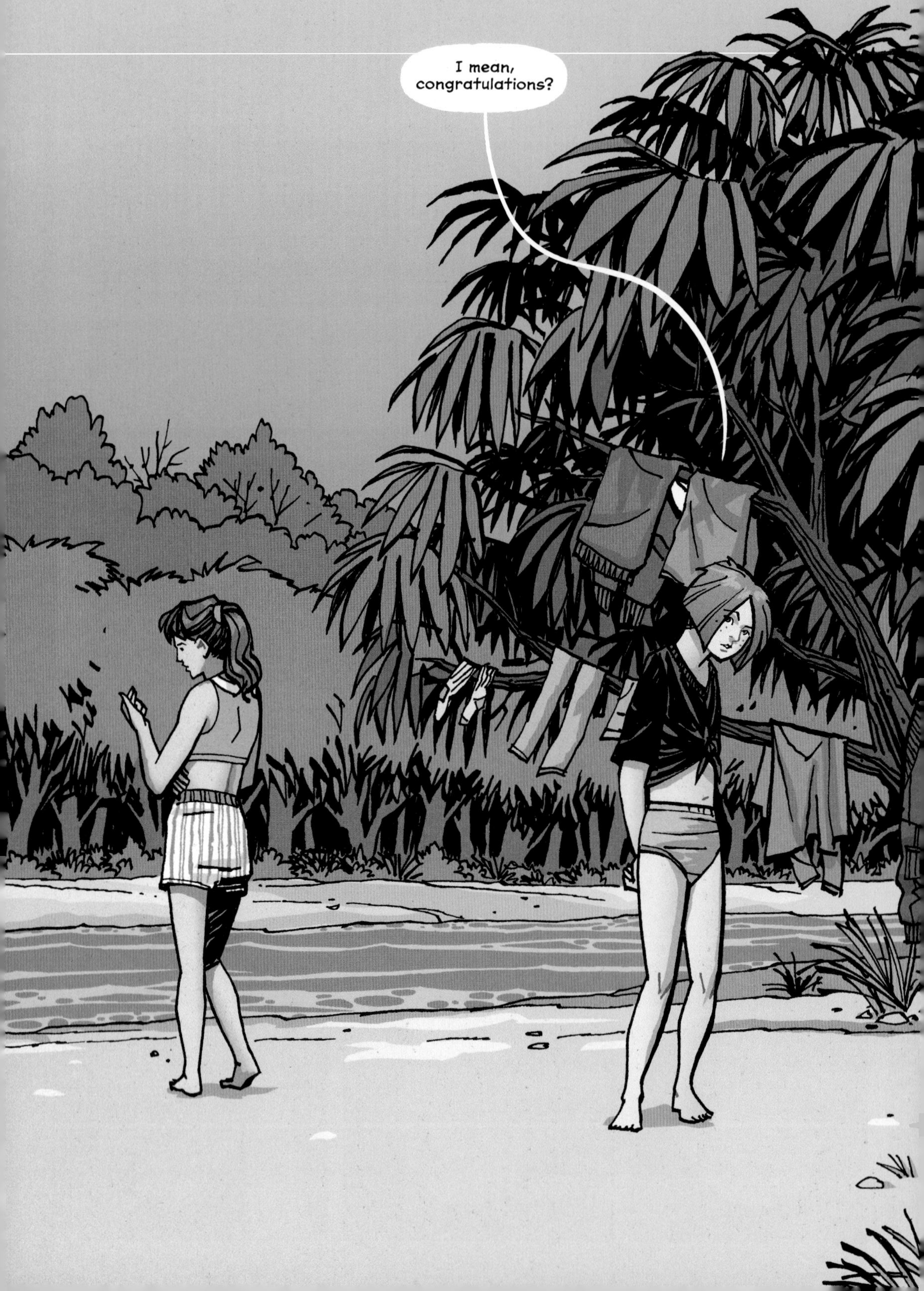
I mean, congratulations?

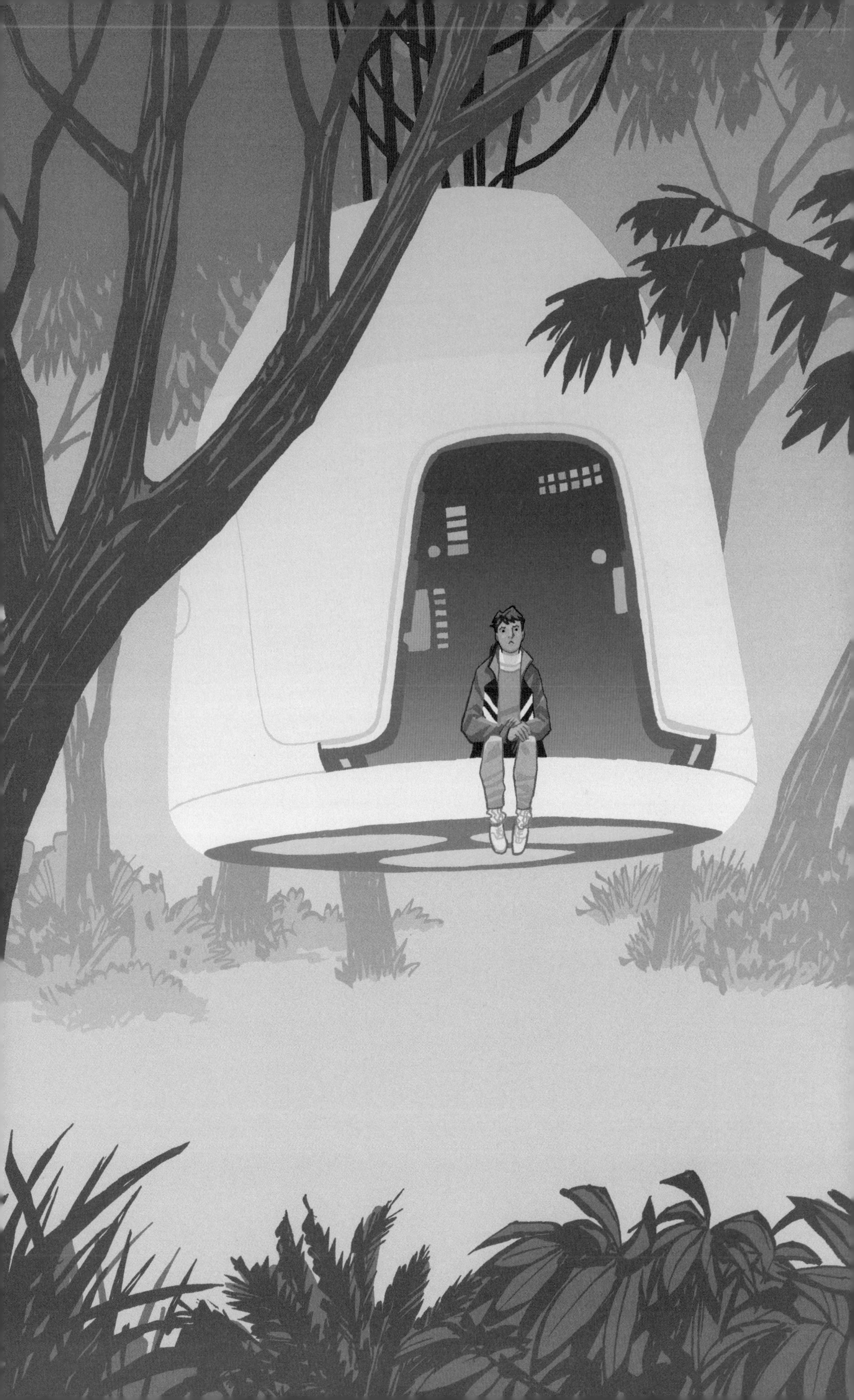

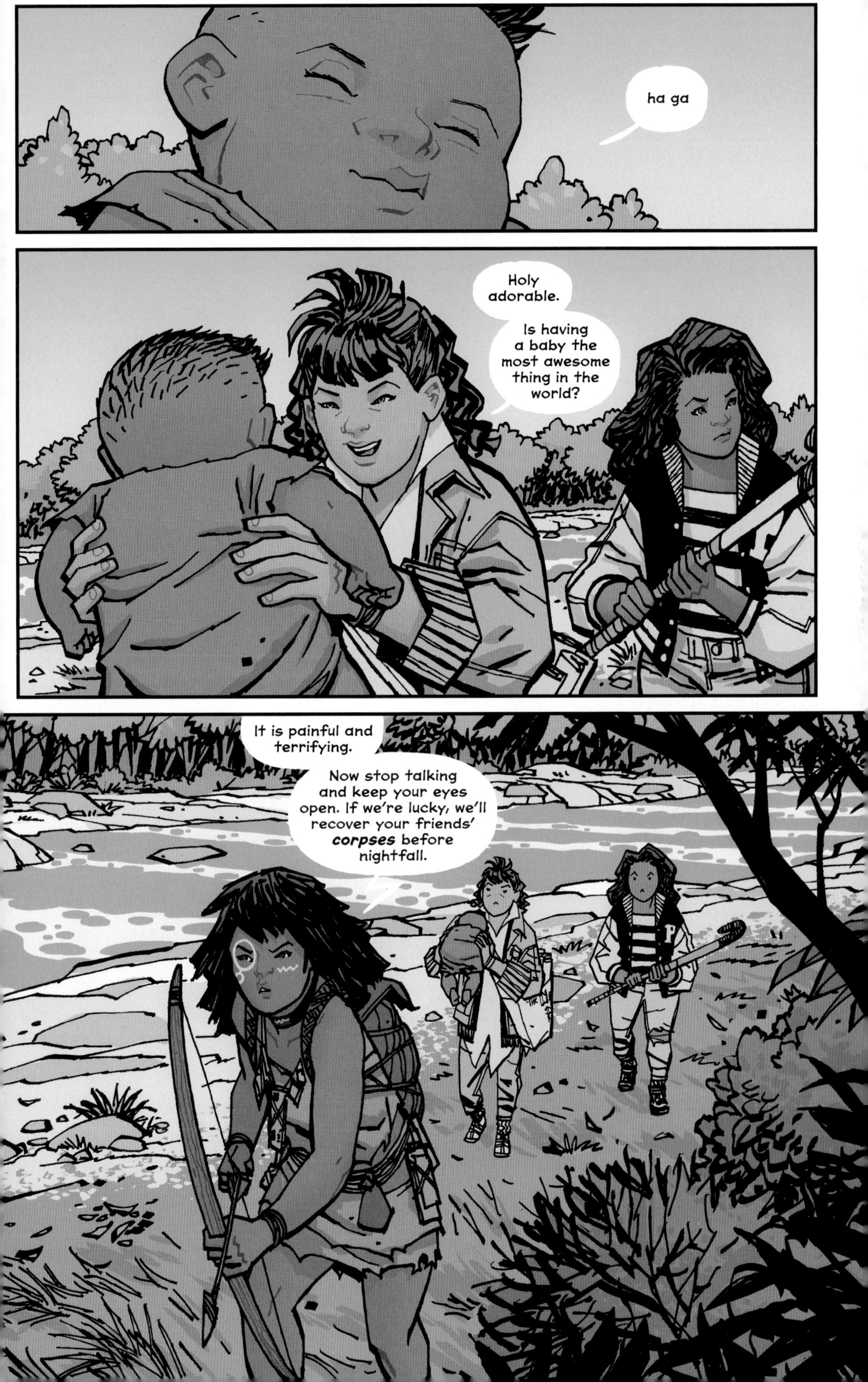
ha ga
Holy adorable.
Is having a baby the most awesome thing in the world?
It is painful and terrifying.
Now stop talking and keep your eyes open. If we're lucky, we'll recover your friends' ***corpses*** before nightfall.

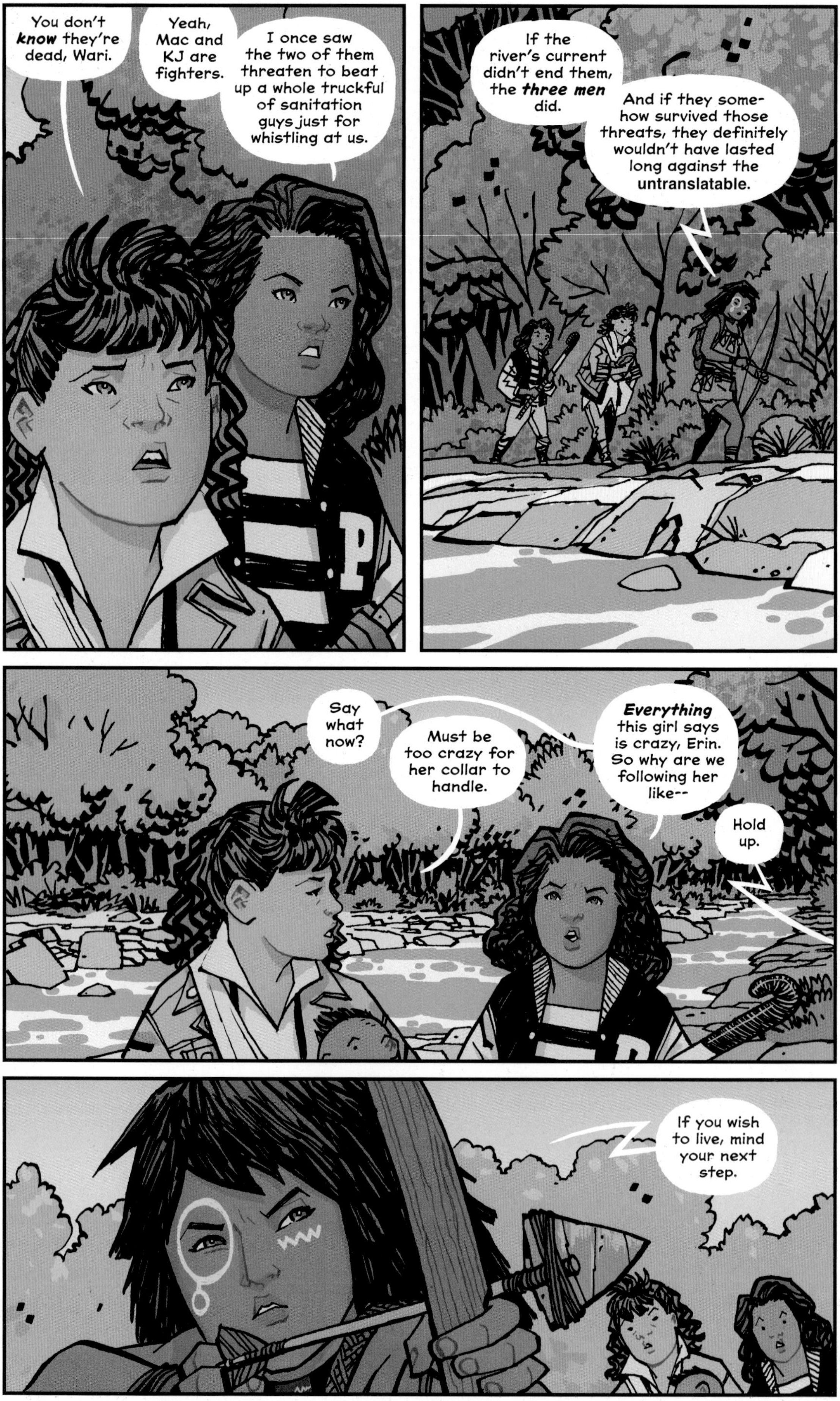
You don't *know* they're dead, Wari.
Yeah, Mac and KJ are fighters.
I once saw the two of them threaten to beat up a whole truckful of sanitation guys just for whistling at us.
If the river's current didn't end them, the *three men* did.
And if they somehow survived those threats, they definitely wouldn't have lasted long against the **untranslatable.**
Everything this girl says is crazy, Erin. So why are we following her like--
Say what now?
Must be too crazy for her collar to handle.
Hold up.
If you wish to live, mind your next step.

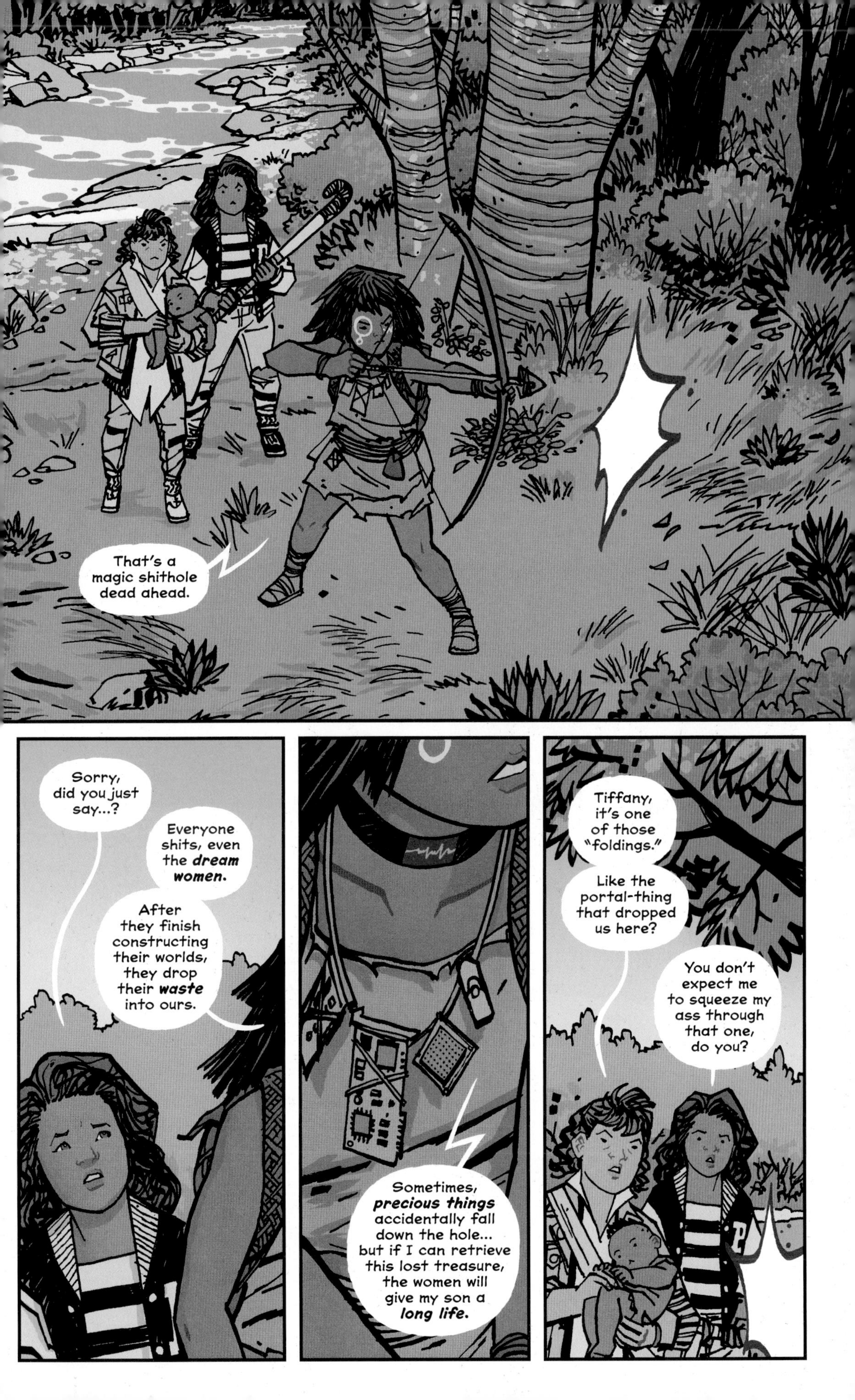
That's a magic shithole dead ahead.
Sorry, did you just say...?
Everyone shits, even the **dream women.**
After they finish constructing their worlds, they drop their **waste** into ours.
Sometimes, **precious things** accidentally fall down the hole... but if I can retrieve this lost treasure, the women will give my son a **long life.**
Tiffany, it's one of those "foldings."
Like the portal-thing that dropped us here?
You don't expect me to squeeze my ass through that one, do you?

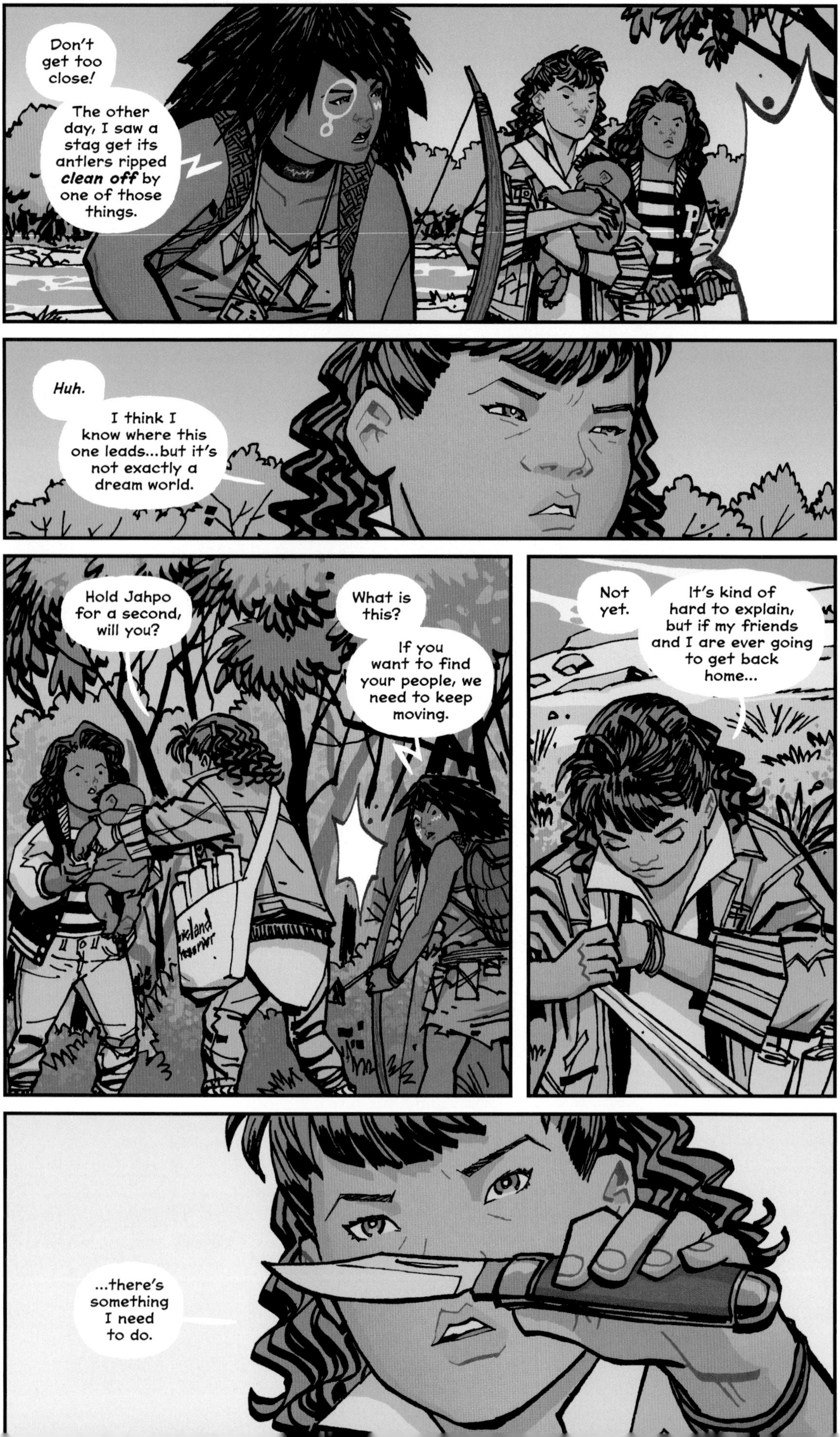
Don't get too close!
The other day, I saw a stag get its antlers ripped **clean off** by one of those things.
Huh.
I think I know where this one leads...but it's not exactly a dream world.
Hold Jahpo for a second, will you?
What is this?
If you want to find your people, we need to keep moving.
Not yet.
It's kind of hard to explain, but if my friends and I are ever going to get back home...
...there's something I need to do.

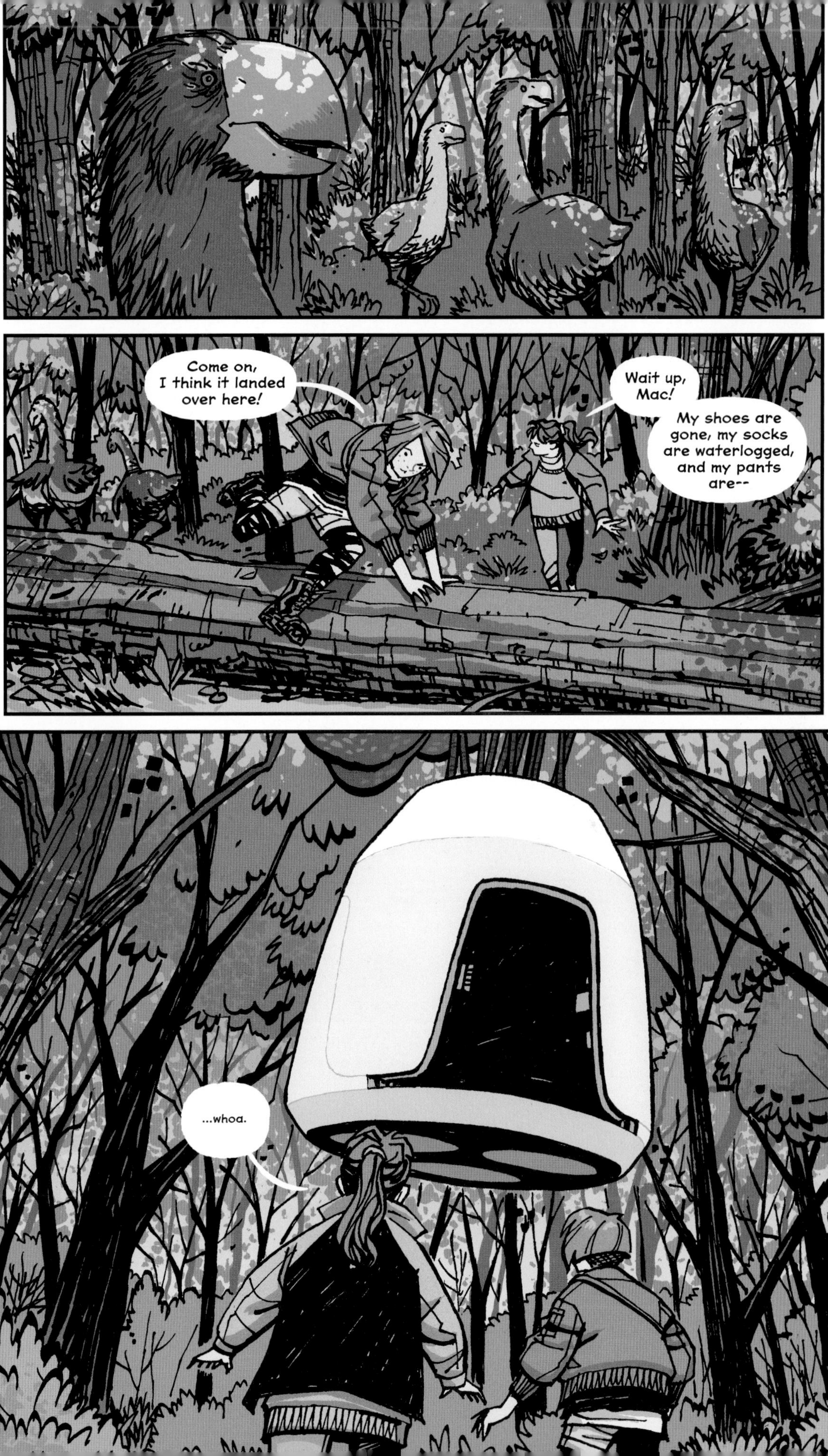
Come on, I think it landed over here!
Wait up, Mac!
My shoes are gone, my socks are waterlogged, and my pants are--
...whoa.

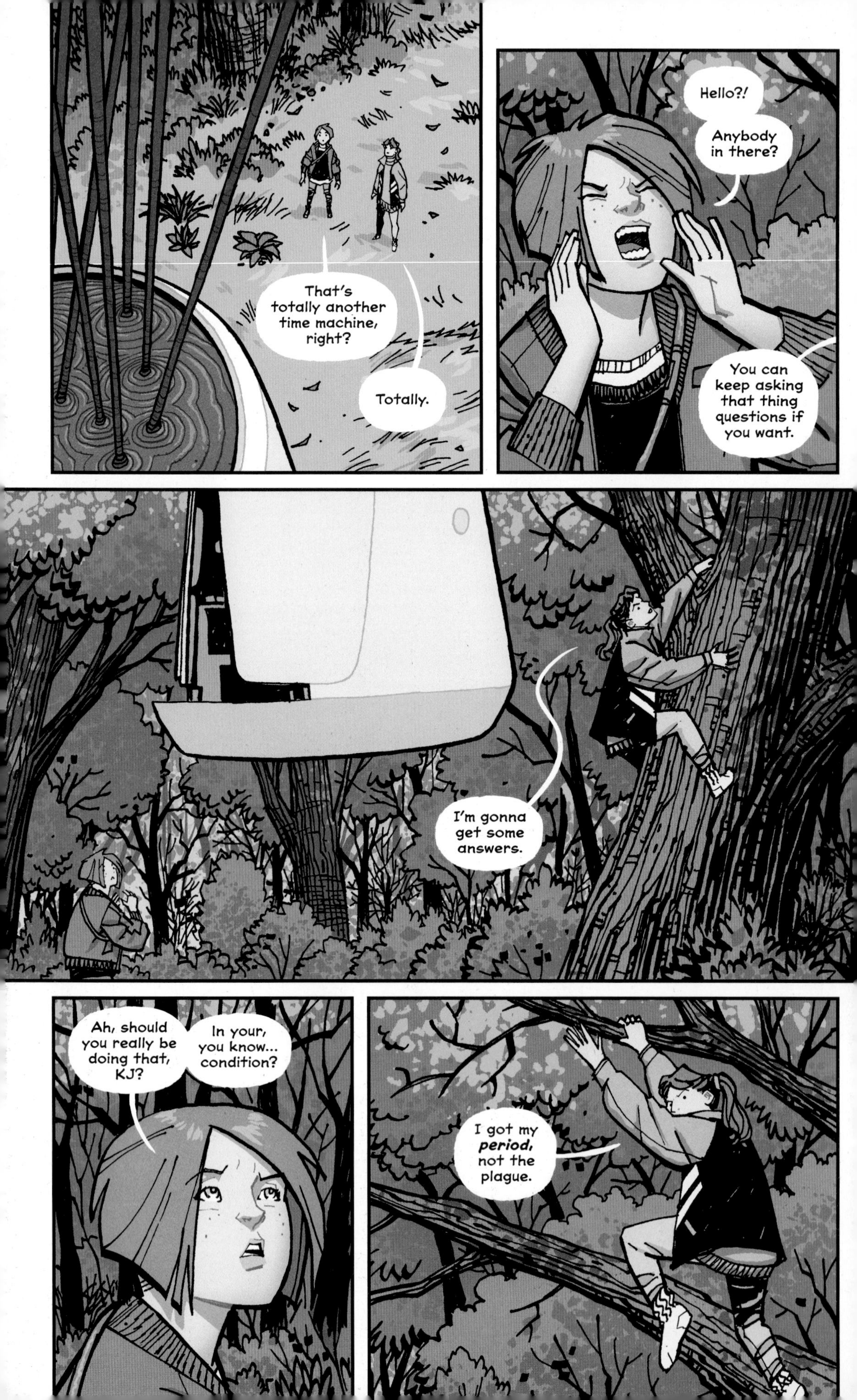
That's totally another time machine, right?
Totally.
Hello?!
Anybody in there?
You can keep asking that thing questions if you want.
I'm gonna get some answers.
Ah, should you really be doing that, KJ?
In your, you know... condition?
I got my *period,* not the plague.

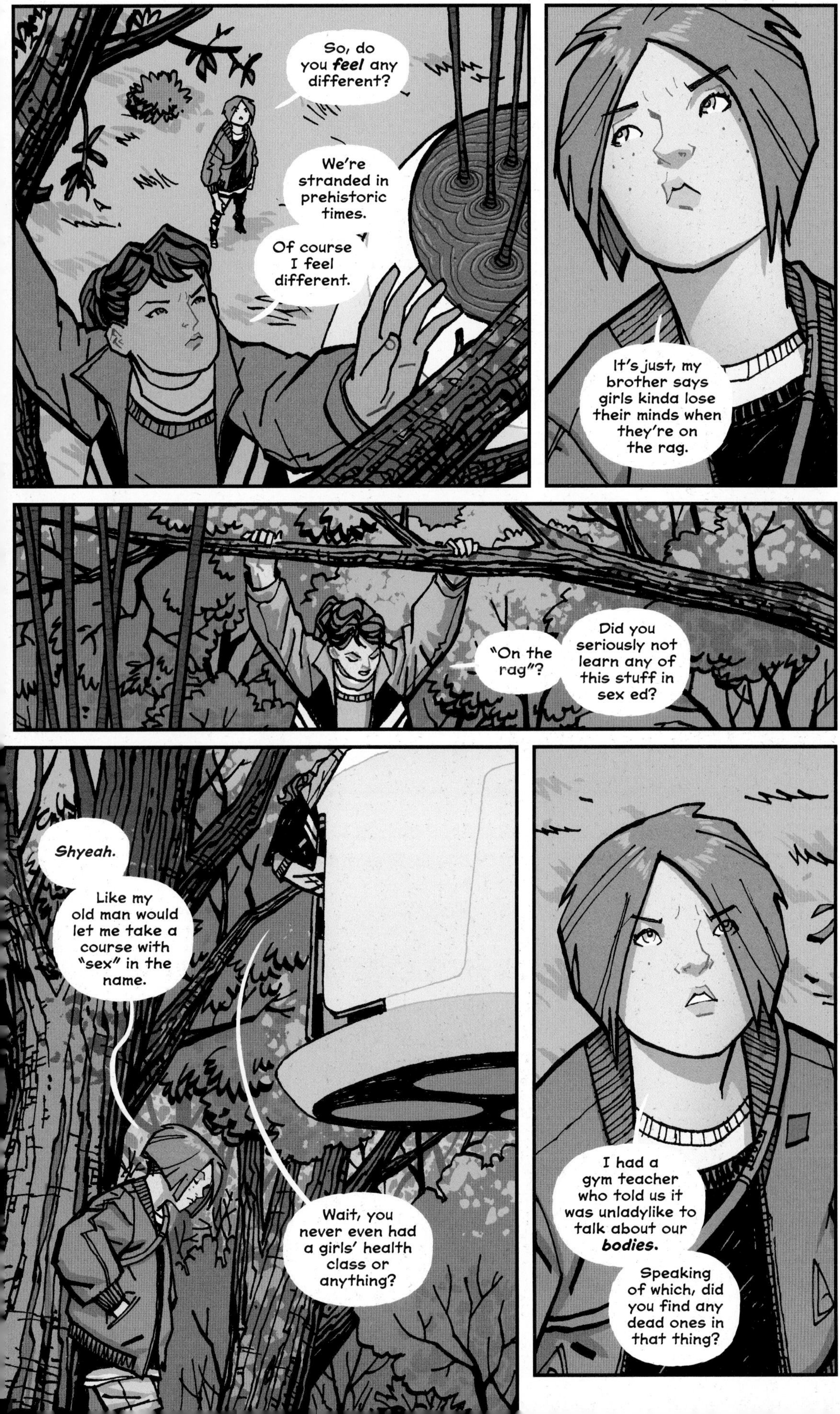
So, do you *feel* any different?
We're stranded in prehistoric times.
Of course I feel different.
It's just, my brother says girls kinda lose their minds when they're on the rag.
"On the rag"?
Did you seriously not learn any of this stuff in sex ed?
Shyeah.
Like my old man would let me take a course with "sex" in the name.
Wait, you never even had a girls' health class or anything?
I had a gym teacher who told us it was unladylike to talk about our ***bodies.***
Speaking of which, did you find any dead ones in that thing?

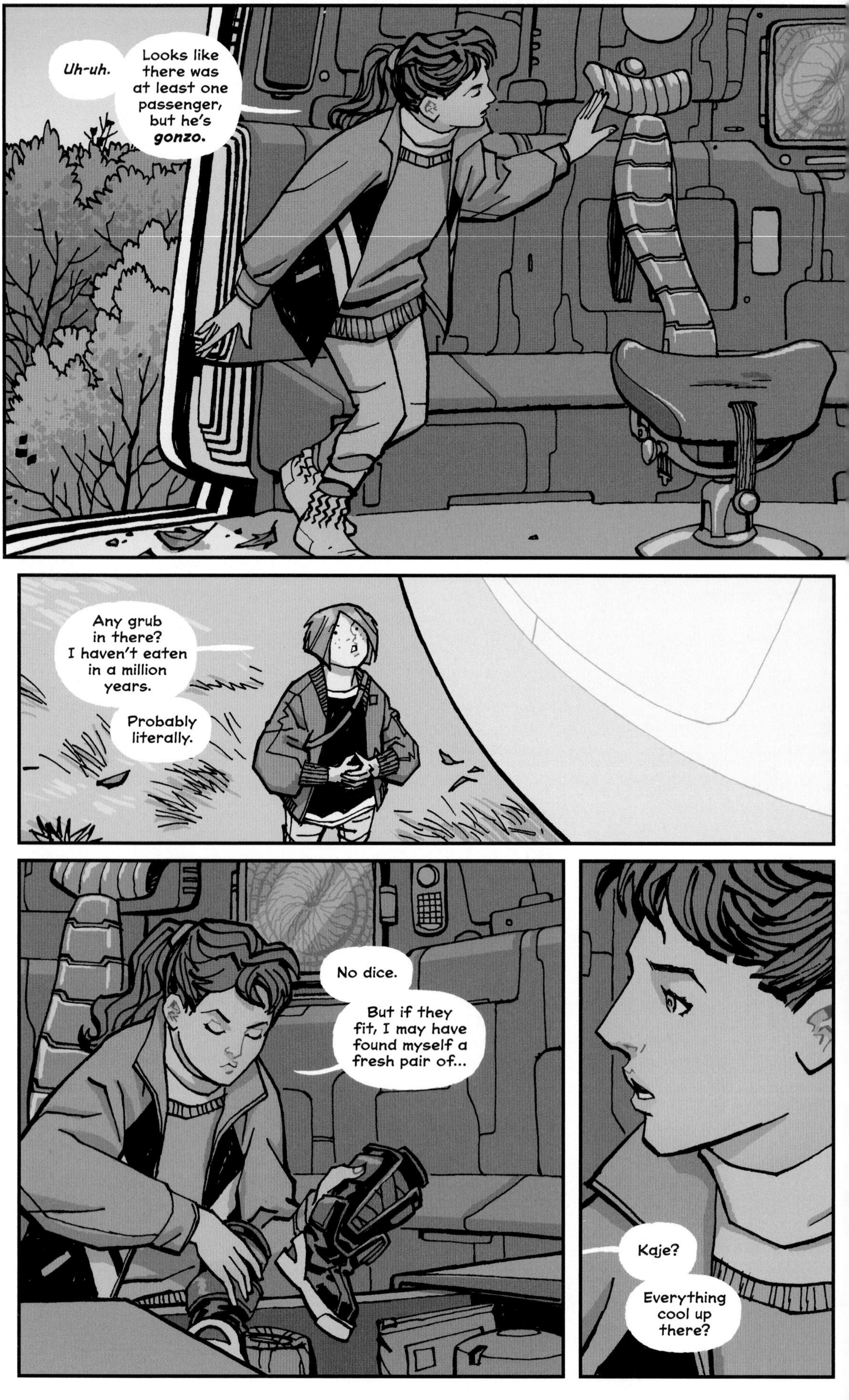
Uh-uh.
Looks like there was at least one passenger, but he's *gonzo.*
Any grub in there? I haven't eaten in a million years.
Probably literally.
No dice.
But if they fit, I may have found myself a fresh pair of...
Kaje?
Everything cool up there?

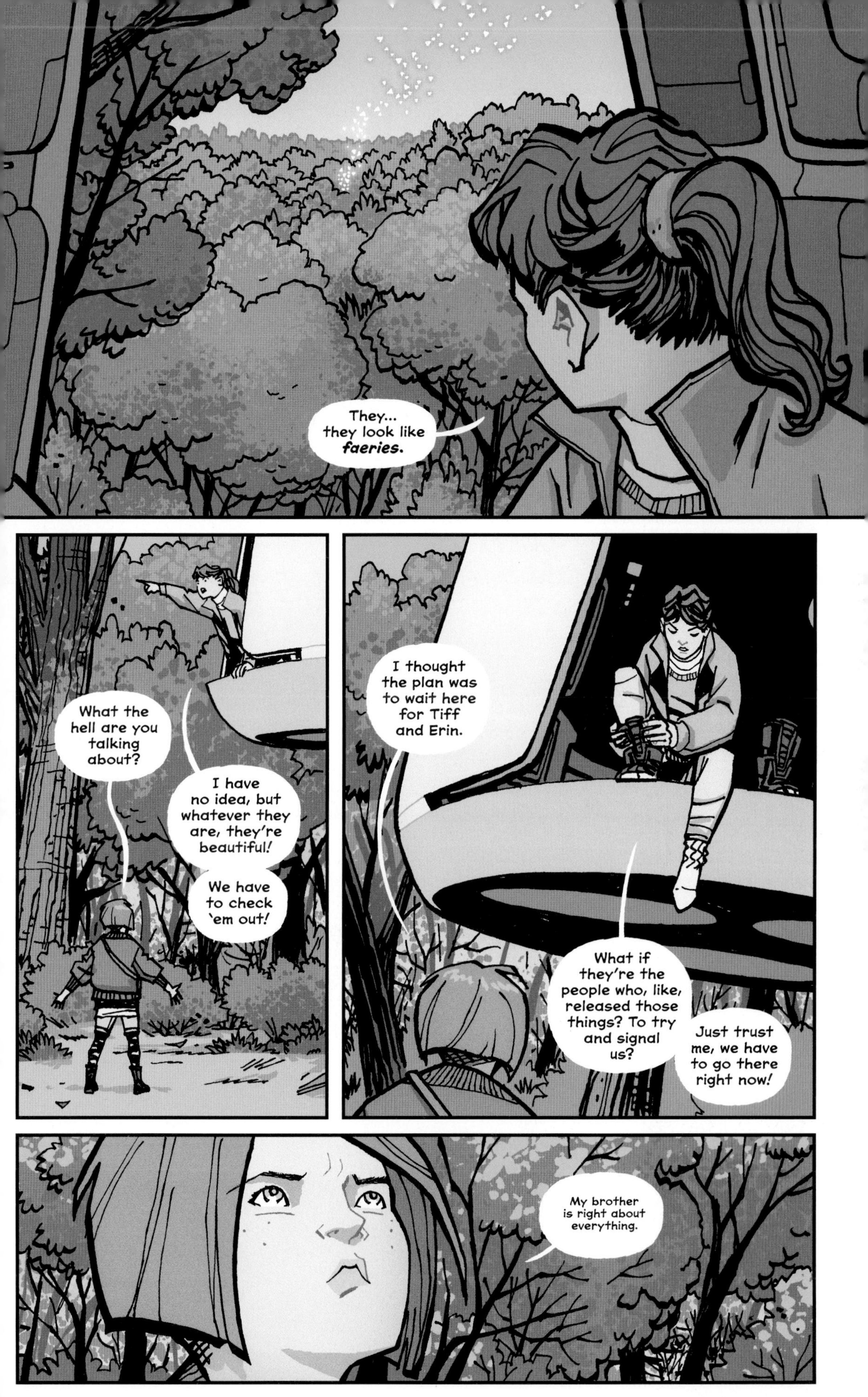
They... they look like *faeries.*
What the hell are you talking about?
I have no idea, but whatever they are, they're beautiful!
We have to check 'em out!
I thought the plan was to wait here for Tiff and Erin.
What if they're the people who, like, released those things? To try and signal us?
Just trust me, we have to go there right now!
My brother is right about everything.

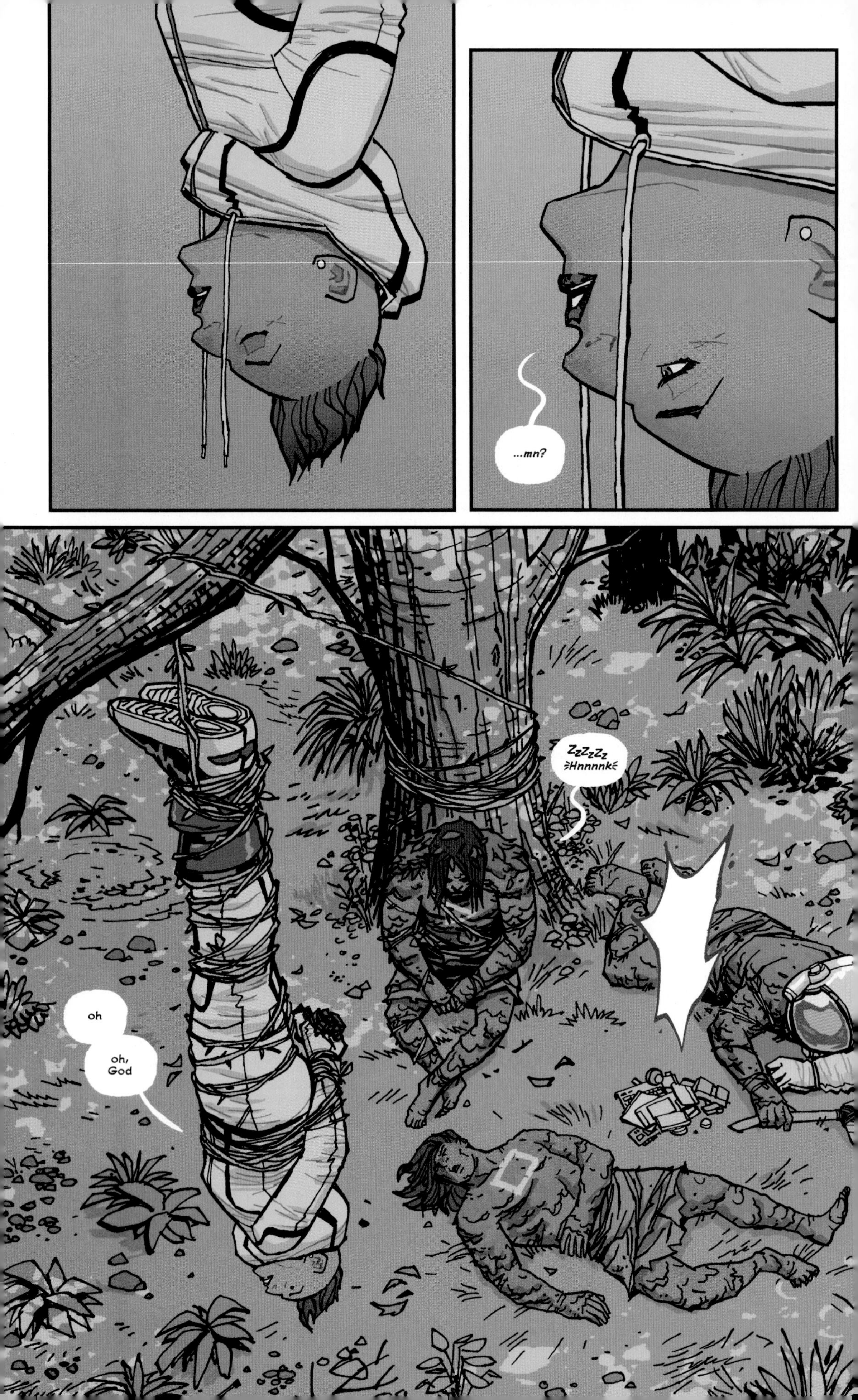
...mn?
ZzZzZz Hnnnnk
oh
oh, God

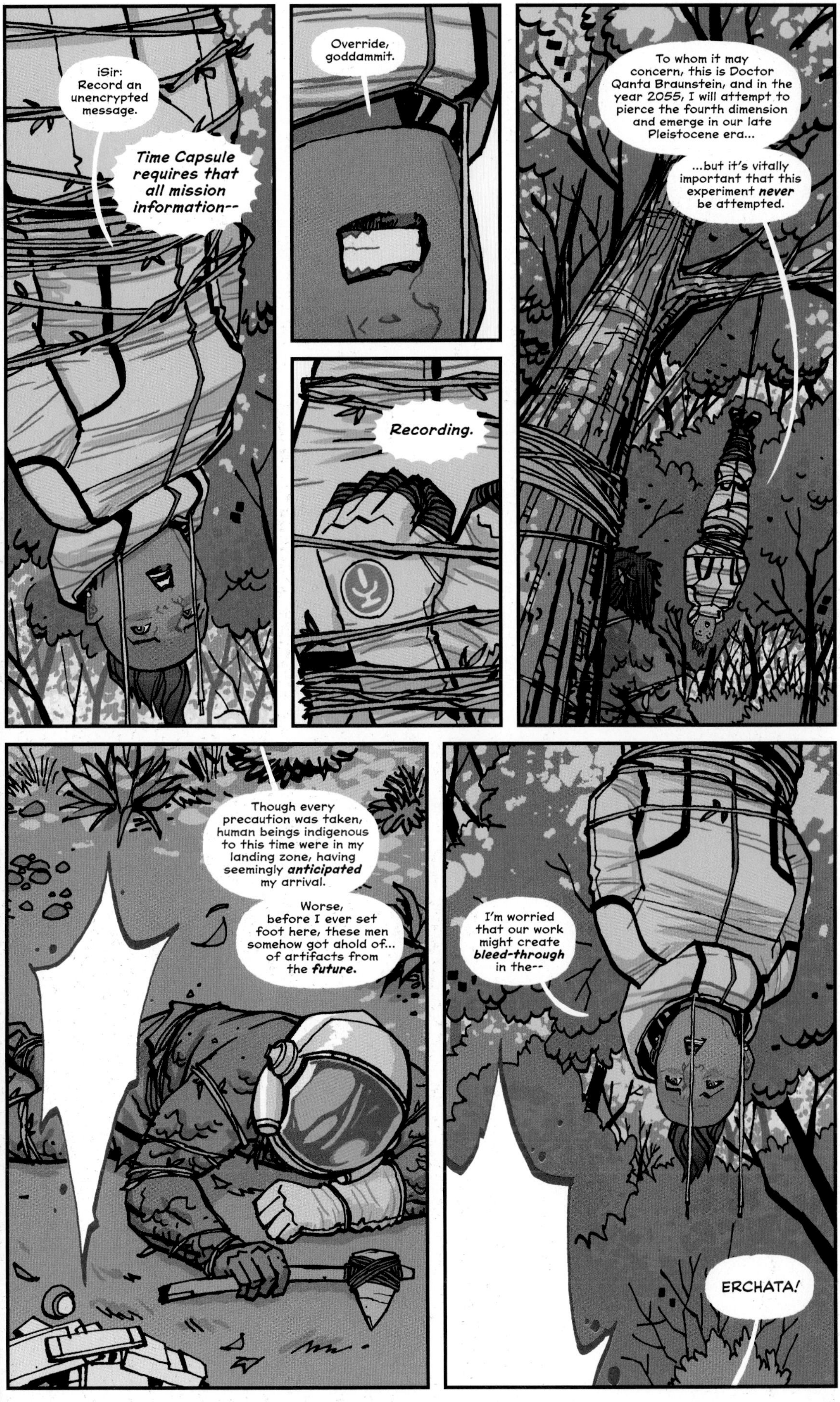
iSir: Record an unencrypted message.
Time Capsule requires that all mission information--
Override, goddammit.
Recording.
To whom it may concern, this is Doctor Qanta Braunstein, and in the year 2055, I will attempt to pierce the fourth dimension and emerge in our late Pleistocene era...
...but it's vitally important that this experiment never be attempted.
Though every precaution was taken, human beings indigenous to this time were in my landing zone, having seemingly anticipated my arrival.
Worse, before I ever set foot here, these men somehow got ahold of... of artifacts from the future.
I'm worried that our work might create bleed-through in the--
ERCHATA!

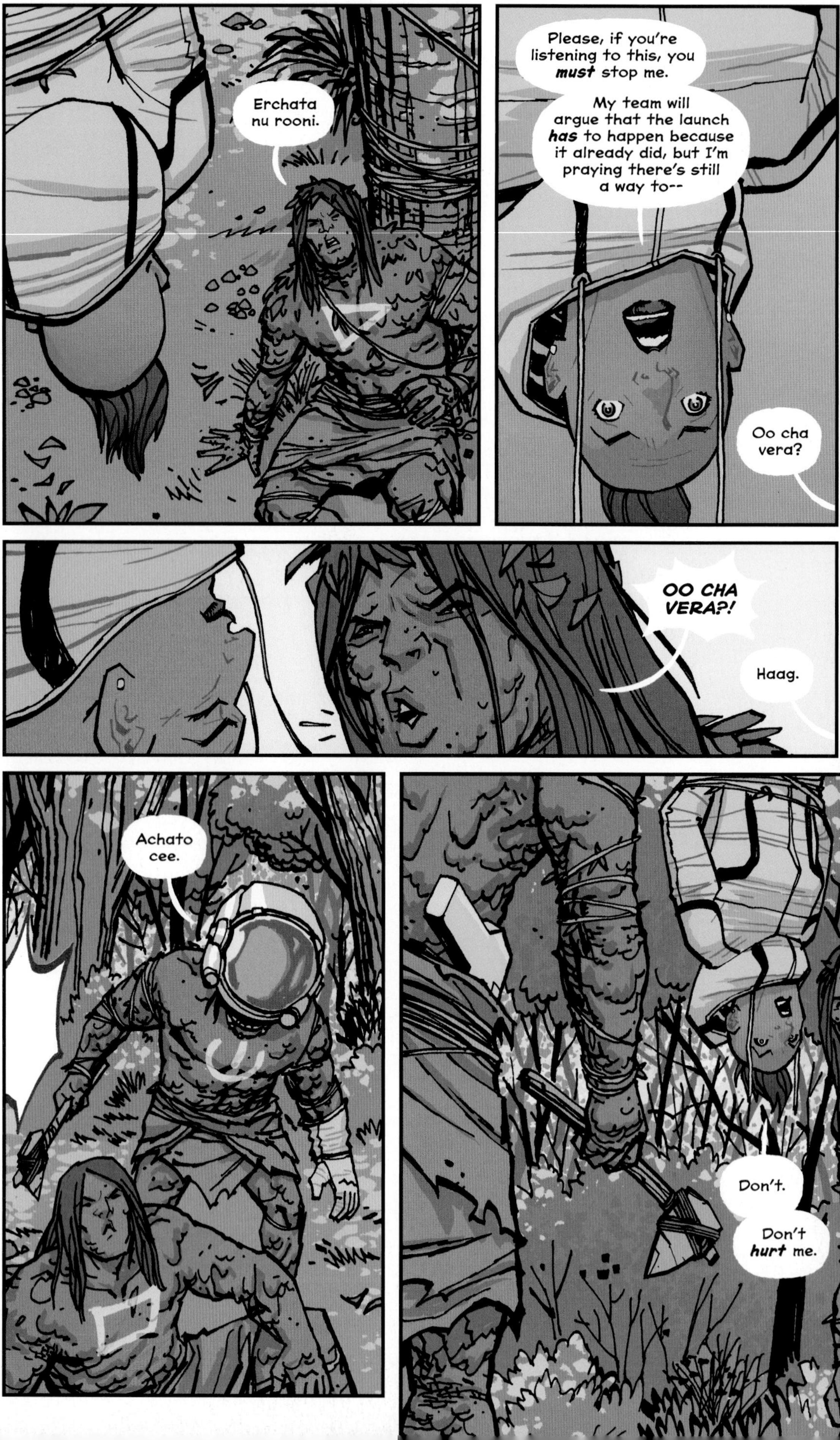
Erchata nu rooni.
Please, if you're listening to this, you **must** stop me.
My team will argue that the launch **has** to happen because it already did, but I'm praying there's still a way to--
Oo cha vera?
OO CHA VERA?!
Haag.
Achato cee.
Don't.
Don't **hurt** me.

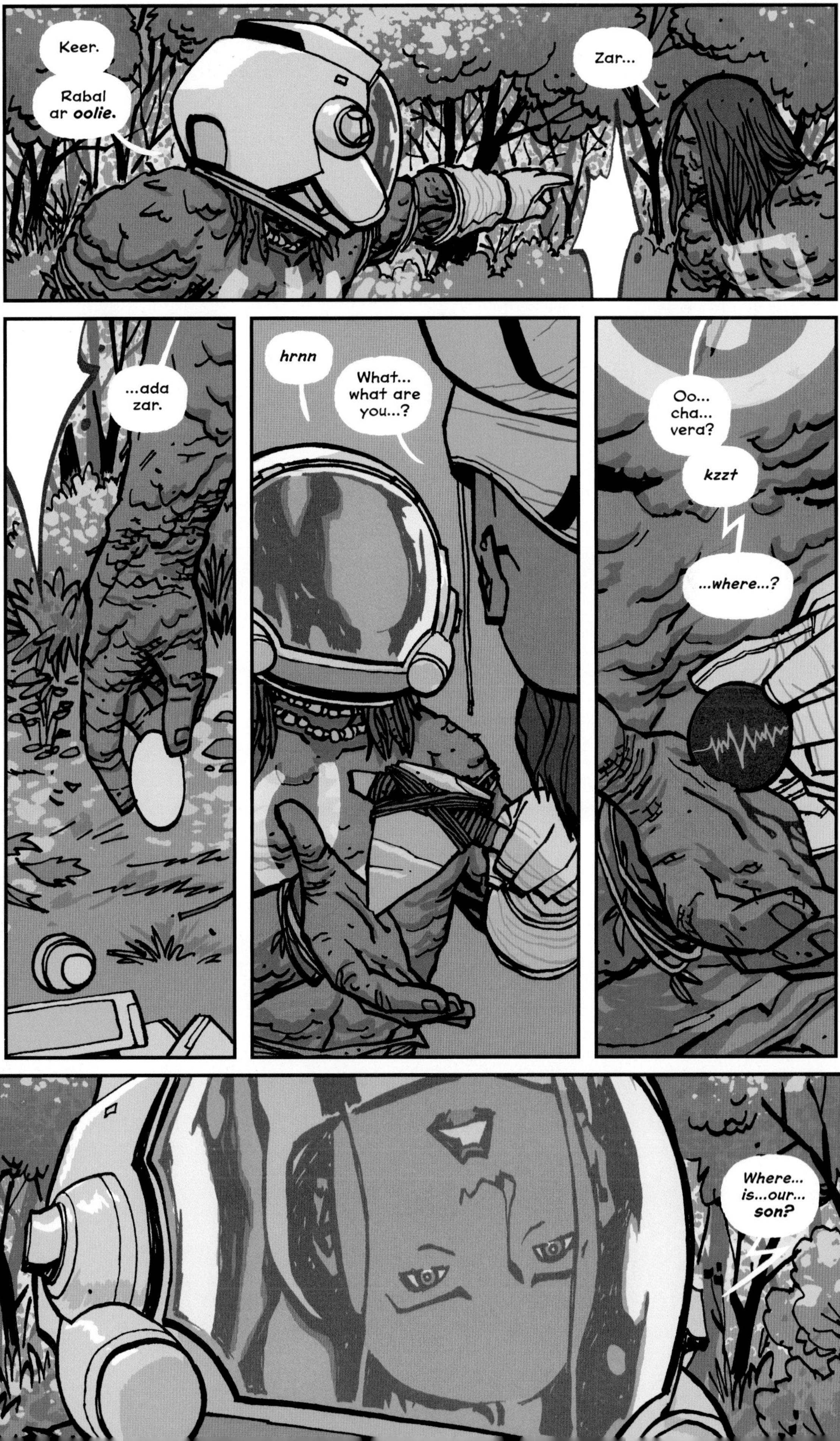
Keer.
Rabal ar *oolie*.
Zar...
...ada zar.
hrnn
What... what are you...?
Oo... cha... vera?
kzzt
...where...?
Where... is...our... son?

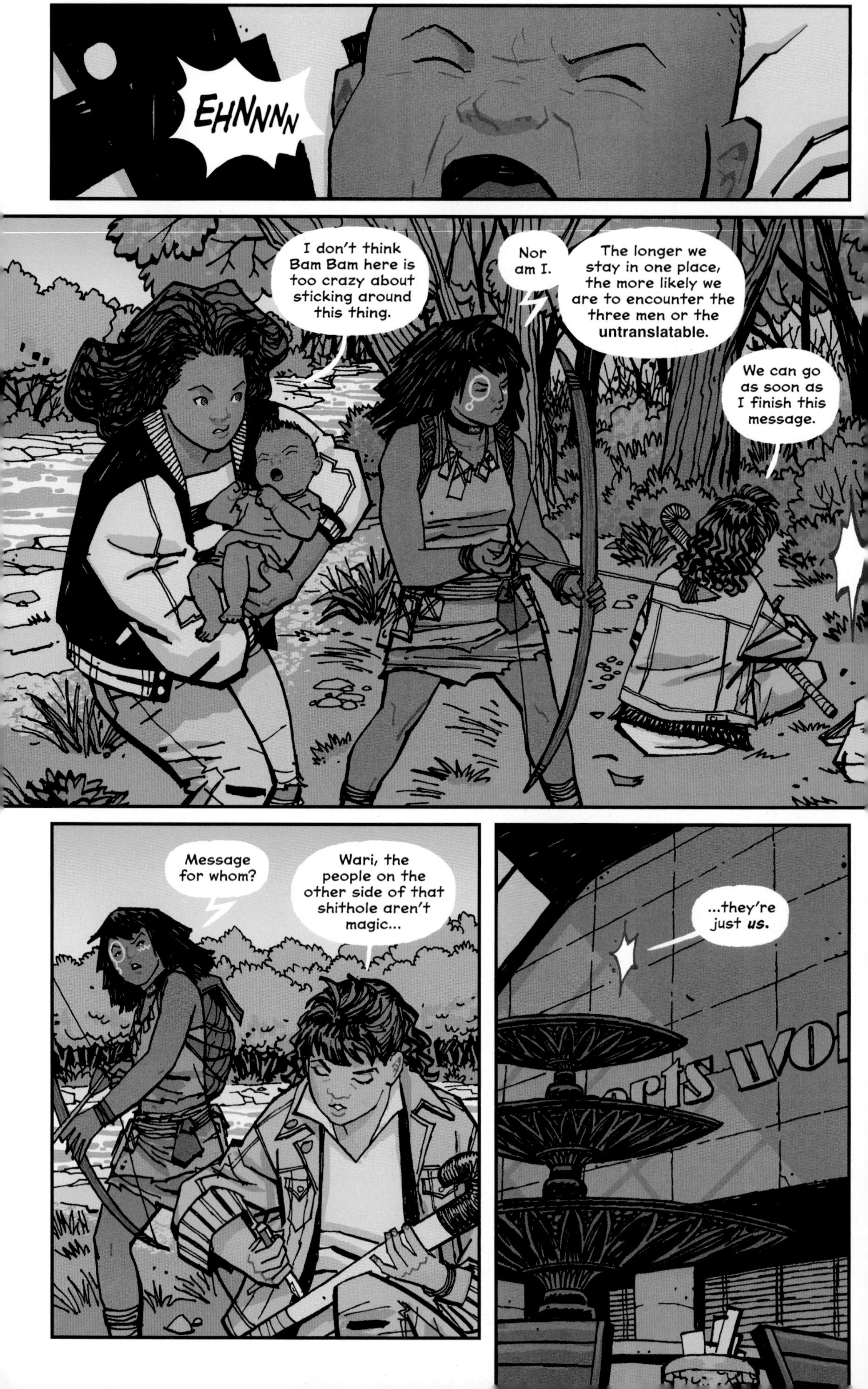
EHNNNN
I don't think Bam Bam here is too crazy about sticking around this thing.
Nor am I.
The longer we stay in one place, the more likely we are to encounter the three men or the **untranslatable.**
We can go as soon as I finish this message.
Message for whom?
Wari, the people on the other side of that shithole aren't magic...
...they're just ***us.***

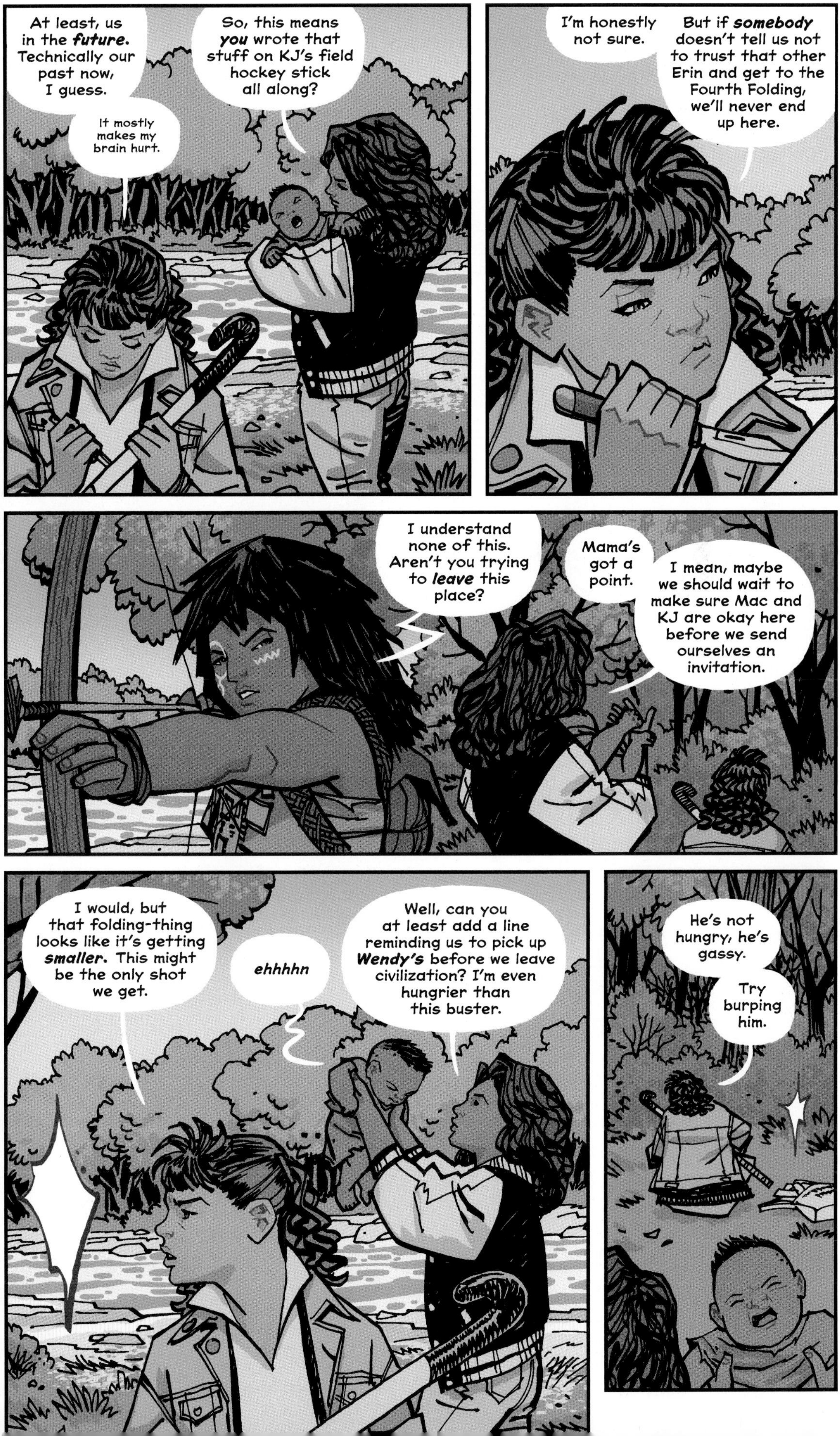
At least, us in the *future.* Technically our past now, I guess.
It mostly makes my brain hurt.
So, this means *you* wrote that stuff on KJ's field hockey stick all along?
I'm honestly not sure.
But if *somebody* doesn't tell us not to trust that other Erin and get to the Fourth Folding, we'll never end up here.
I understand none of this. Aren't you trying to *leave* this place?
Mama's got a point.
I mean, maybe we should wait to make sure Mac and KJ are okay here before we send ourselves an invitation.
I would, but that folding-thing looks like it's getting *smaller.* This might be the only shot we get.
ehhhhn
Well, can you at least add a line reminding us to pick up *Wendy's* before we leave civilization? I'm even hungrier than this buster.
He's not hungry, he's gassy.
Try burping him.

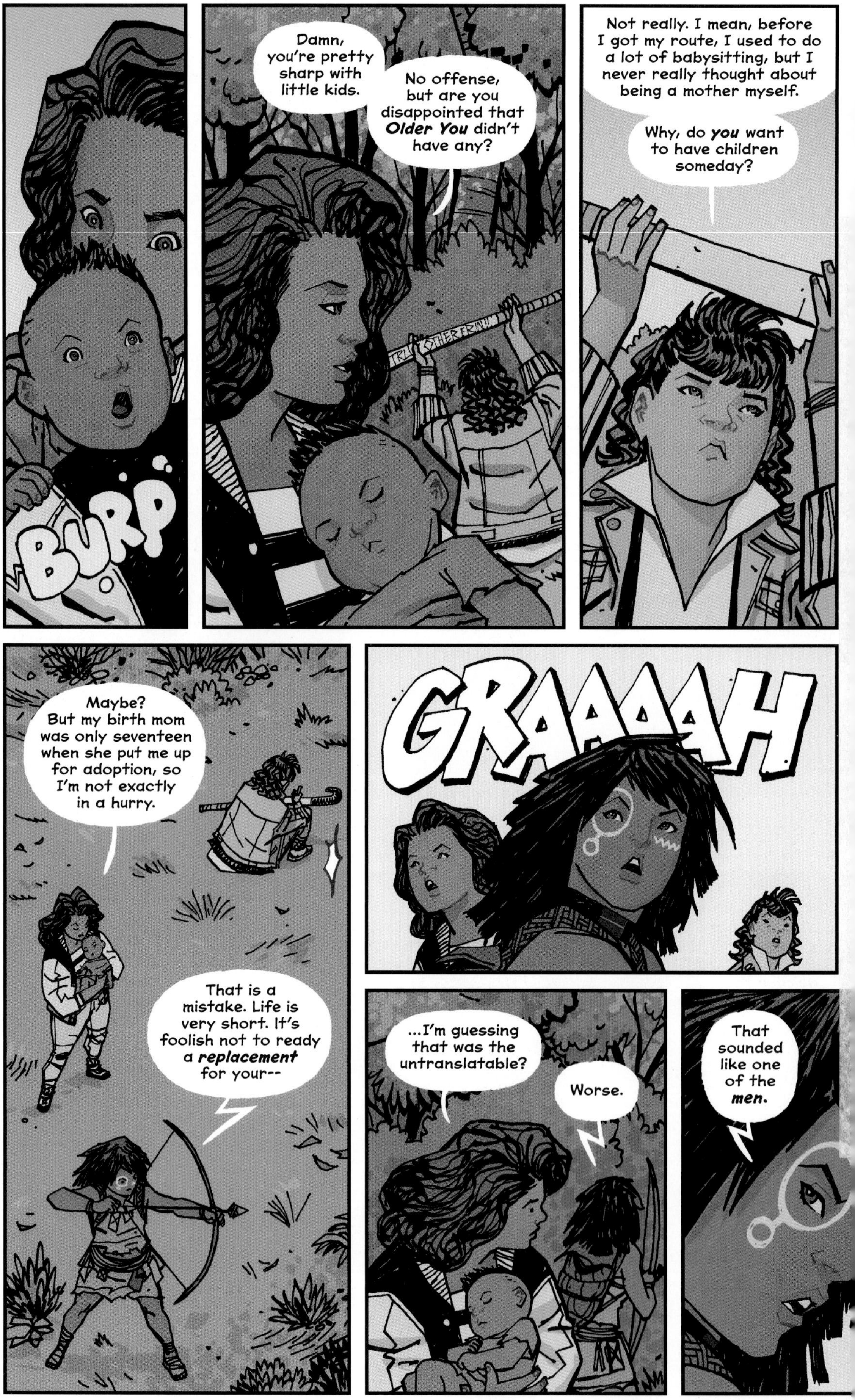
BURP
Damn, you're pretty sharp with little kids.
No offense, but are you disappointed that Older You didn't have any?
Not really. I mean, before I got my route, I used to do a lot of babysitting, but I never really thought about being a mother myself.
Why, do you want to have children someday?
Maybe? But my birth mom was only seventeen when she put me up for adoption, so I'm not exactly in a hurry.
That is a mistake. Life is very short. It's foolish not to ready a replacement for your--
GRAAAAH
...I'm guessing that was the untranslatable?
Worse.
That sounded like one of the men.

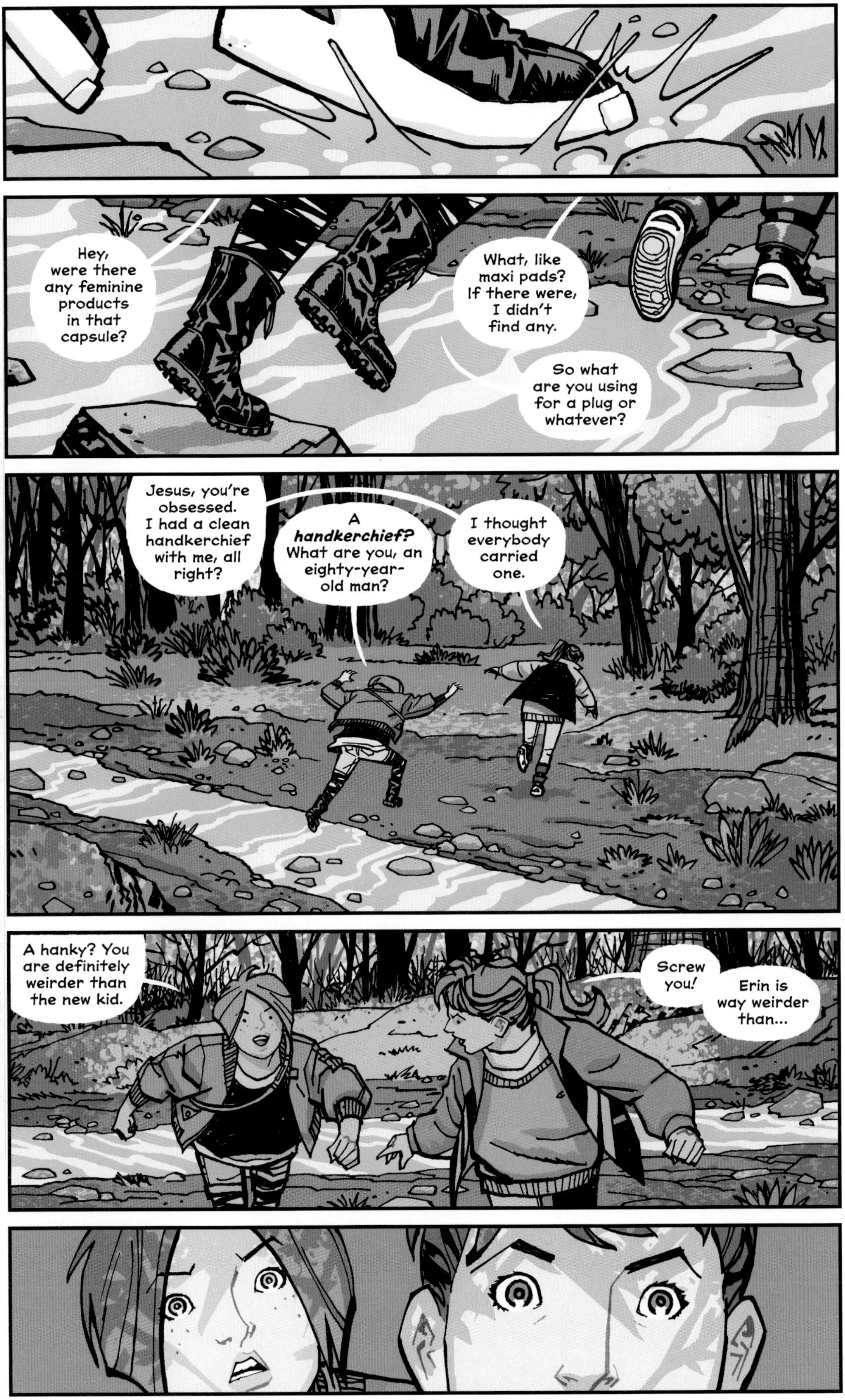
Hey, were there any feminine products in that capsule?
What, like maxi pads? If there were, I didn't find any.
So what are you using for a plug or whatever?
Jesus, you're obsessed. I had a clean handkerchief with me, all right?
A ***handkerchief?*** What are you, an eighty-year-old man?
I thought everybody carried one.
A hanky? You are definitely weirder than the new kid.
Screw you!
Erin is way weirder than...

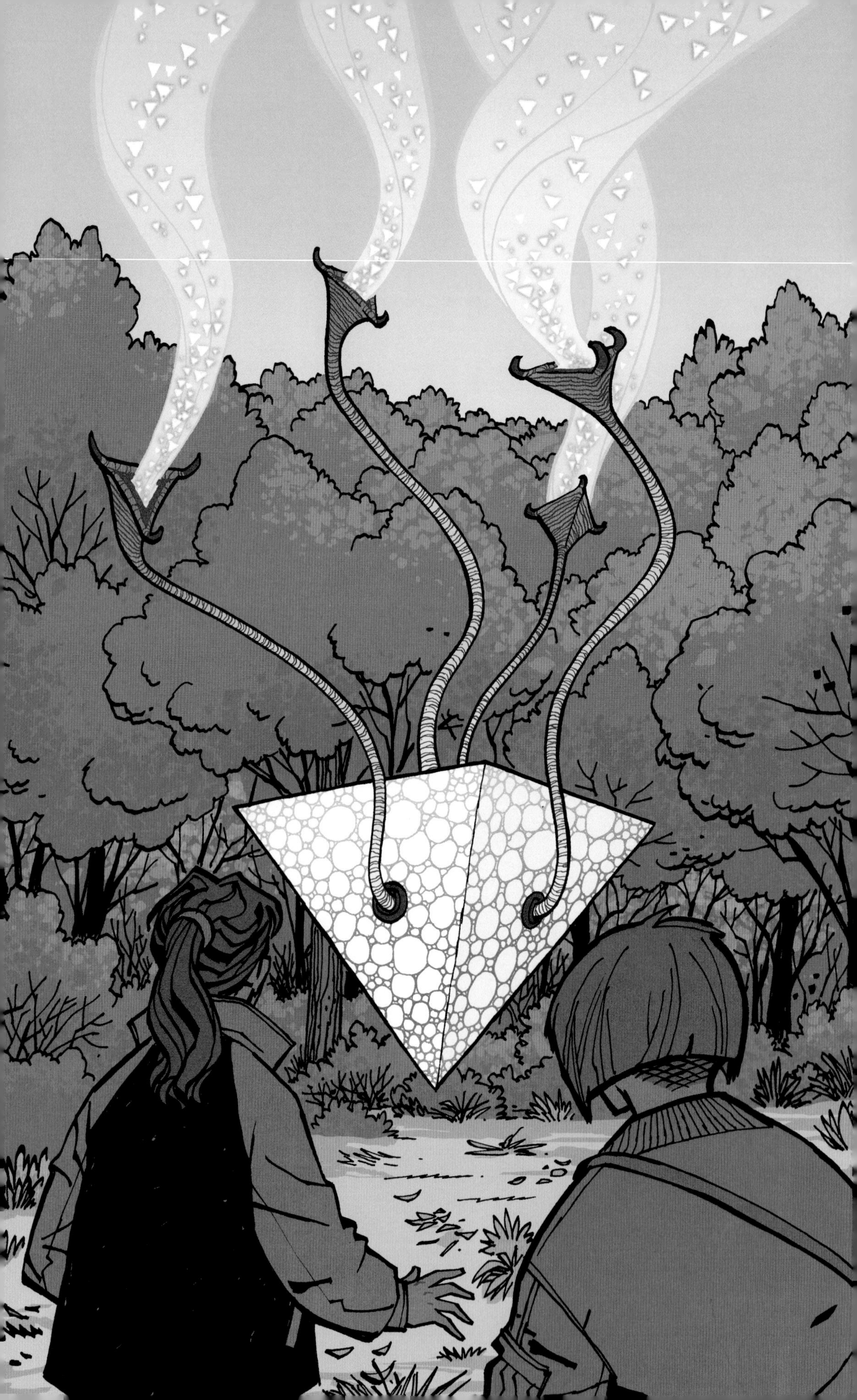

It's....it's another *monster*.

Like the thing that attacked Tiff.

This isn't a monster.

This is magnificent.

What the hell are you doing?!

I wonder what it feels like.

Don't you want to know how it...

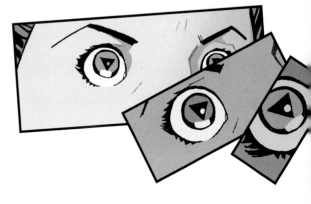

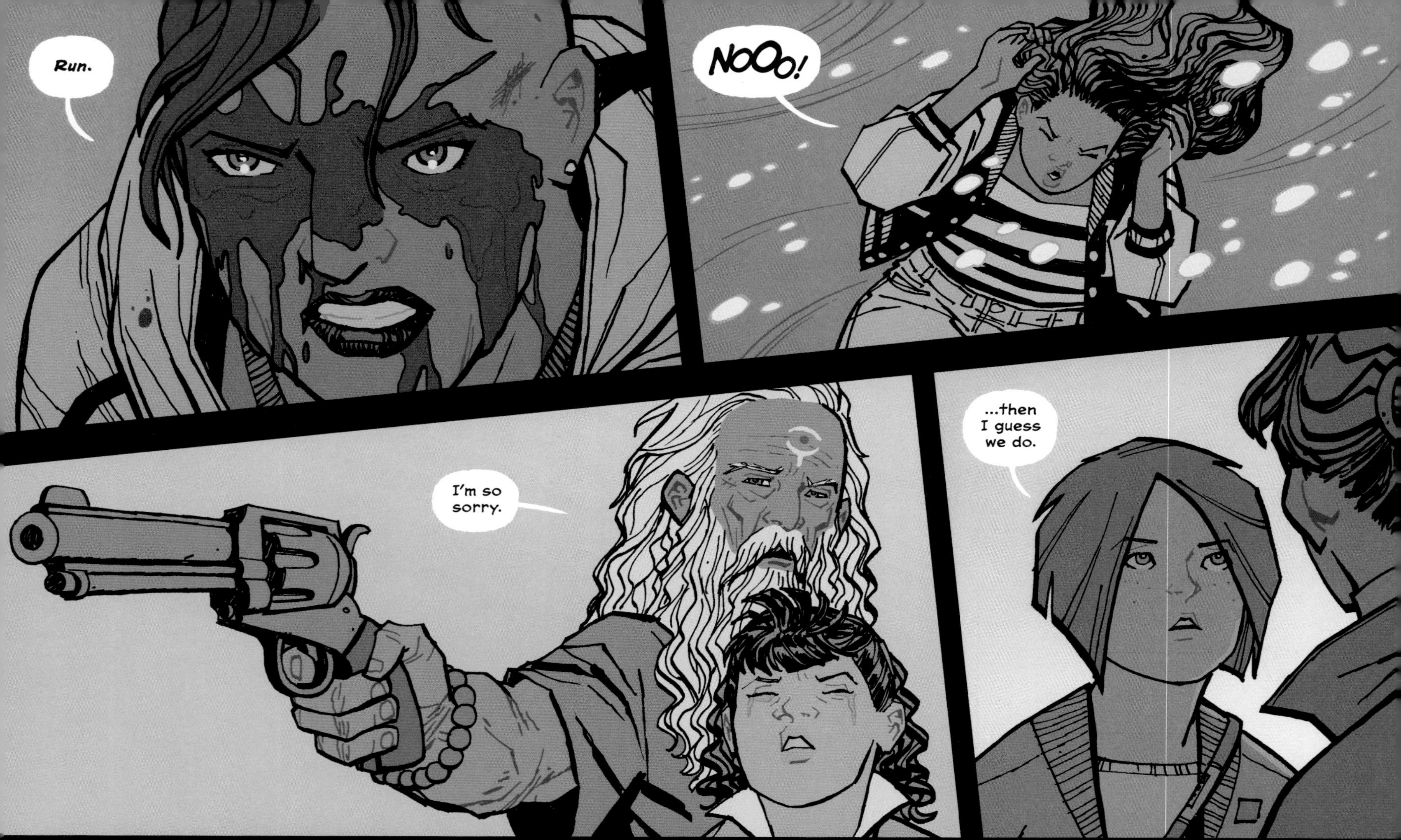
Run.
NOOo!
...then I guess we do.
I'm so sorry.

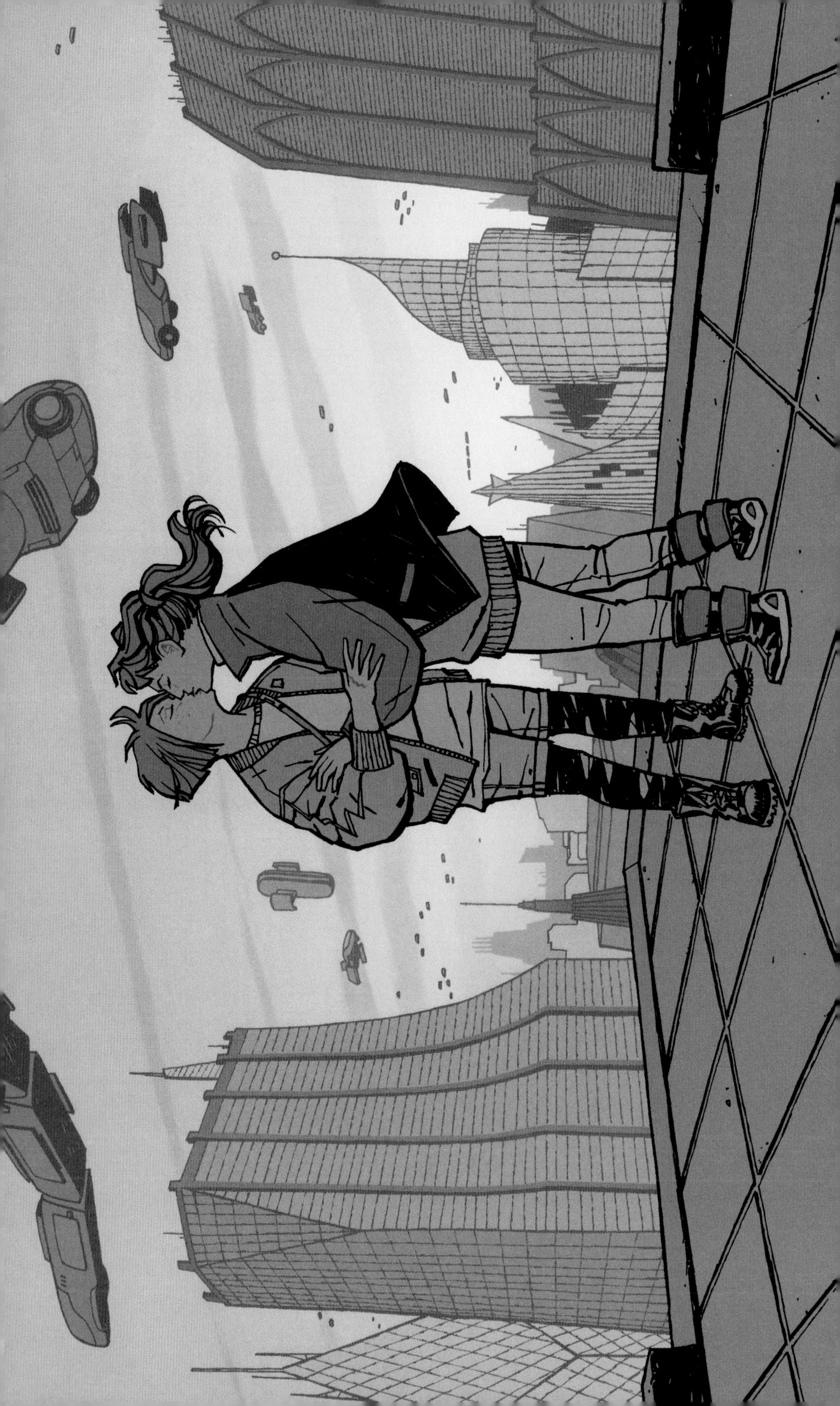

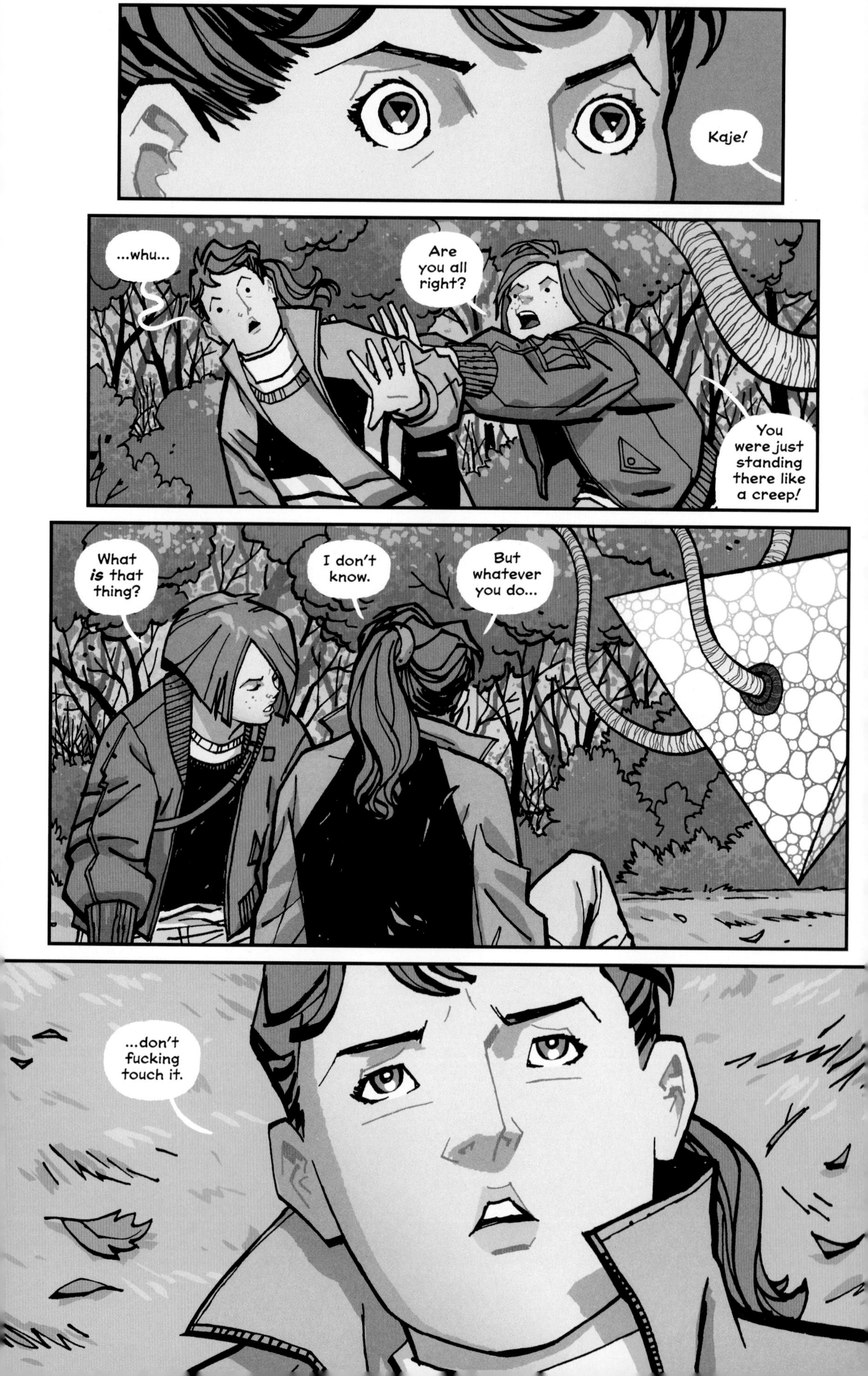
Kaje!
...whu...
Are you all right?
You were just standing there like a creep!
What *is* that thing?
I don't know.
But whatever you do...
...don't fucking touch it.

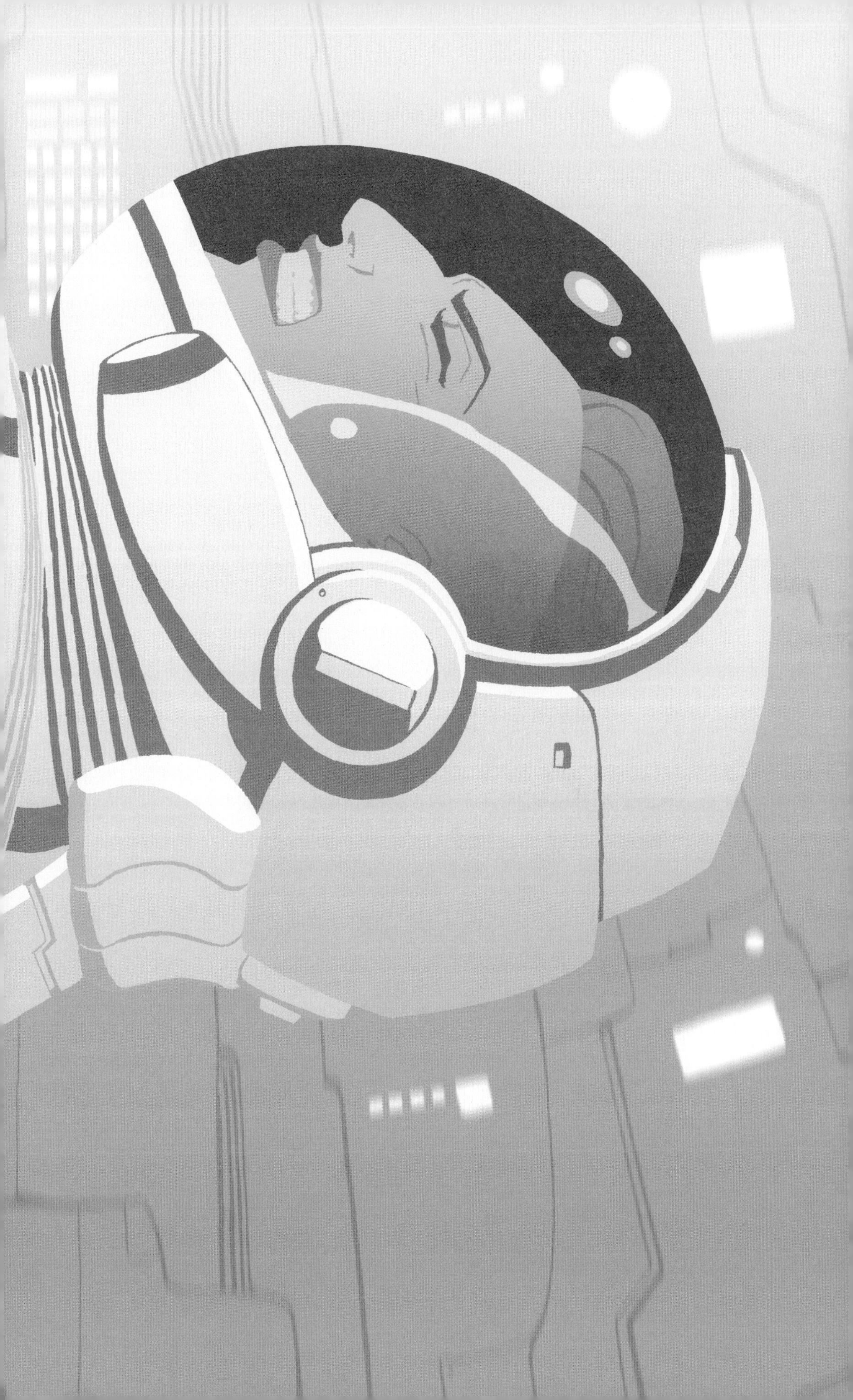

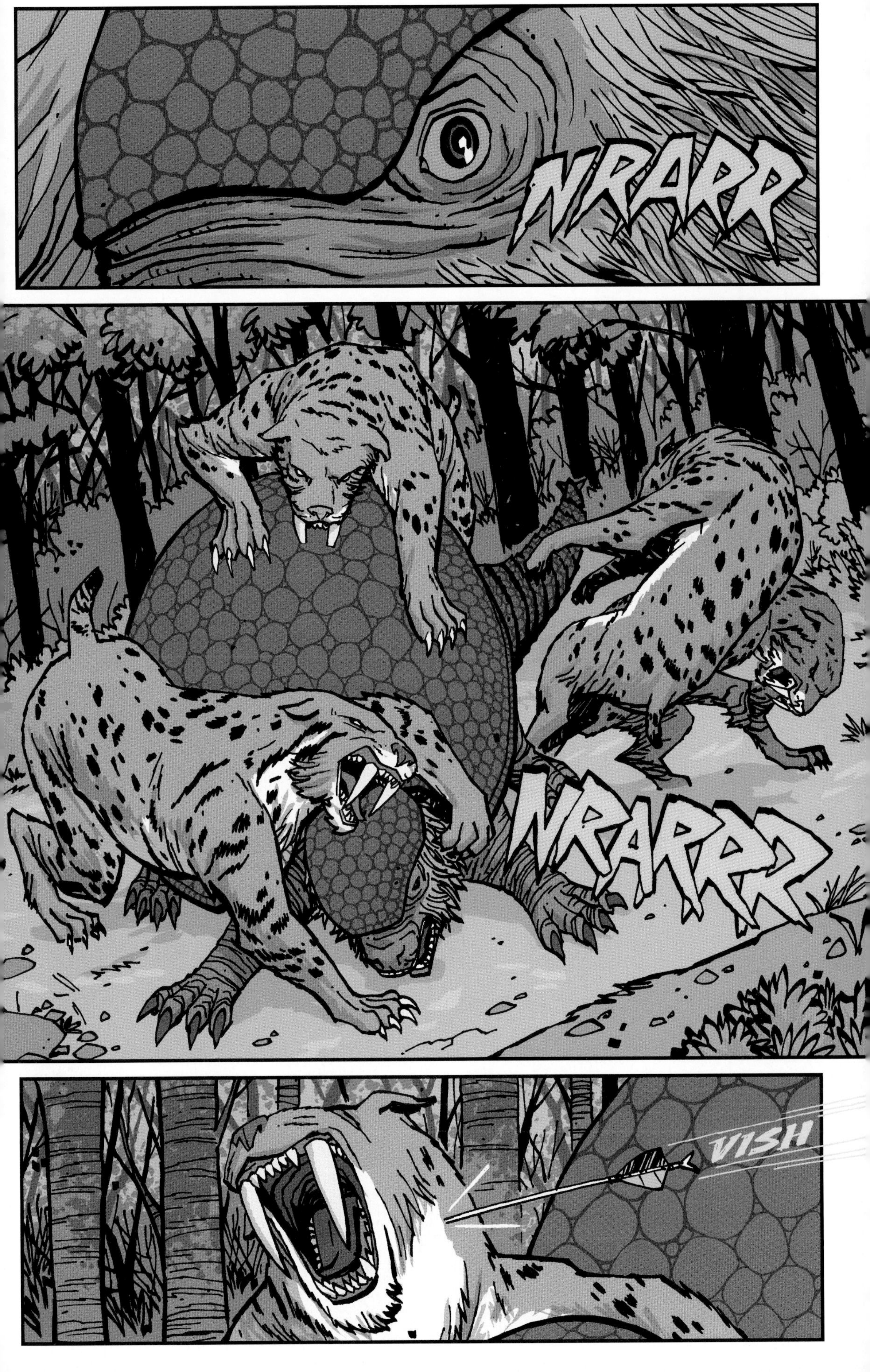

NRARR
NRARRR
VISH

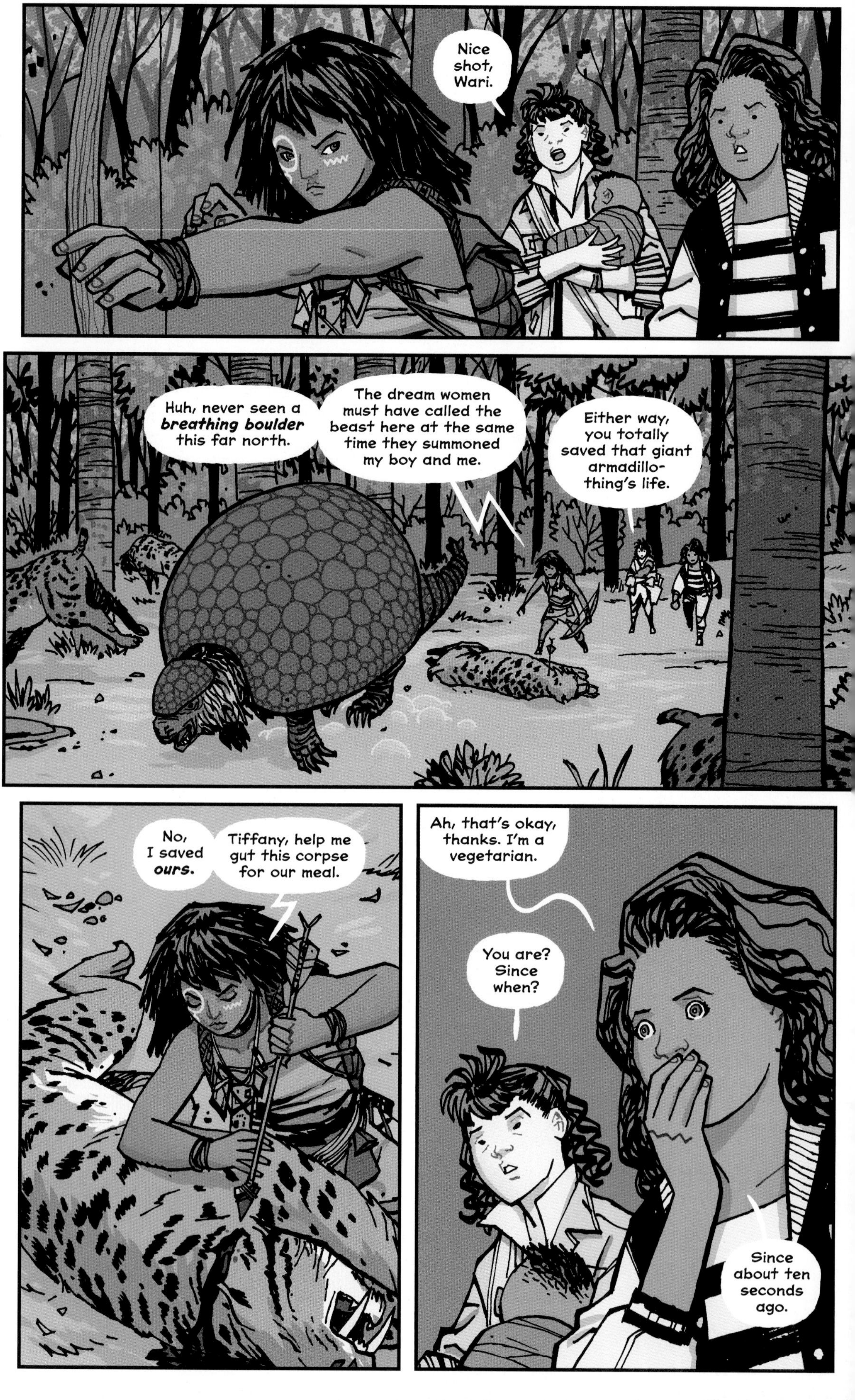
Nice shot, Wari.
Huh, never seen a **breathing boulder** this far north.
The dream women must have called the beast here at the same time they summoned my boy and me.
Either way, you totally saved that giant armadillo-thing's life.
No, I saved **ours.**
Tiffany, help me gut this corpse for our meal.
Ah, that's okay, thanks. I'm a vegetarian.
You are? Since when?
Since about ten seconds ago.

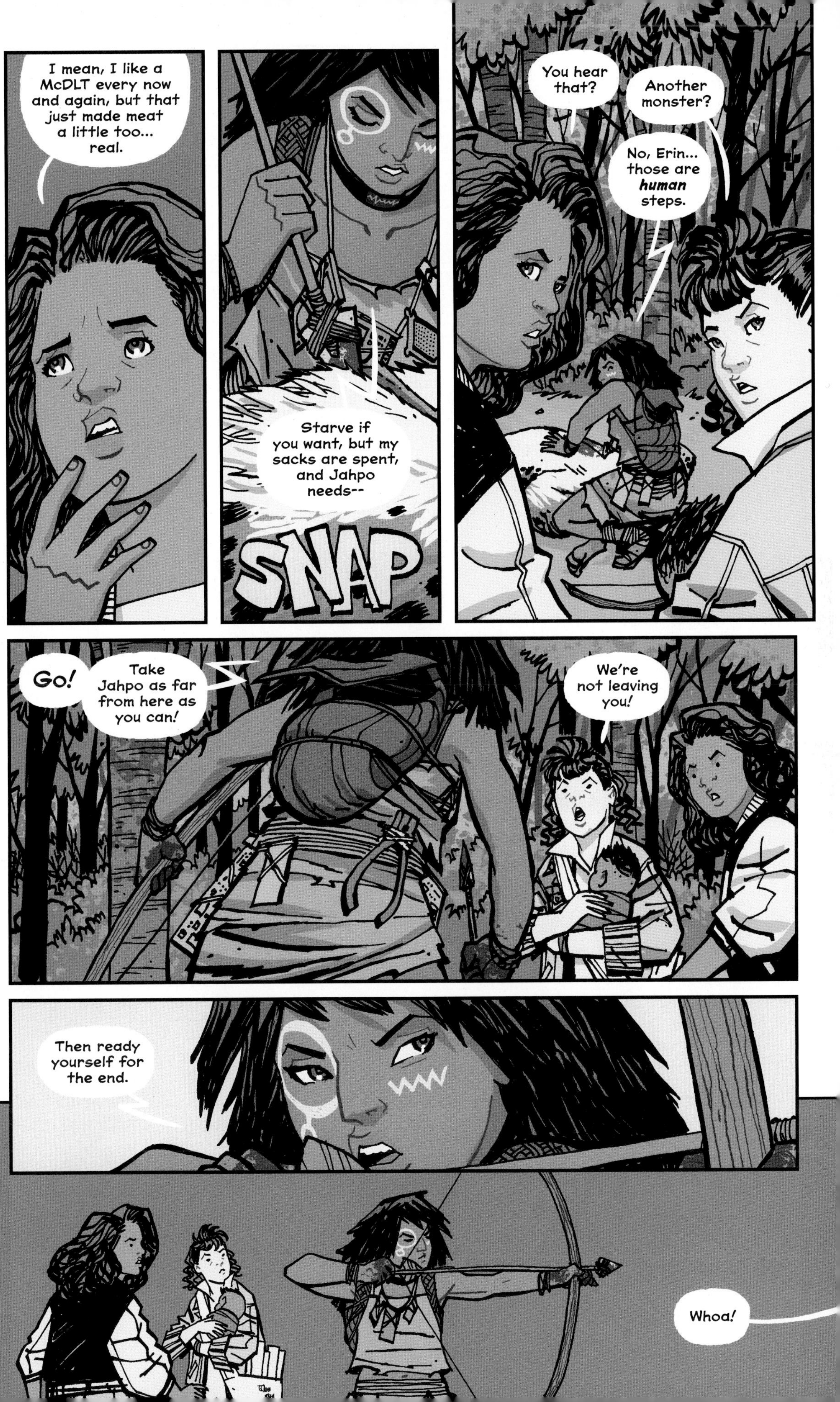

I mean, I like a McDLT every now and again, but that just made meat a little too... real.
Starve if you want, but my sacks are spent, and Jahpo needs--
SNAP
You hear that?
Another monster?
No, Erin... those are **human** steps.
Go!
Take Jahpo as far from here as you can!
We're not leaving you!
Then ready yourself for the end.
Whoa!

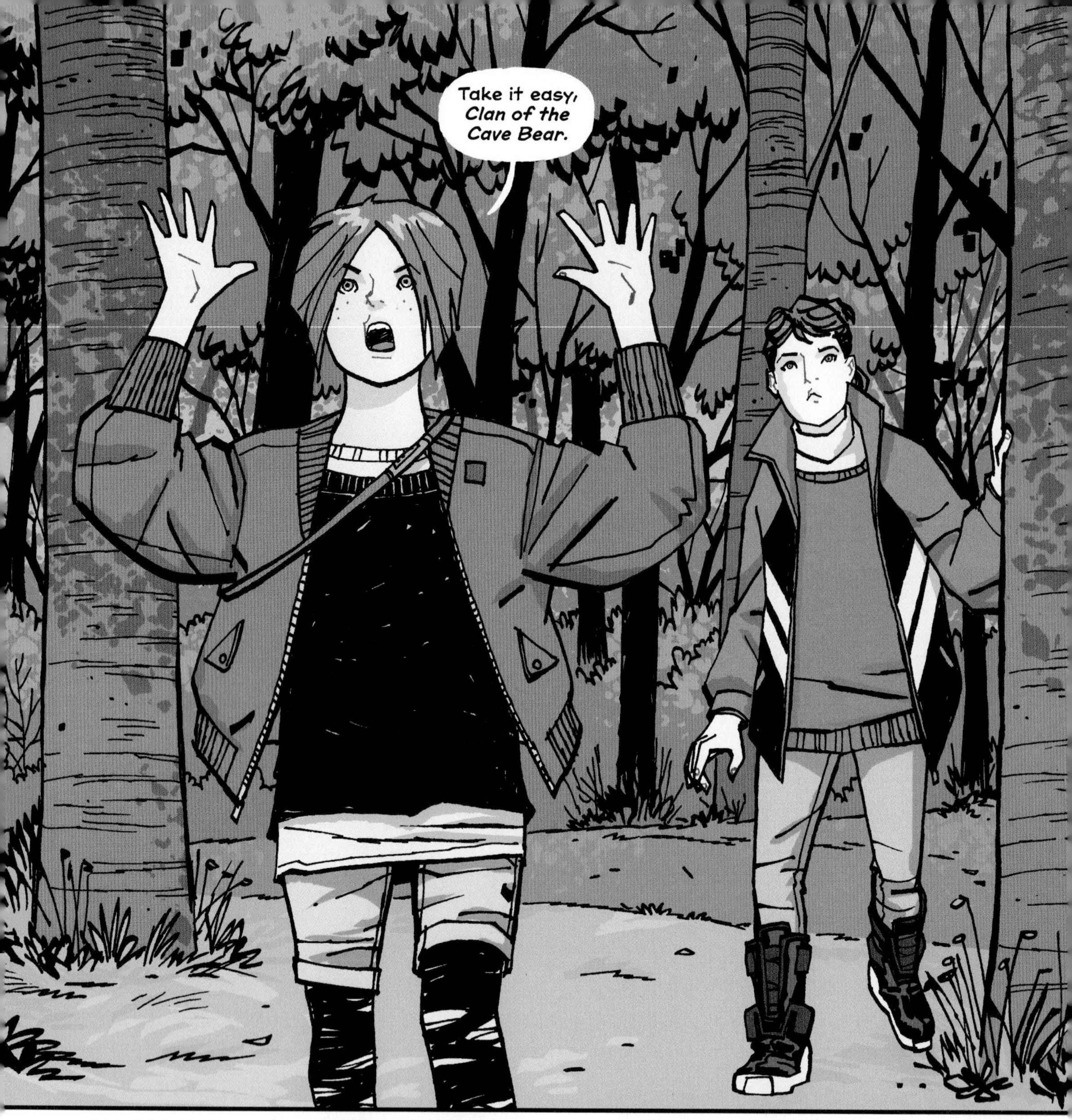
Take it easy, Clan of the Cave Bear.

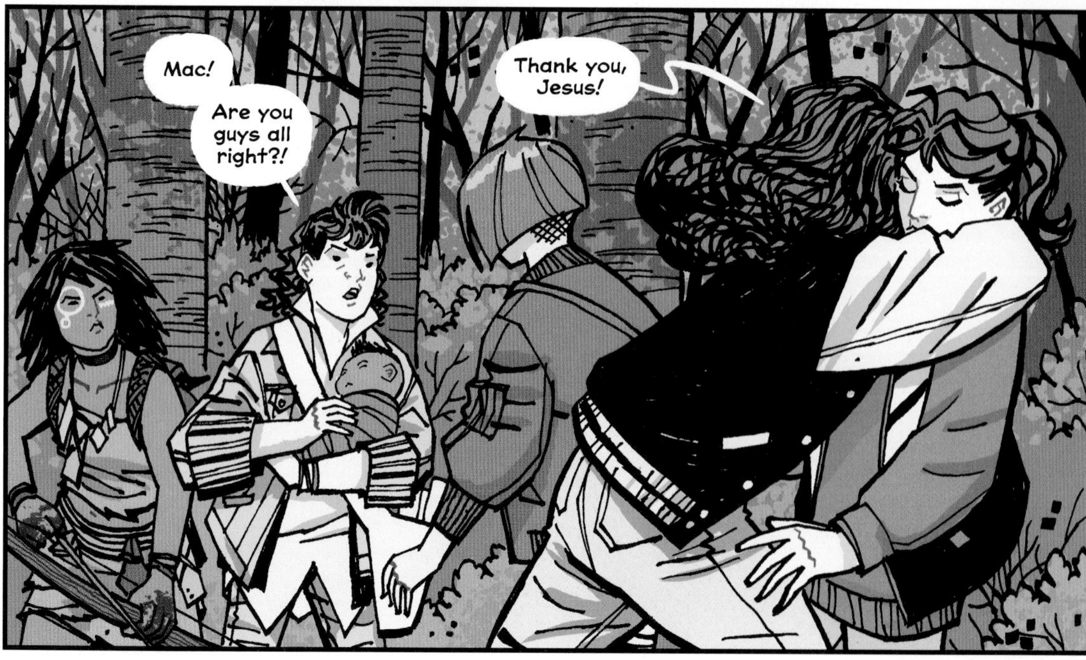
Mac!
Are you guys all right?!
Thank you, Jesus!

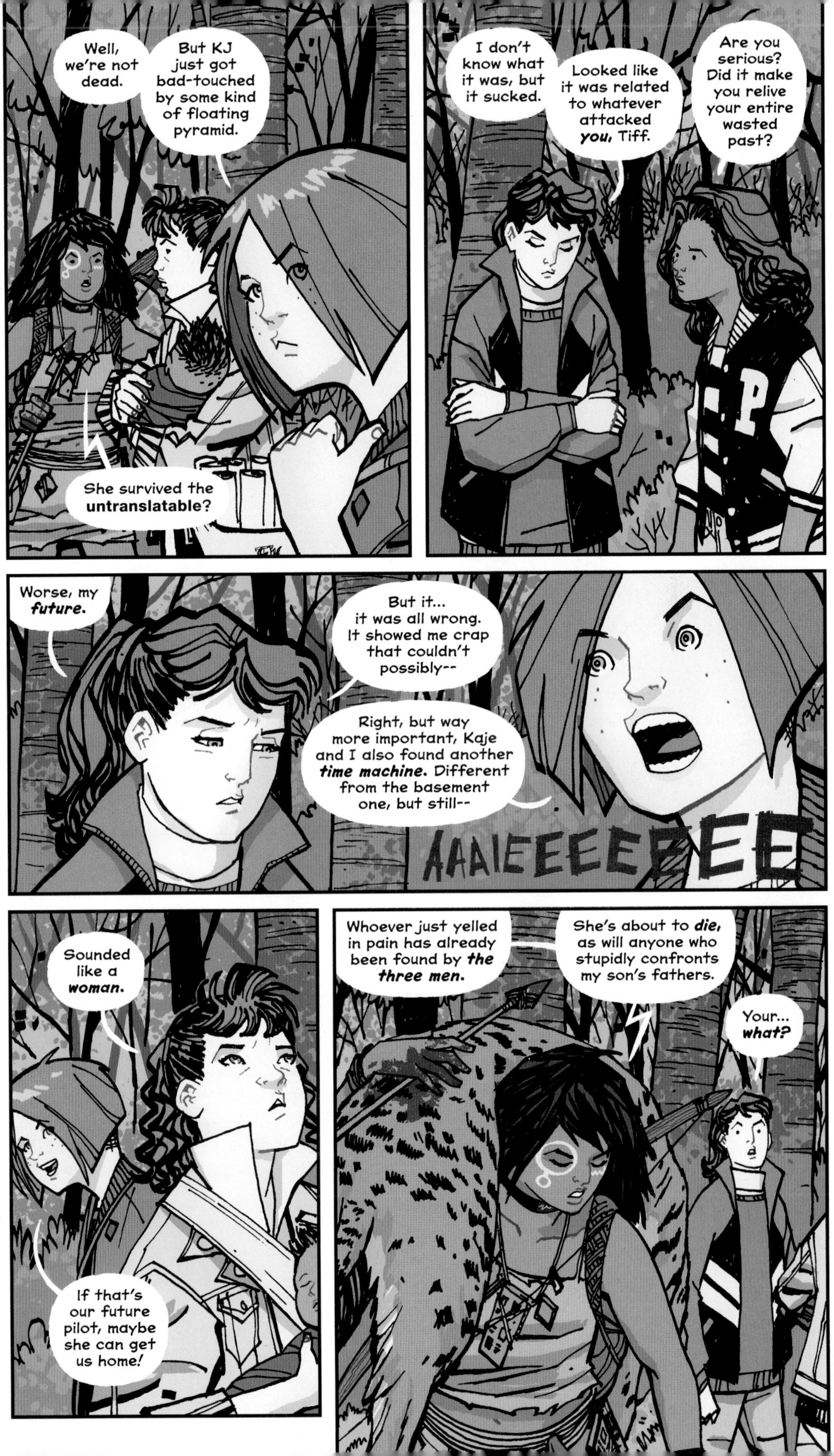
Well, we're not dead.
But KJ just got bad-touched by some kind of floating pyramid.
She survived the **untranslatable?**
I don't know what it was, but it sucked.
Looked like it was related to whatever attacked ***you,*** Tiff.
Are you serious? Did it make you relive your entire wasted past?
Worse, my ***future.***
But it... it was all wrong. It showed me crap that couldn't possibly--
Right, but way more important, Kaje and I also found another ***time machine.*** Different from the basement one, but still--
AAAIEEEEEEE
Sounded like a ***woman.***
If that's our future pilot, maybe she can get us home!
Whoever just yelled in pain has already been found by ***the three men.***
She's about to ***die,*** as will anyone who stupidly confronts my son's fathers.
Your... ***what?***

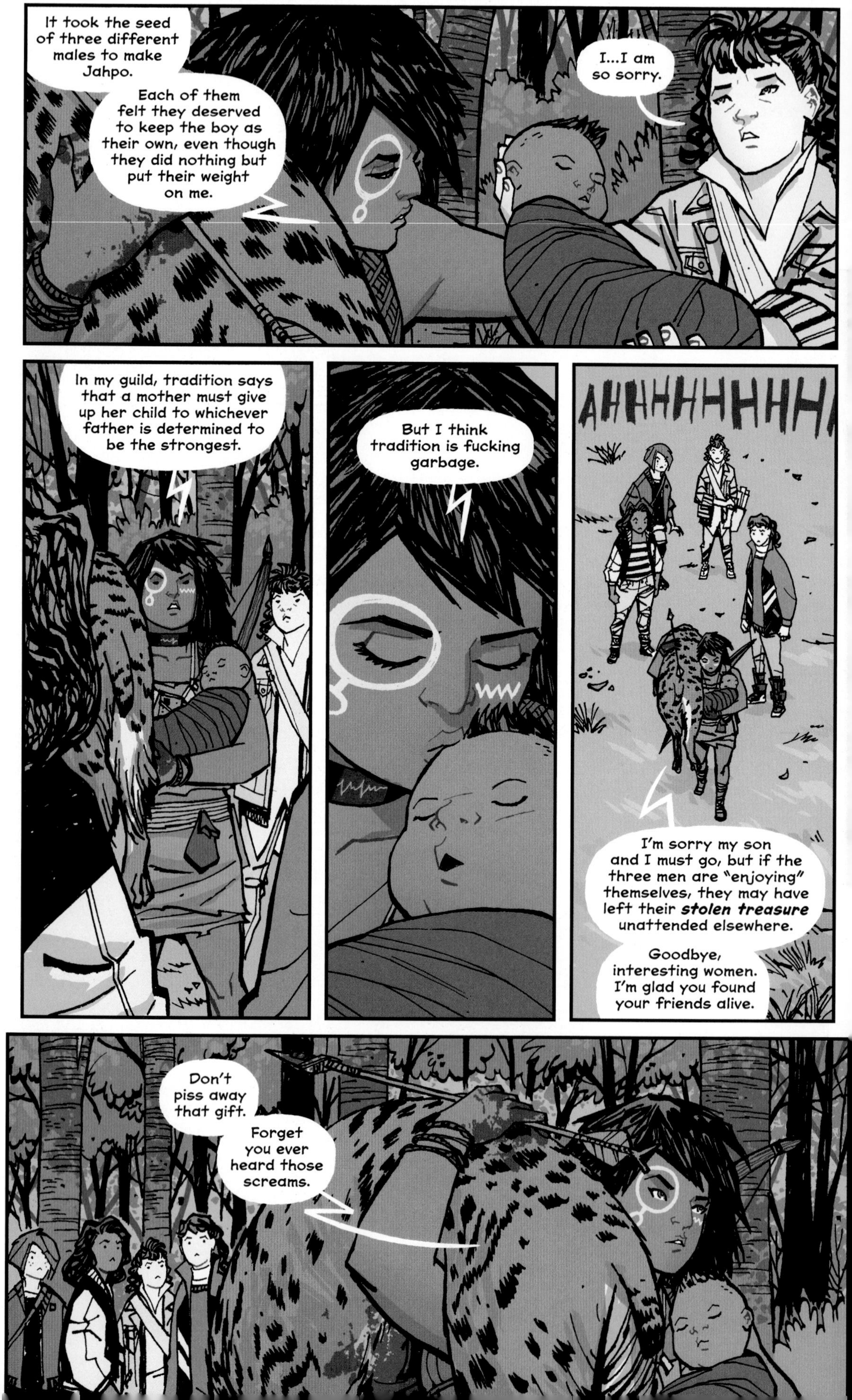

It took the seed of three different males to make Jahpo.
Each of them felt they deserved to keep the boy as their own, even though they did nothing but put their weight on me.
I...I am so sorry.
In my guild, tradition says that a mother must give up her child to whichever father is determined to be the strongest.
But I think tradition is fucking garbage.
AHHHHHHHH
I'm sorry my son and I must go, but if the three men are "enjoying" themselves, they may have left their **stolen treasure** unattended elsewhere.
Goodbye, interesting women. I'm glad you found your friends alive.
Don't piss away that gift.
Forget you ever heard those screams.

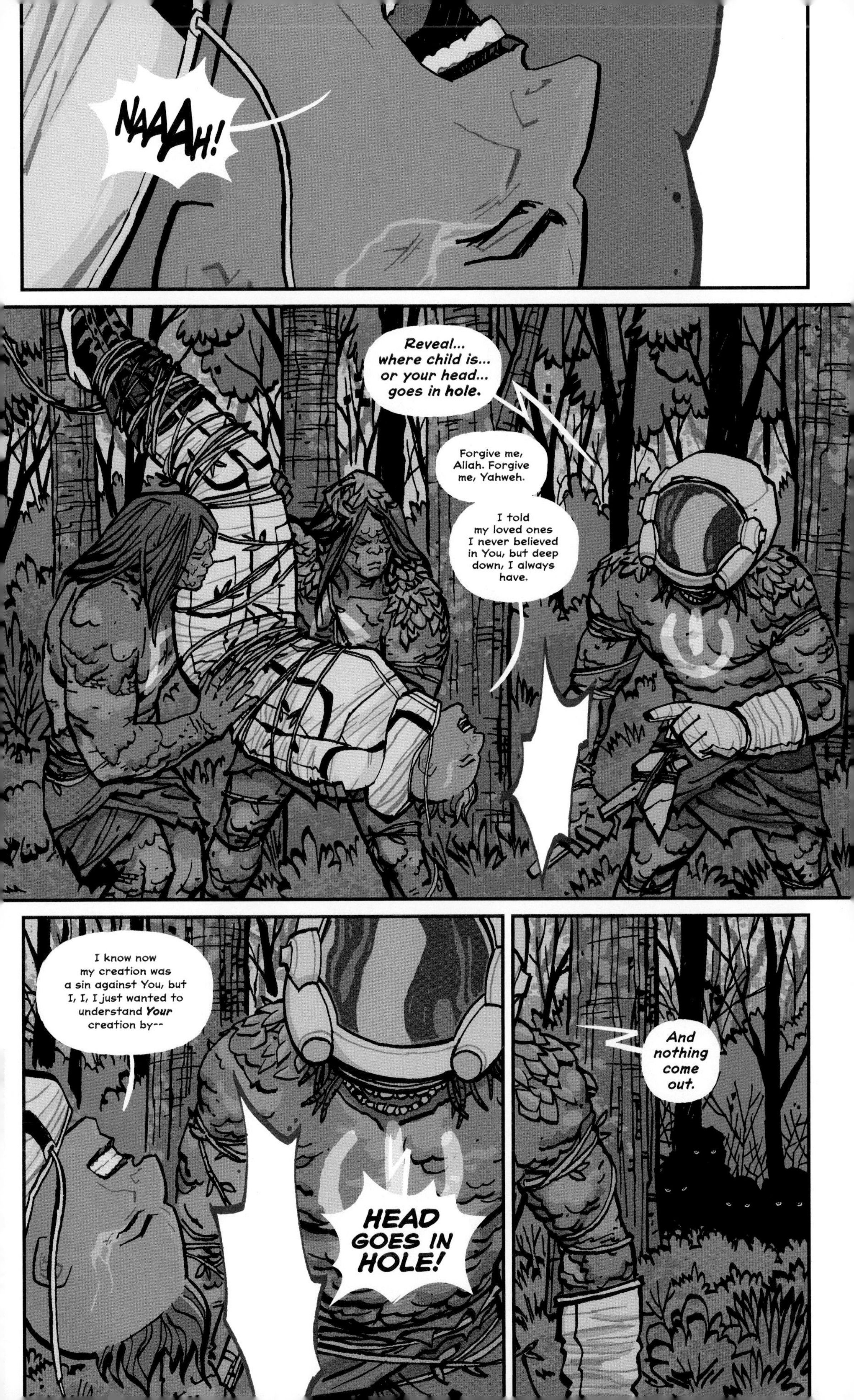
NAAAAH!
Reveal... where child is... or your head... goes in hole.
Forgive me, Allah. Forgive me, Yahweh.
I told my loved ones I never believed in You, but deep down, I always have.
I know now my creation was a sin against You, but I, I, I just wanted to understand Your creation by--
HEAD GOES IN HOLE!
And nothing come out.

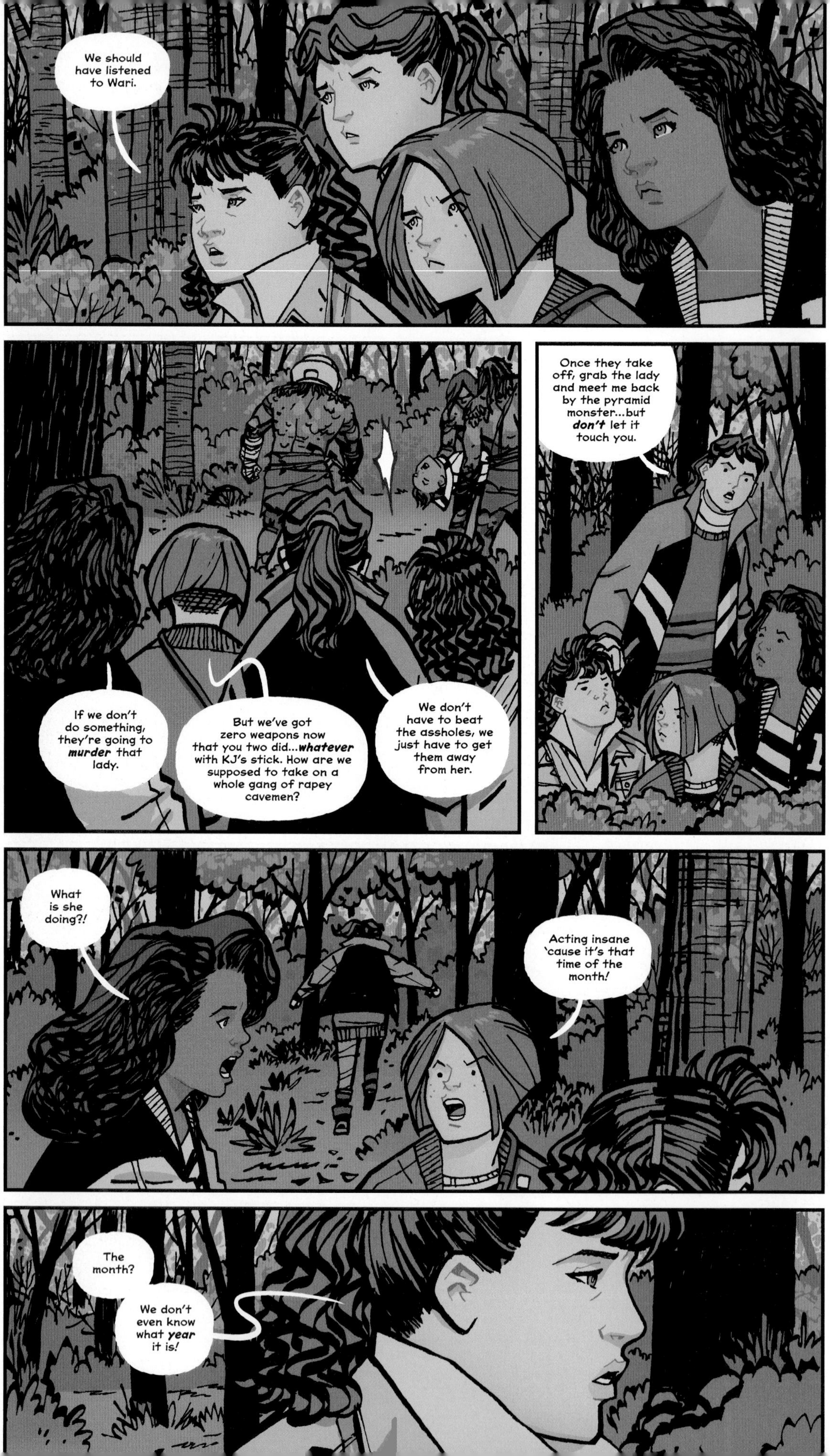
We should have listened to Wari.
If we don't do something, they're going to *murder* that lady.
But we've got zero weapons now that you two did...*whatever* with KJ's stick. How are we supposed to take on a whole gang of rapey cavemen?
We don't have to beat the assholes, we just have to get them away from her.
Once they take off, grab the lady and meet me back by the pyramid monster...but *don't* let it touch you.
What is she doing?!
Acting insane 'cause it's that time of the month!
The month?
We don't even know what *year* it is!

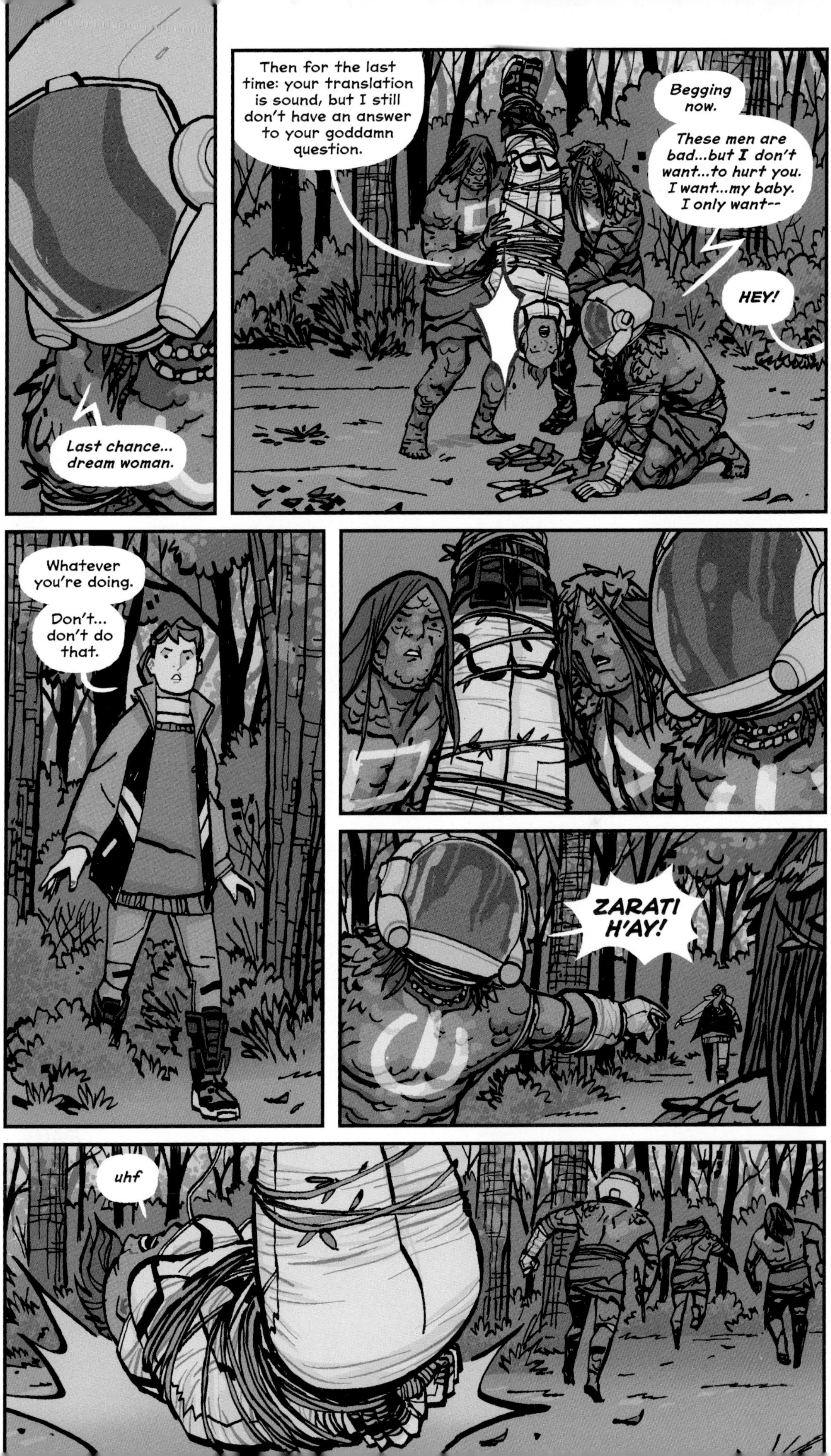
Last chance... dream woman.
Then for the last time: your translation is sound, but I still don't have an answer to your goddamn question.
Begging now.
These men are bad...but I don't want...to hurt you. I want...my baby. I only want--
HEY!
Whatever you're doing.
Don't... don't do that.
ZARATI H'AY!
uhf

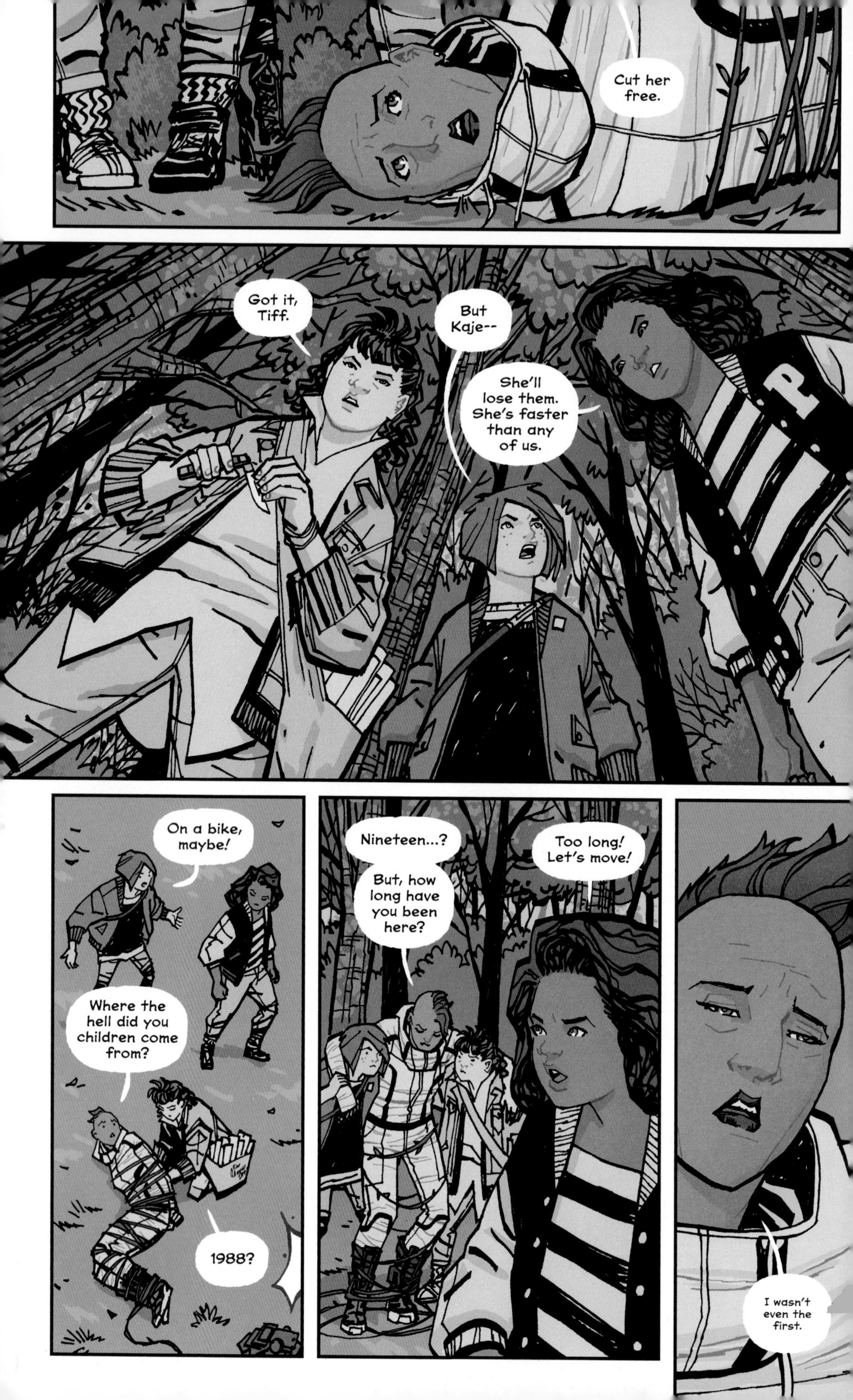

Cut her free.
Got it, Tiff.
But Kaje--
She'll lose them. She's faster than any of us.
On a bike, maybe!
Where the hell did you children come from?
1988?
Nineteen...?
But, how long have you been here?
Too long! Let's move!
I wasn't even the first.

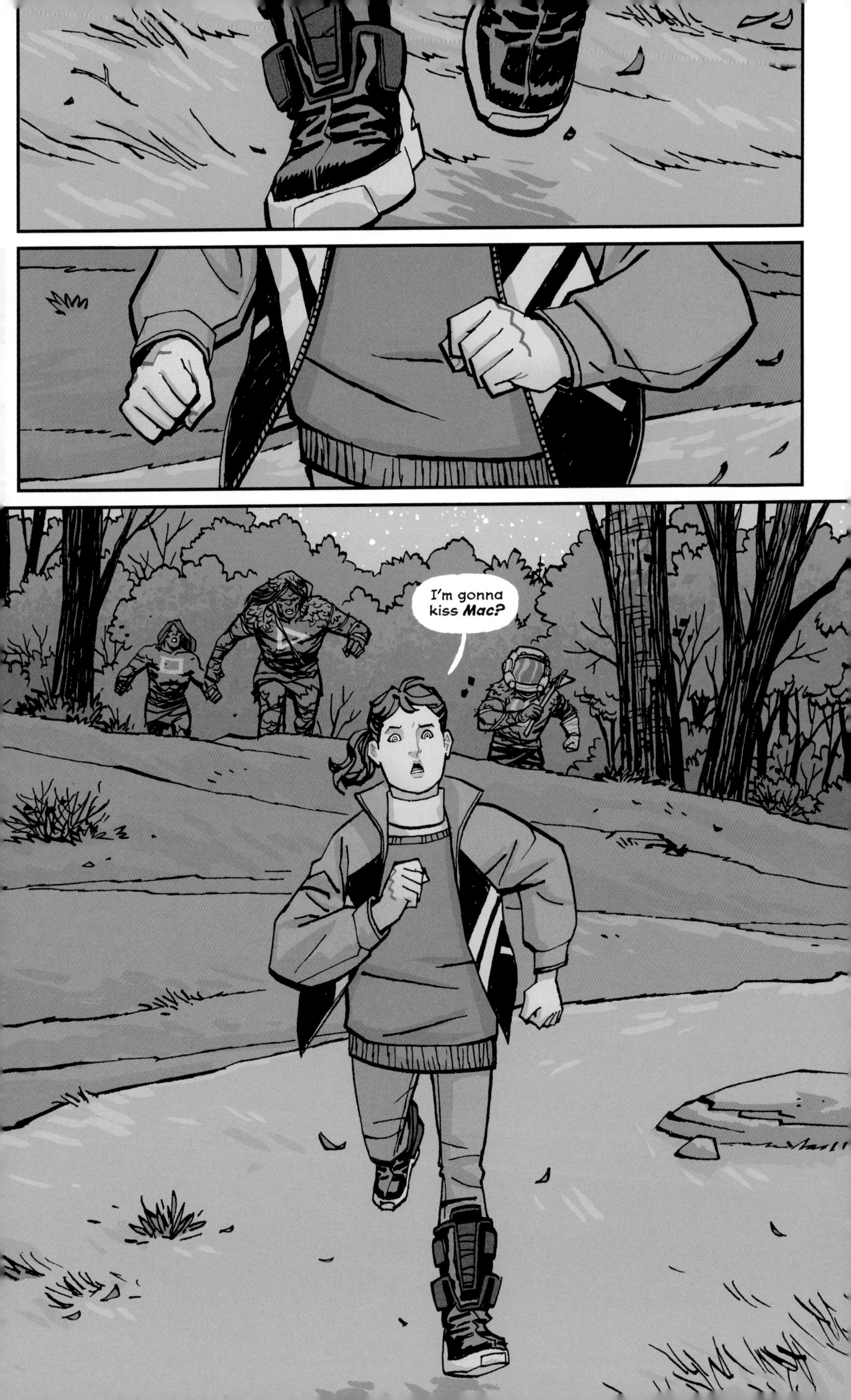
I'm gonna kiss **Mac?**

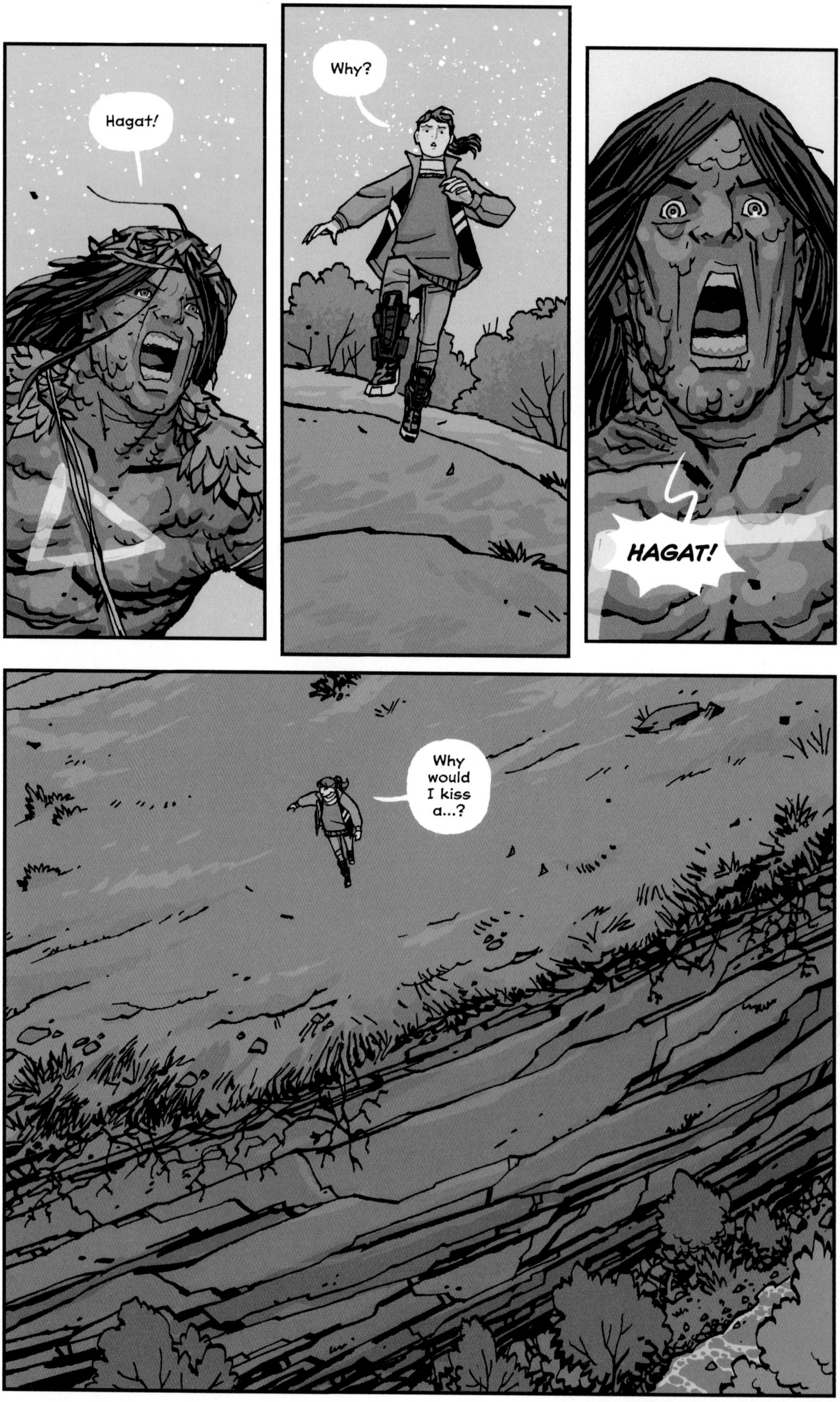
Hagat!
Why?
HAGAT!
Why would I kiss a...?

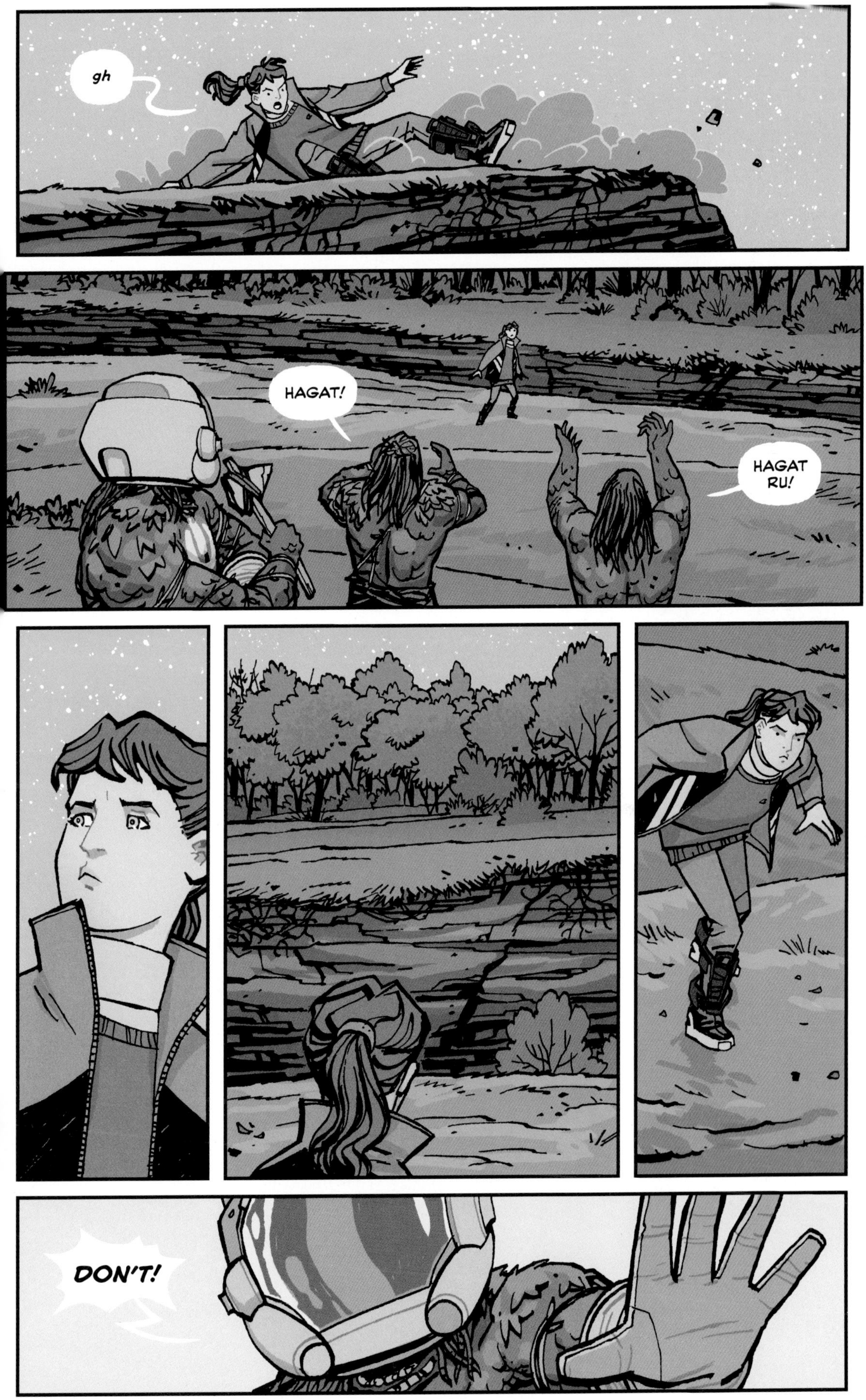
gh
HAGAT!
HAGAT RU!
DON'T!

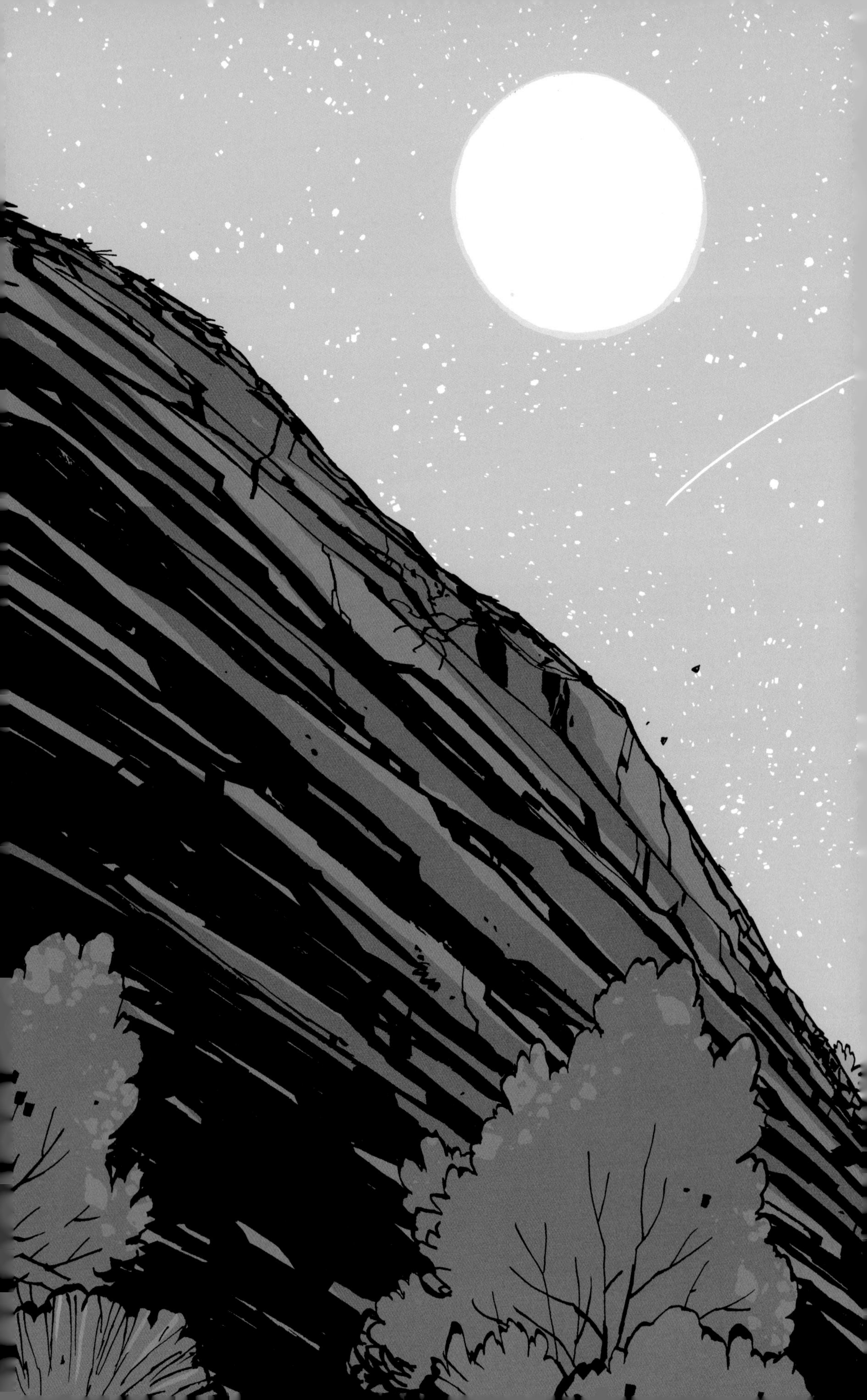

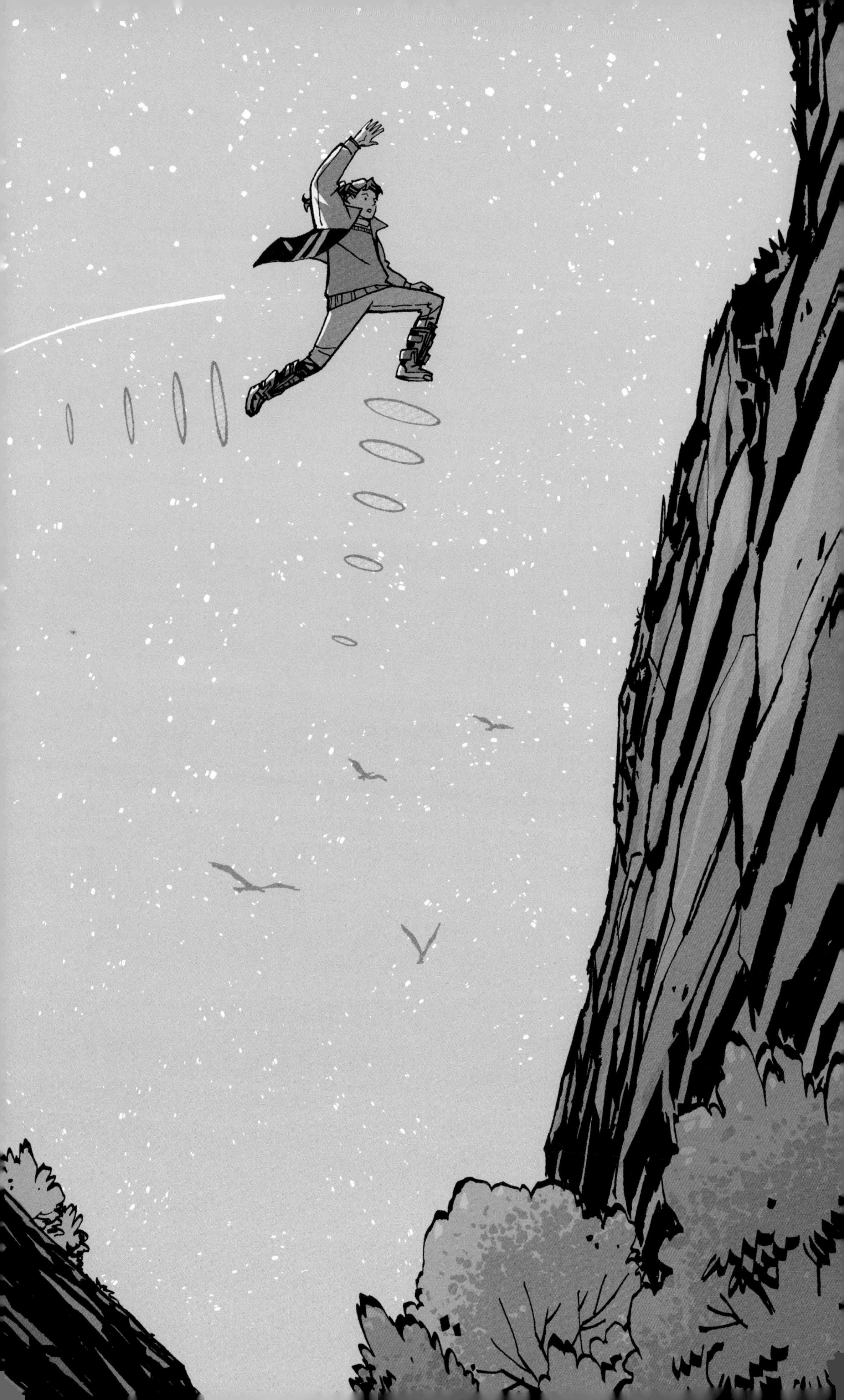

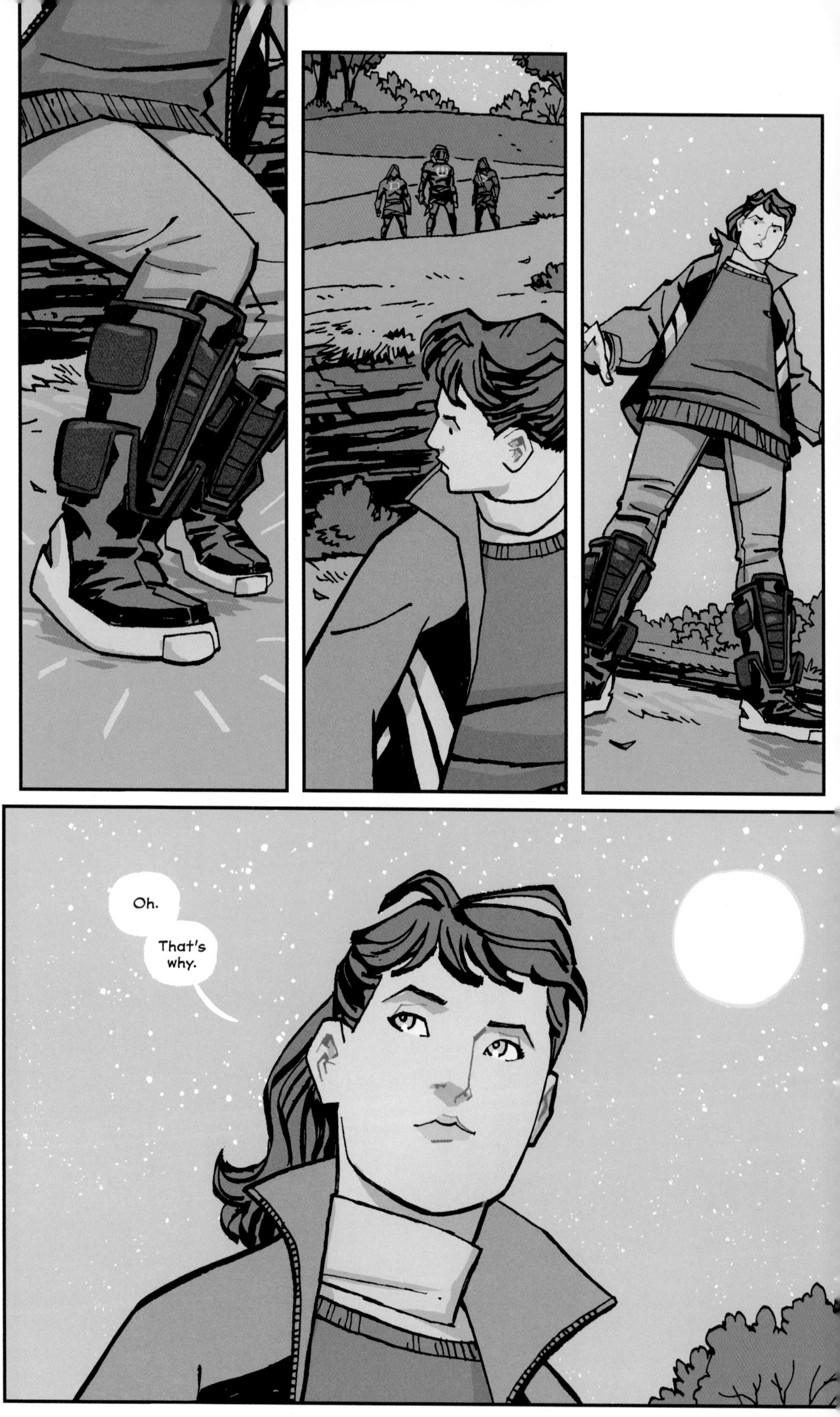
Oh.
That's why.

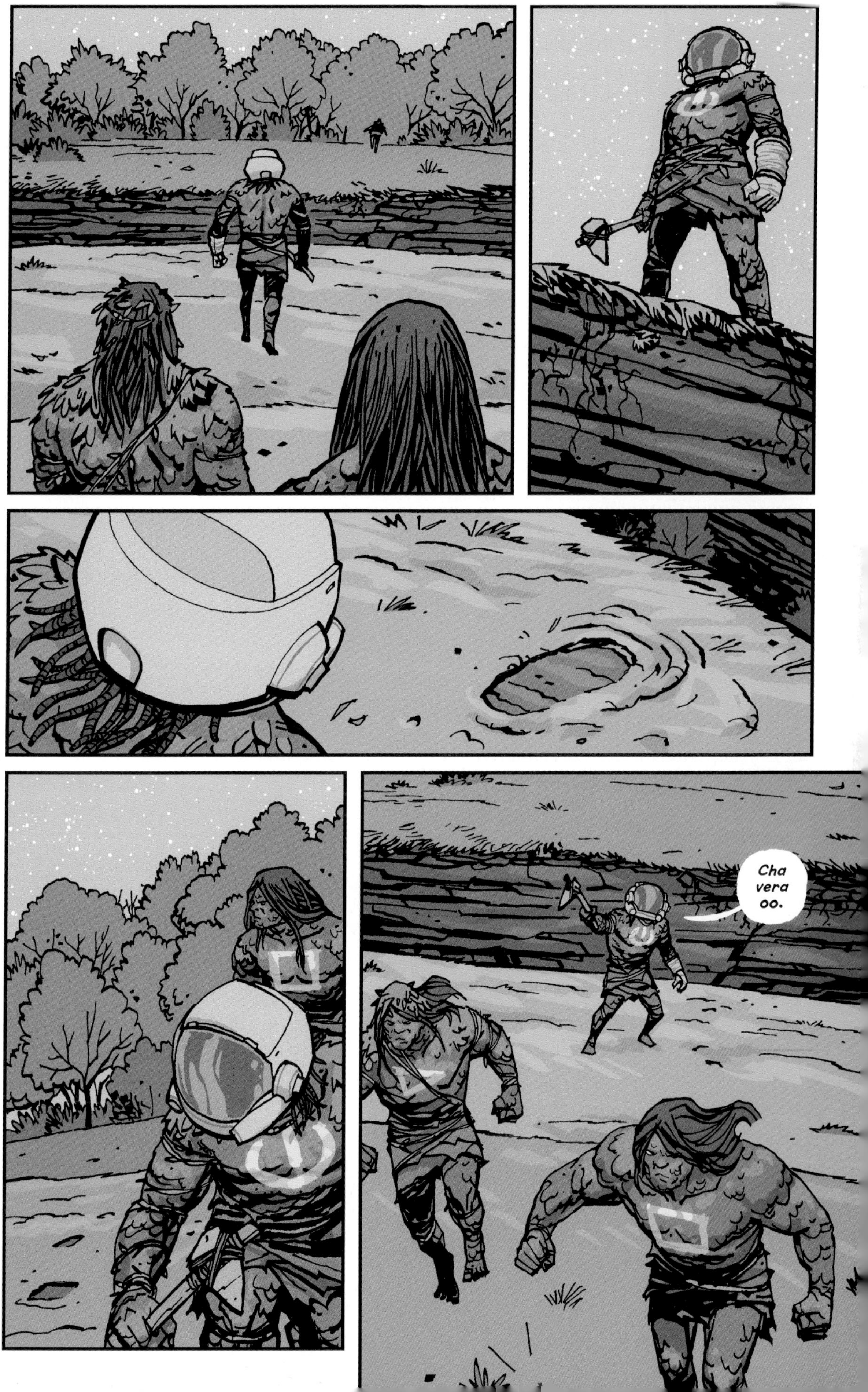
Cha vera oo.

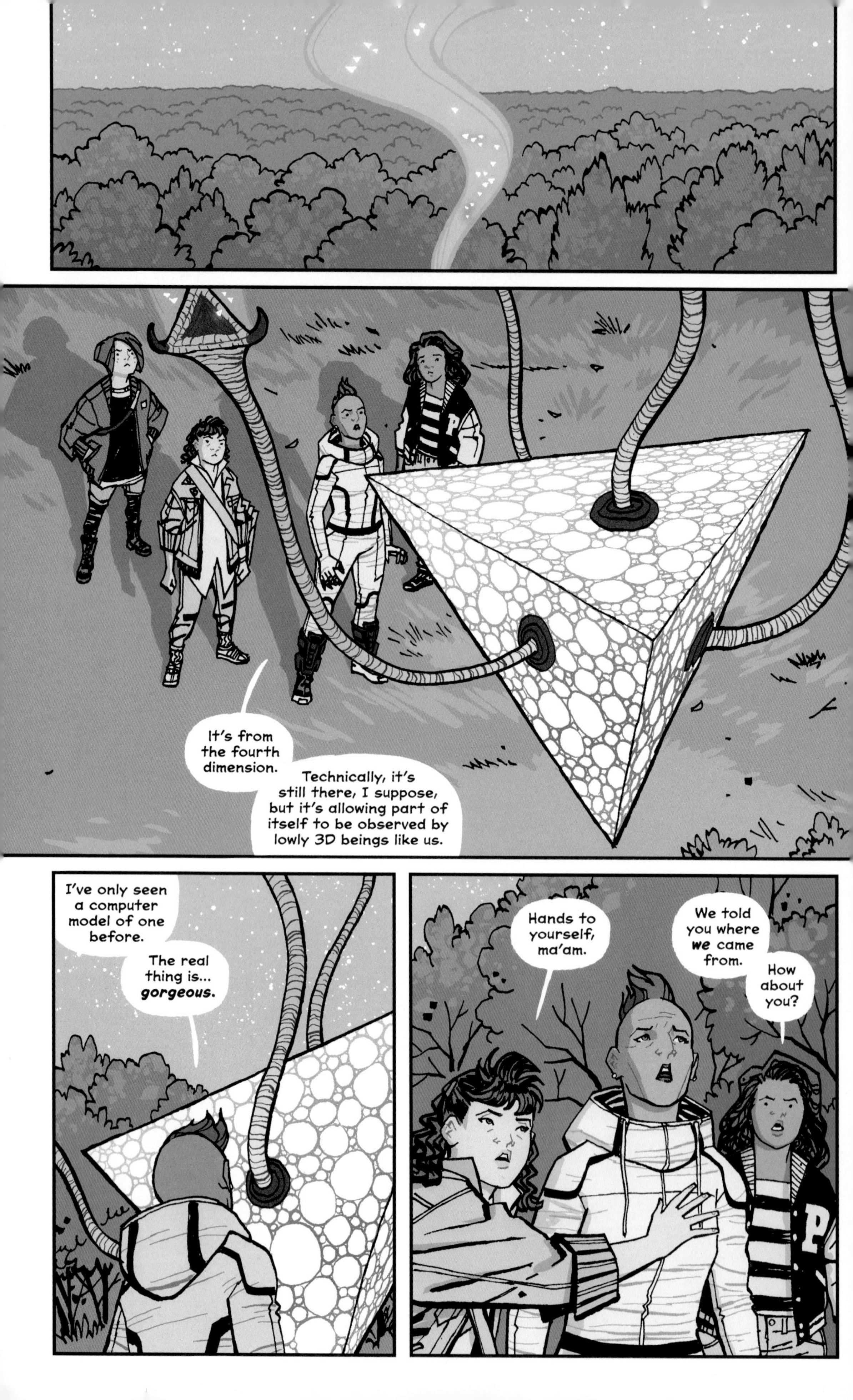

It's from the fourth dimension.
Technically, it's still there, I suppose, but it's allowing part of itself to be observed by lowly 3D beings like us.
I've only seen a computer model of one before.
The real thing is... **gorgeous.**
Hands to yourself, ma'am.
We told you where **we** came from.
How about you?

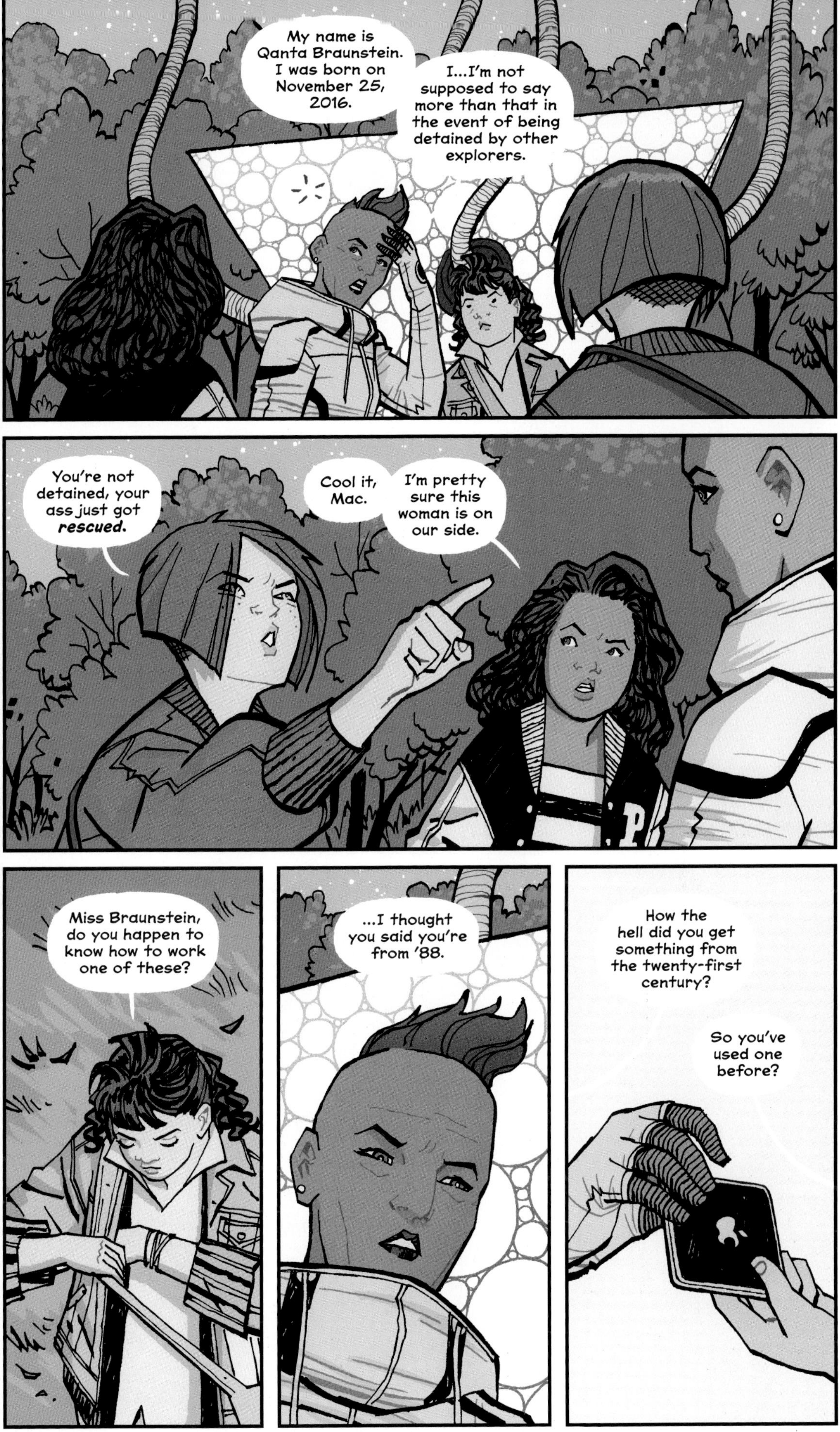
My name is Qanta Braunstein. I was born on November 25, 2016.
I...I'm not supposed to say more than that in the event of being detained by other explorers.
You're not detained, your ass just got *rescued.*
Cool it, Mac.
I'm pretty sure this woman is on our side.
Miss Braunstein, do you happen to know how to work one of these?
...I thought you said you're from '88.
How the hell did you get something from the twenty-first century?
So you've used one before?

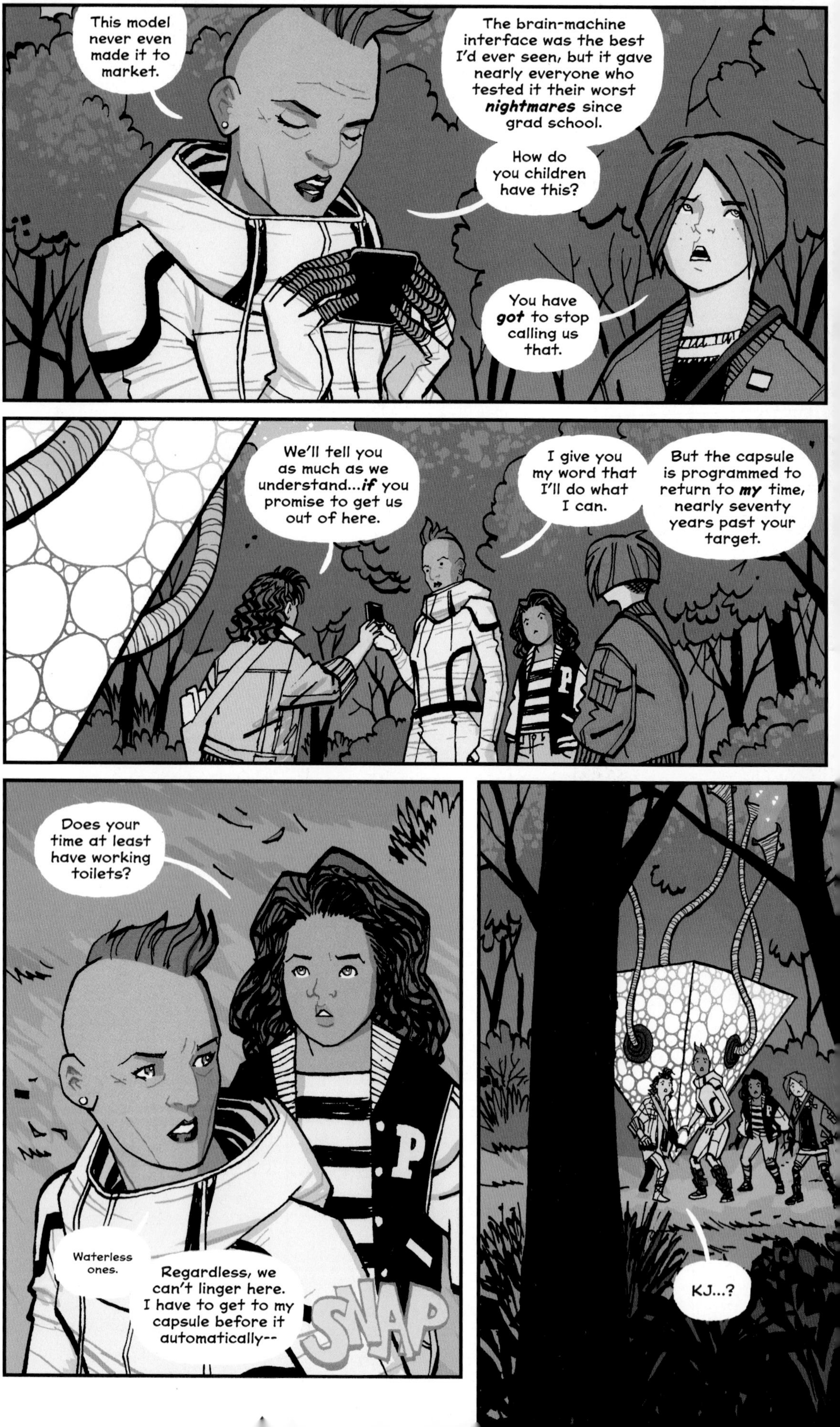
This model never even made it to market.
The brain-machine interface was the best I'd ever seen, but it gave nearly everyone who tested it their worst *nightmares* since grad school.
How do you children have this?
You have *got* to stop calling us that.
We'll tell you as much as we understand...*if* you promise to get us out of here.
I give you my word that I'll do what I can.
But the capsule is programmed to return to *my* time, nearly seventy years past your target.
Does your time at least have working toilets?
Waterless ones.
Regardless, we can't linger here. I have to get to my capsule before it automatically--
SNAP
KJ...?

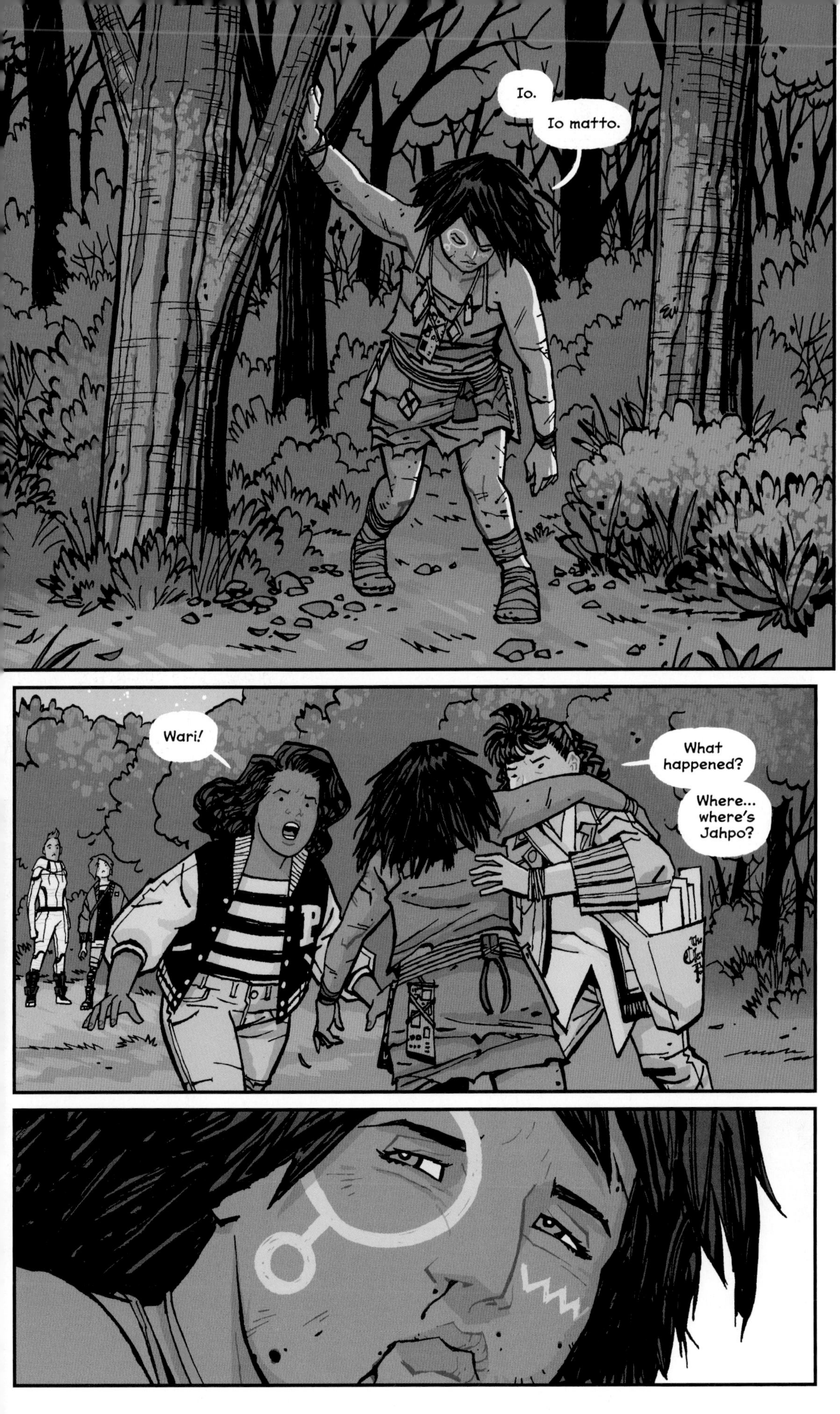
Io.
Io matto.
Wari!
What happened?
Where... where's Jahpo?

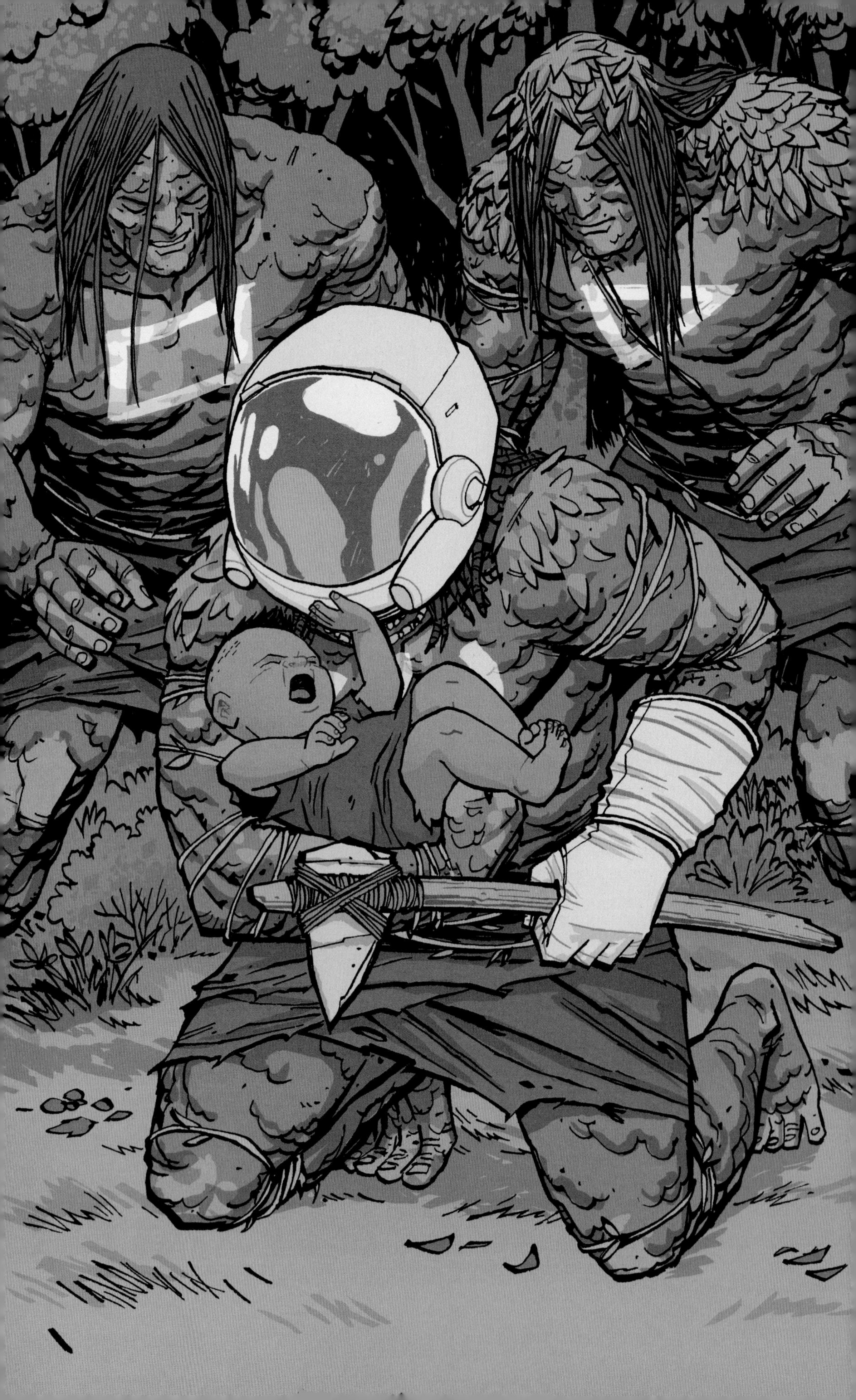

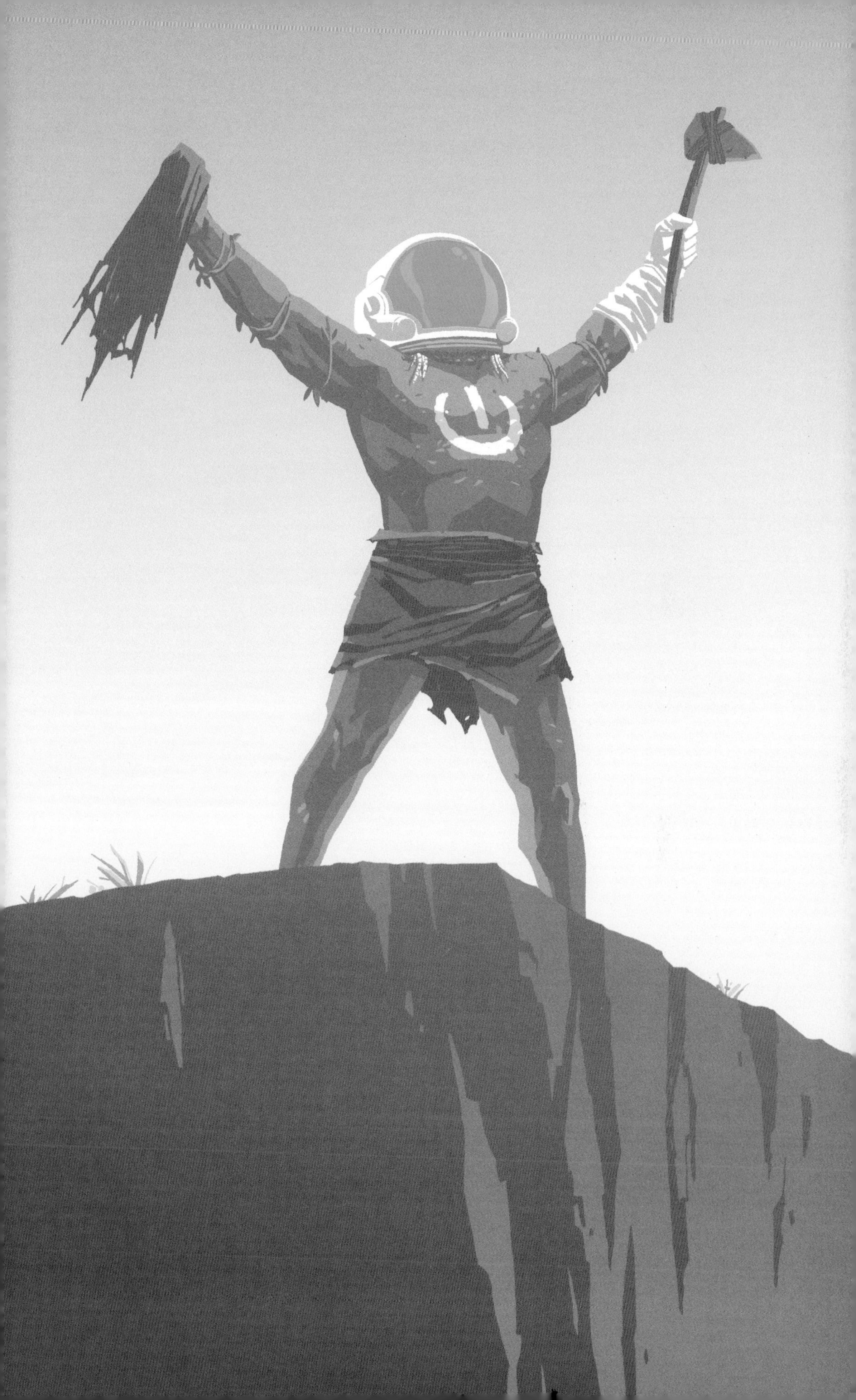

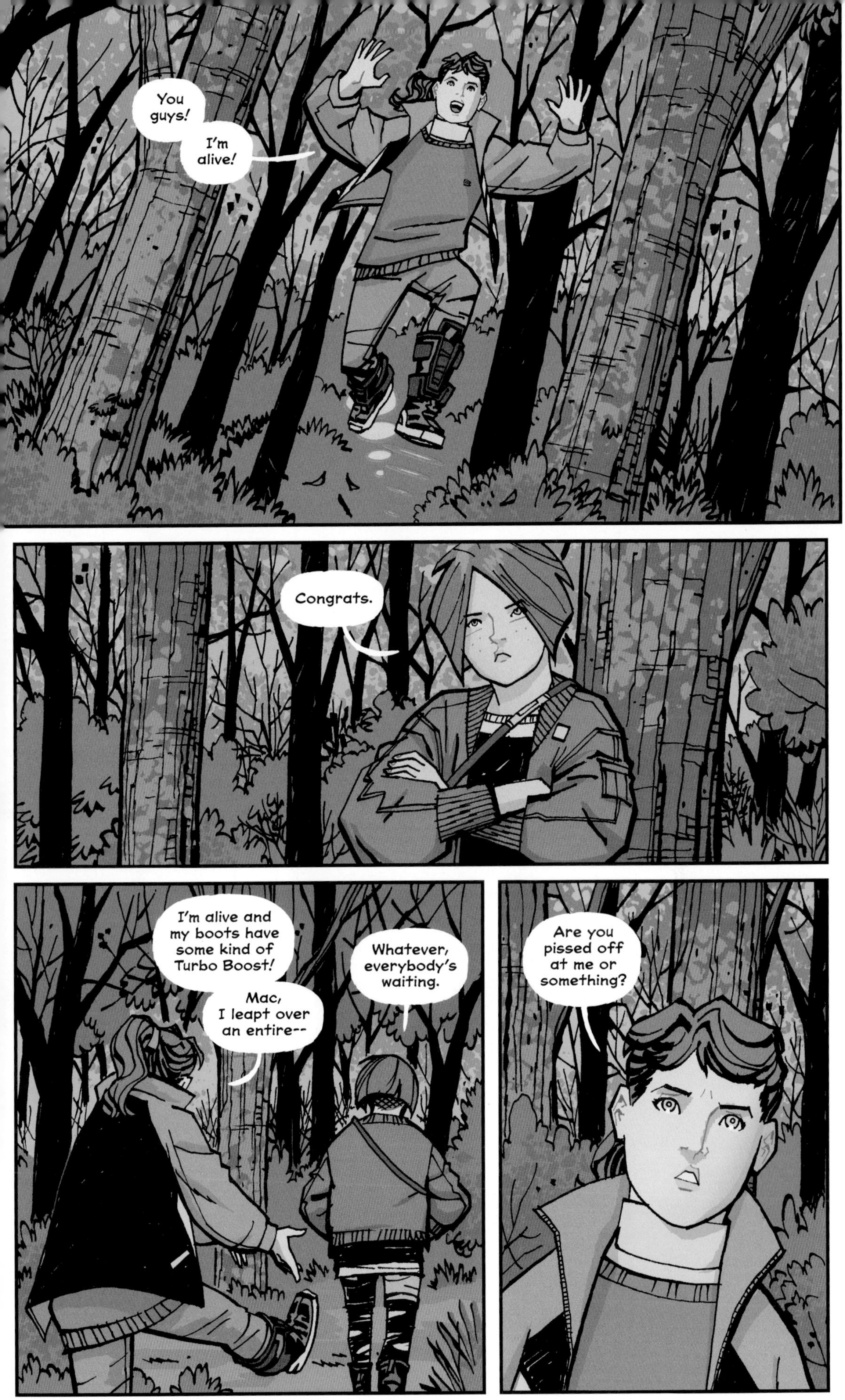
You guys!
I'm alive!
Congrats.
I'm alive and my boots have some kind of Turbo Boost!
Mac, I leapt over an entire--
Whatever, everybody's waiting.
Are you pissed off at me or something?

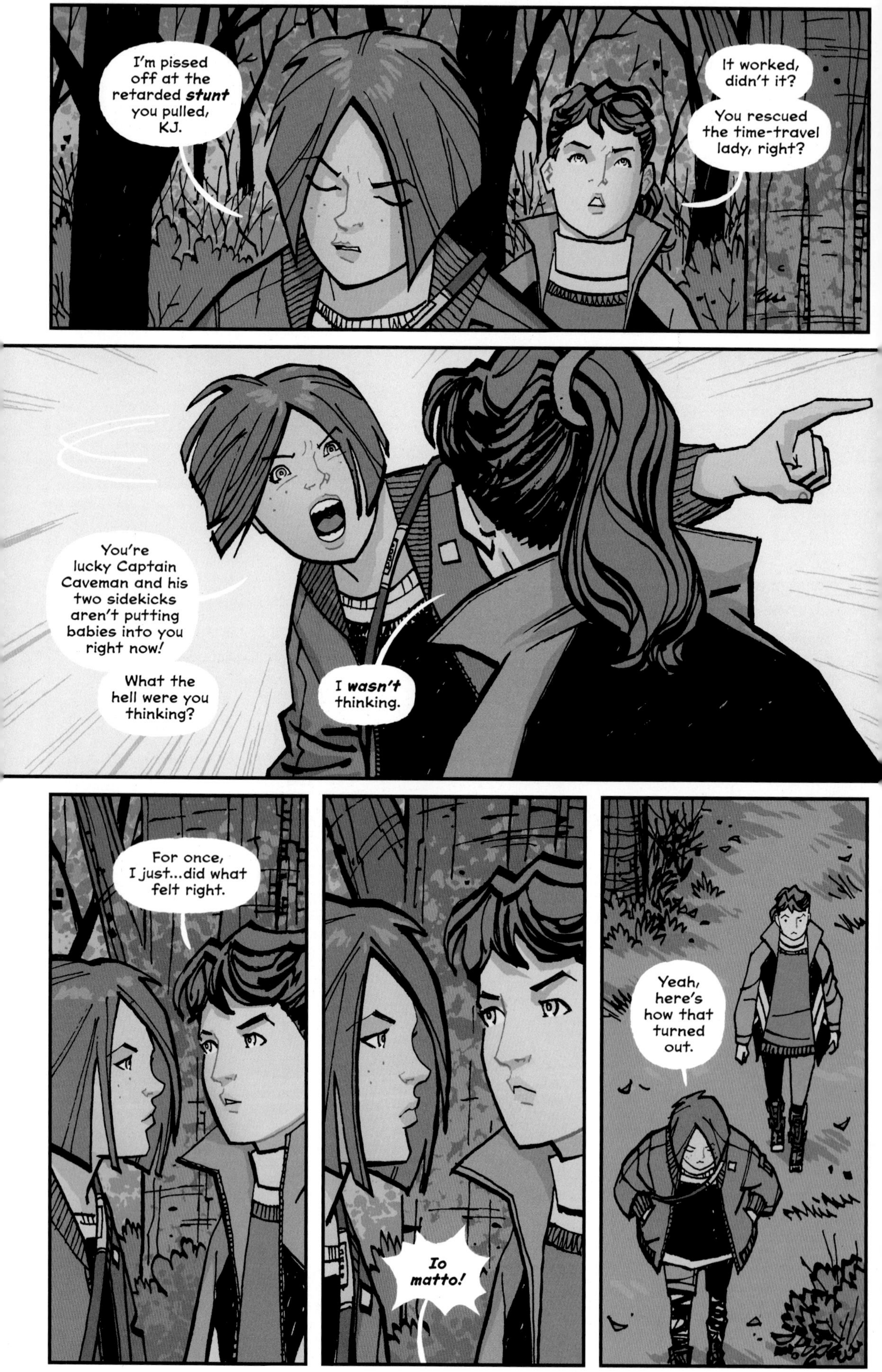
I'm pissed off at the retarded *stunt* you pulled, KJ.
It worked, didn't it?
You rescued the time-travel lady, right?
You're lucky Captain Caveman and his two sidekicks aren't putting babies into you right now!
What the hell were you thinking?
I *wasn't* thinking.
For once, I just...did what felt right.
Io matto!
Yeah, here's how that turned out.

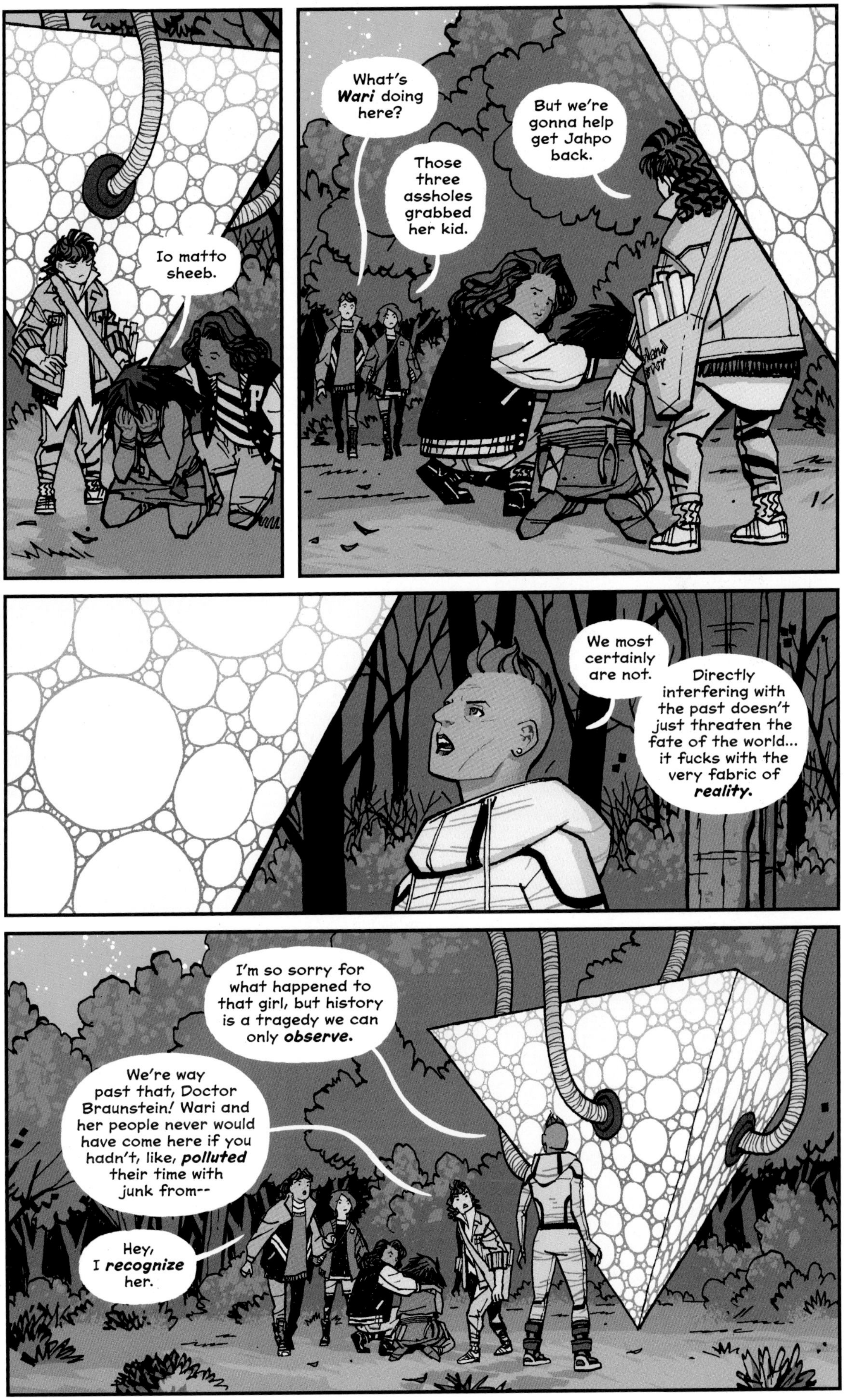
Io matto sheeb.
What's Wari doing here?
Those three assholes grabbed her kid.
But we're gonna help get Jahpo back.
We most certainly are not.
Directly interfering with the past doesn't just threaten the fate of the world... it fucks with the very fabric of reality.
I'm so sorry for what happened to that girl, but history is a tragedy we can only observe.
We're way past that, Doctor Braunstein! Wari and her people never would have come here if you hadn't, like, polluted their time with junk from--
Hey, I recognize her.

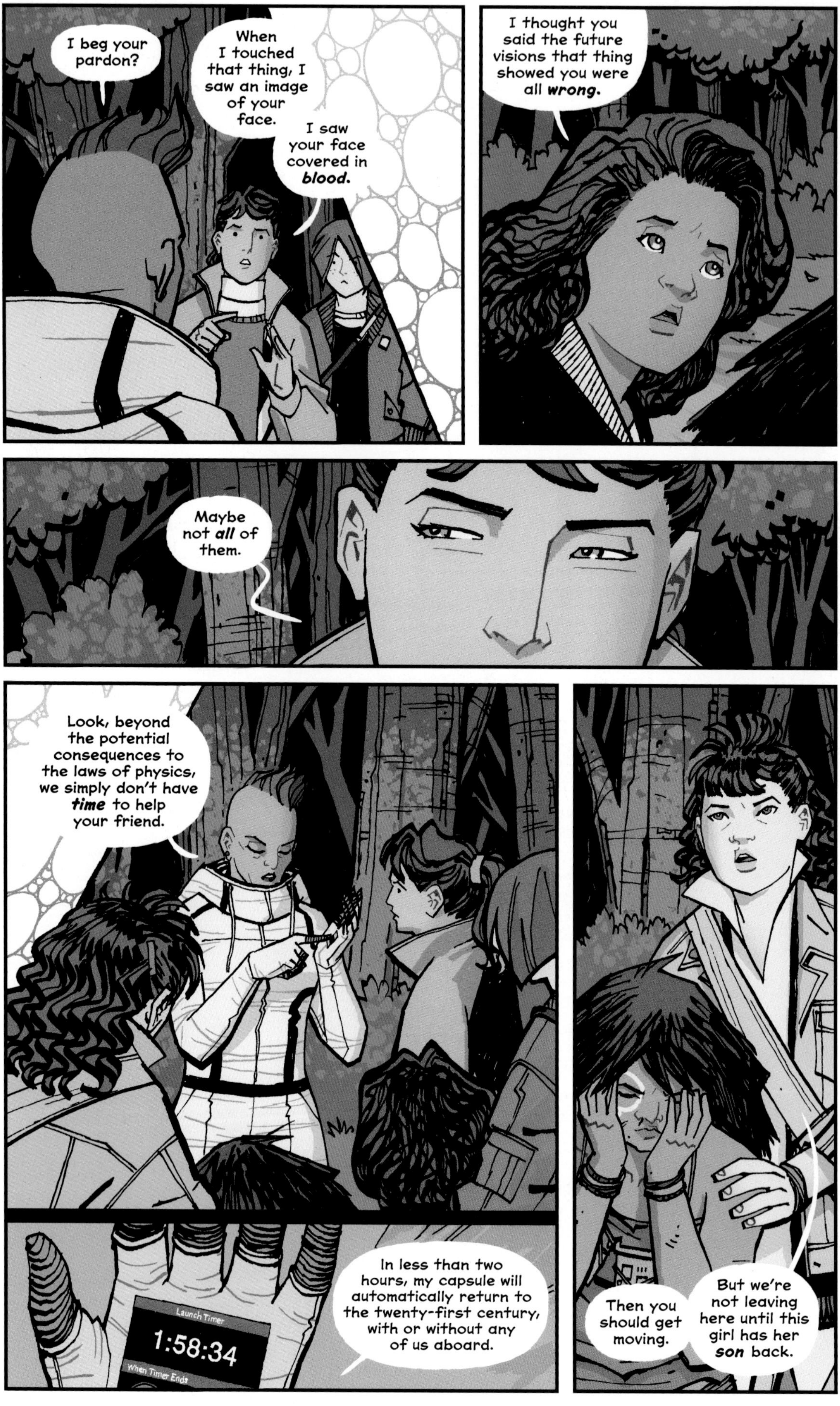
I beg your pardon?
When I touched that thing, I saw an image of your face.
I saw your face covered in *blood.*
I thought you said the future visions that thing showed you were all *wrong.*
Maybe not *all* of them.
Look, beyond the potential consequences to the laws of physics, we simply don't have *time* to help your friend.
Launch Timer
1:58:34
When Timer Ends
In less than two hours, my capsule will automatically return to the twenty-first century, with or without any of us aboard.
Then you should get moving.
But we're not leaving here until this girl has her *son* back.

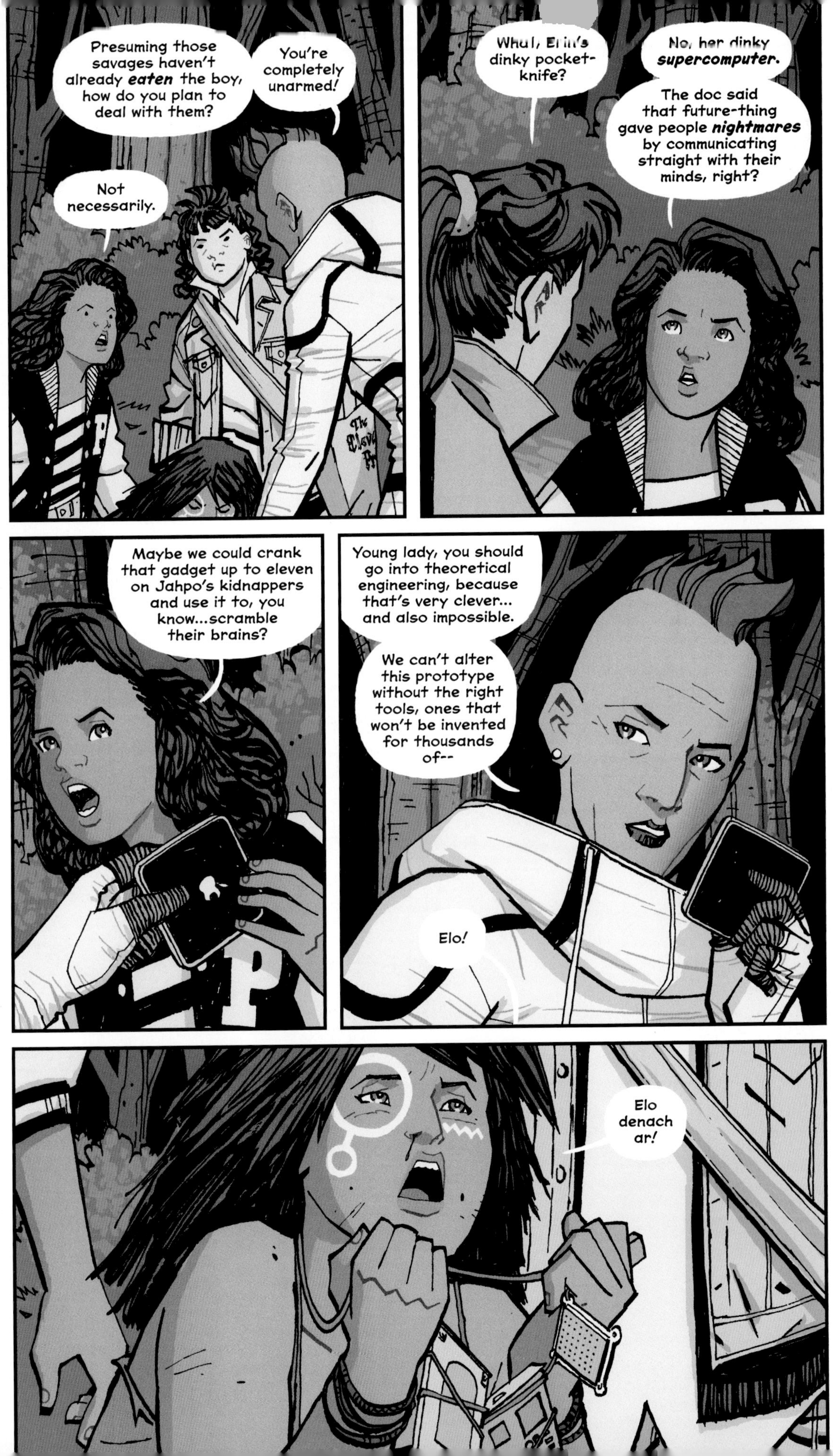

Presuming those savages haven't already *eaten* the boy, how do you plan to deal with them?
You're completely unarmed!
Not necessarily.
What, Erin's dinky pocket-knife?
No, her dinky ***supercomputer.***
The doc said that future-thing gave people ***nightmares*** by communicating straight with their minds, right?
Maybe we could crank that gadget up to eleven on Jahpo's kidnappers and use it to, you know...scramble their brains?
Young lady, you should go into theoretical engineering, because that's very clever... and also impossible.
We can't alter this prototype without the right tools, ones that won't be invented for thousands of--
Elo!
Elo denach ar!

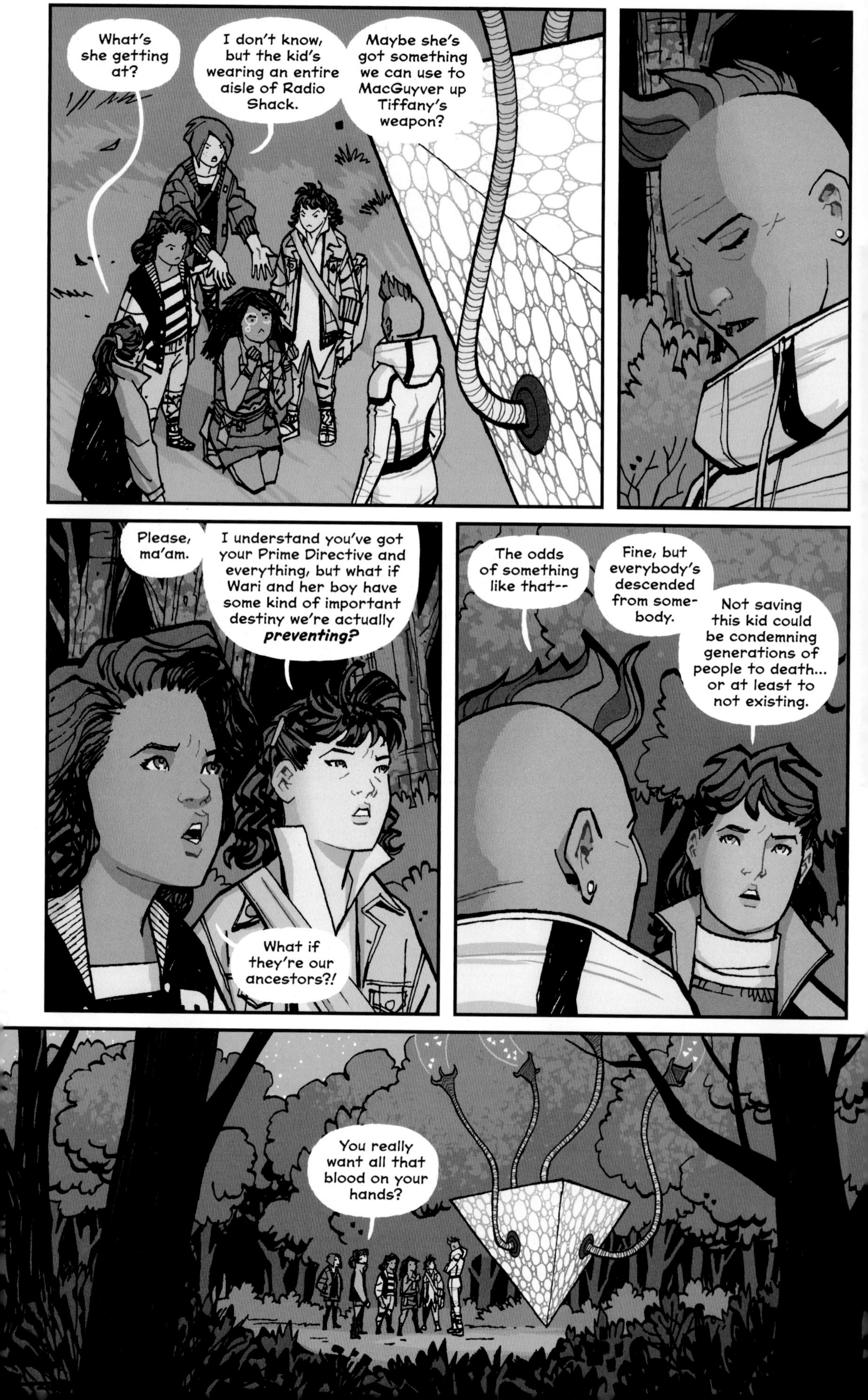
What's she getting at?
I don't know, but the kid's wearing an entire aisle of Radio Shack.
Maybe she's got something we can use to MacGuyver up Tiffany's weapon?
Please, ma'am.
I understand you've got your Prime Directive and everything, but what if Wari and her boy have some kind of important destiny we're actually *preventing?*
What if they're our ancestors?!
The odds of something like that--
Fine, but everybody's descended from some-body.
Not saving this kid could be condemning generations of people to death... or at least to not existing.
You really want all that blood on your hands?

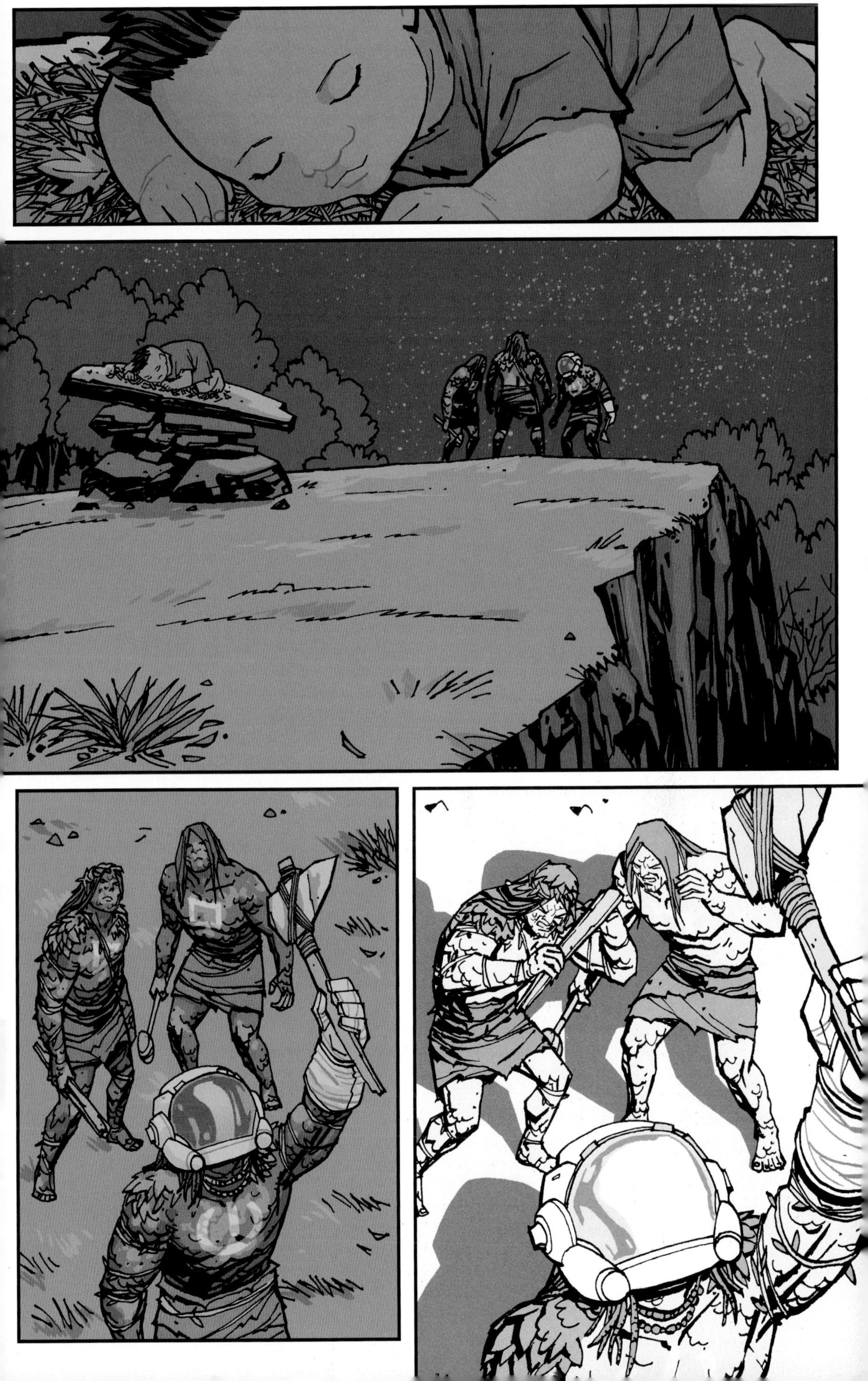

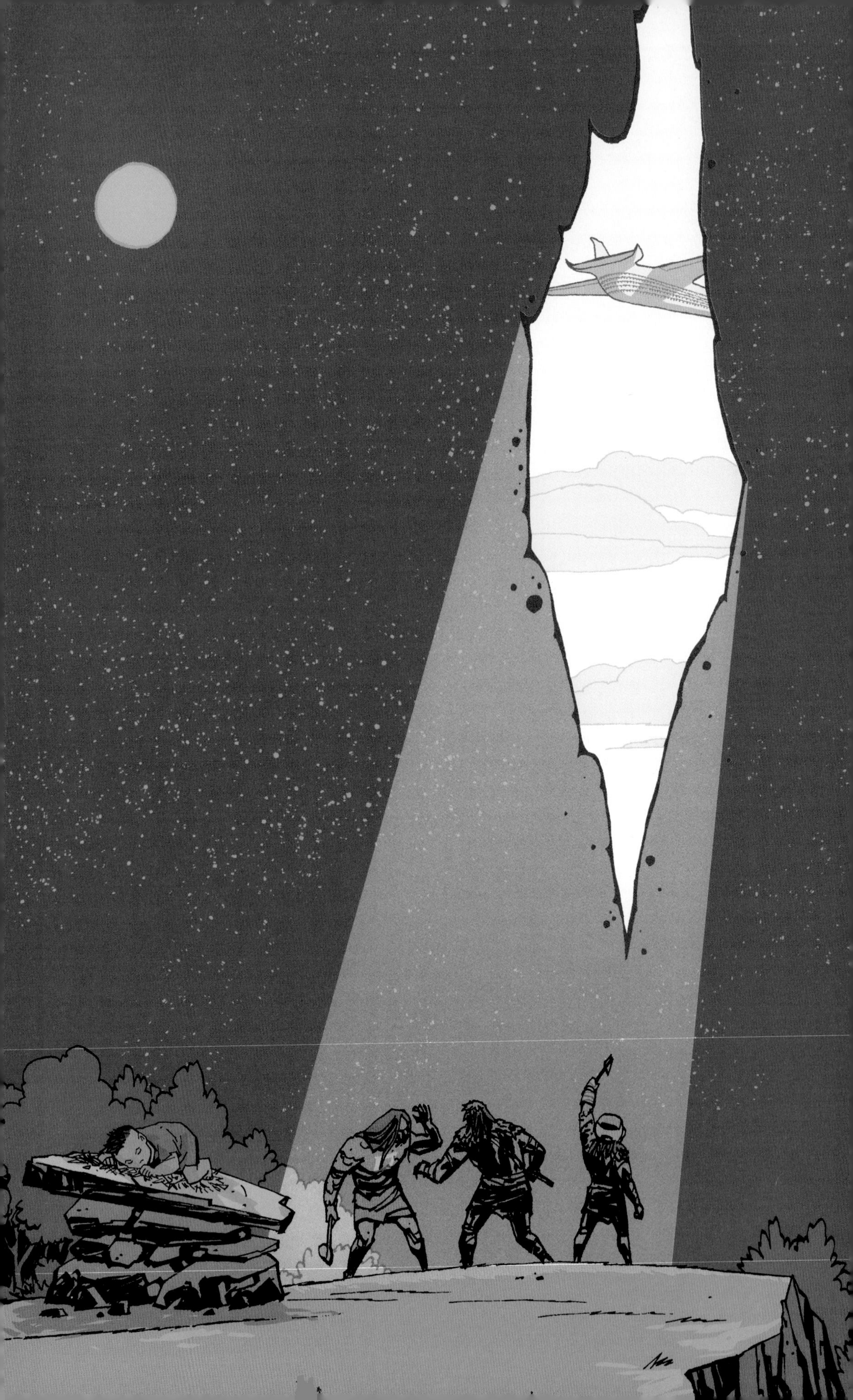

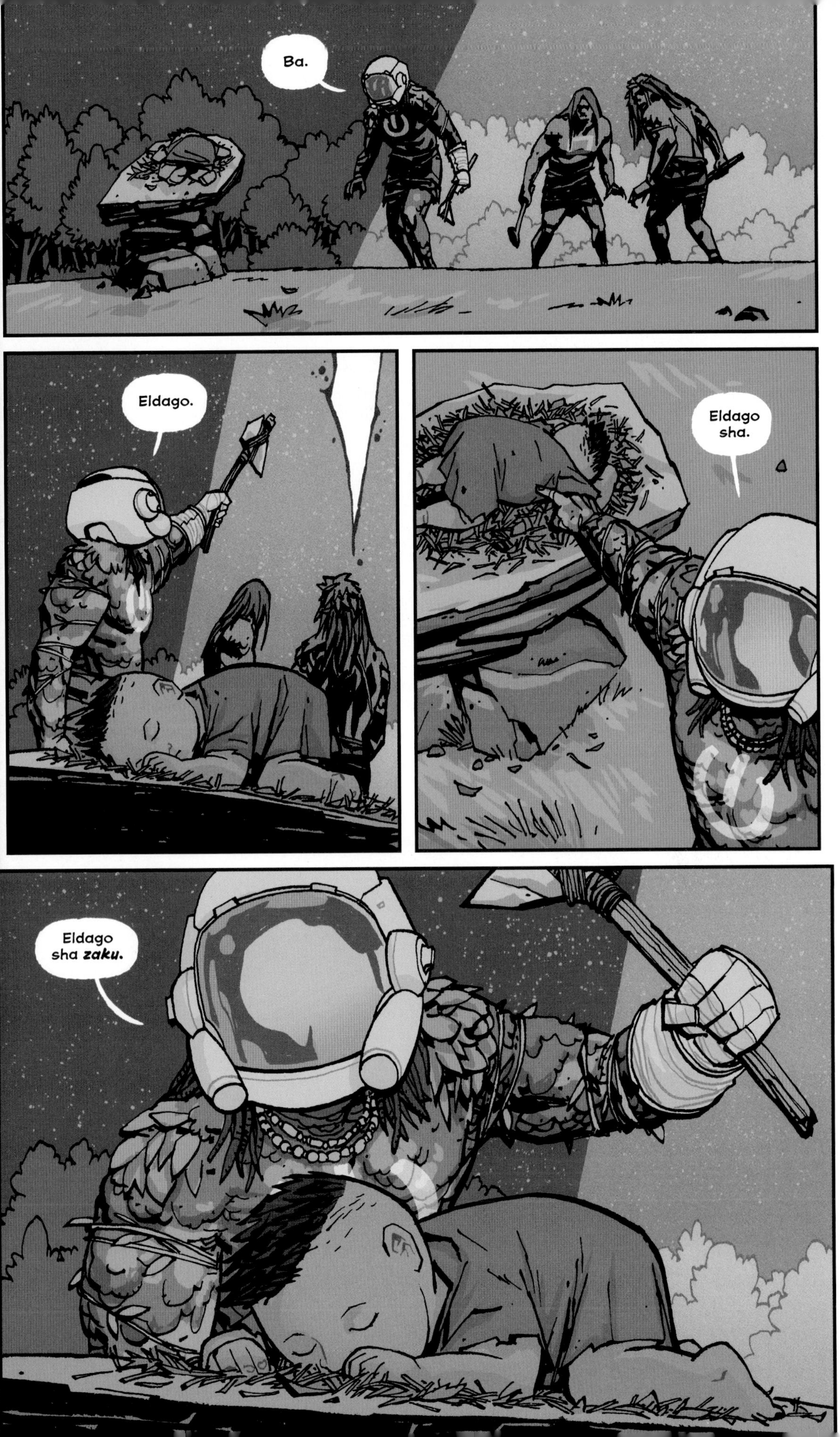
Ba.
Eldago.
Eldago sha.
Eldago sha *zaku*.

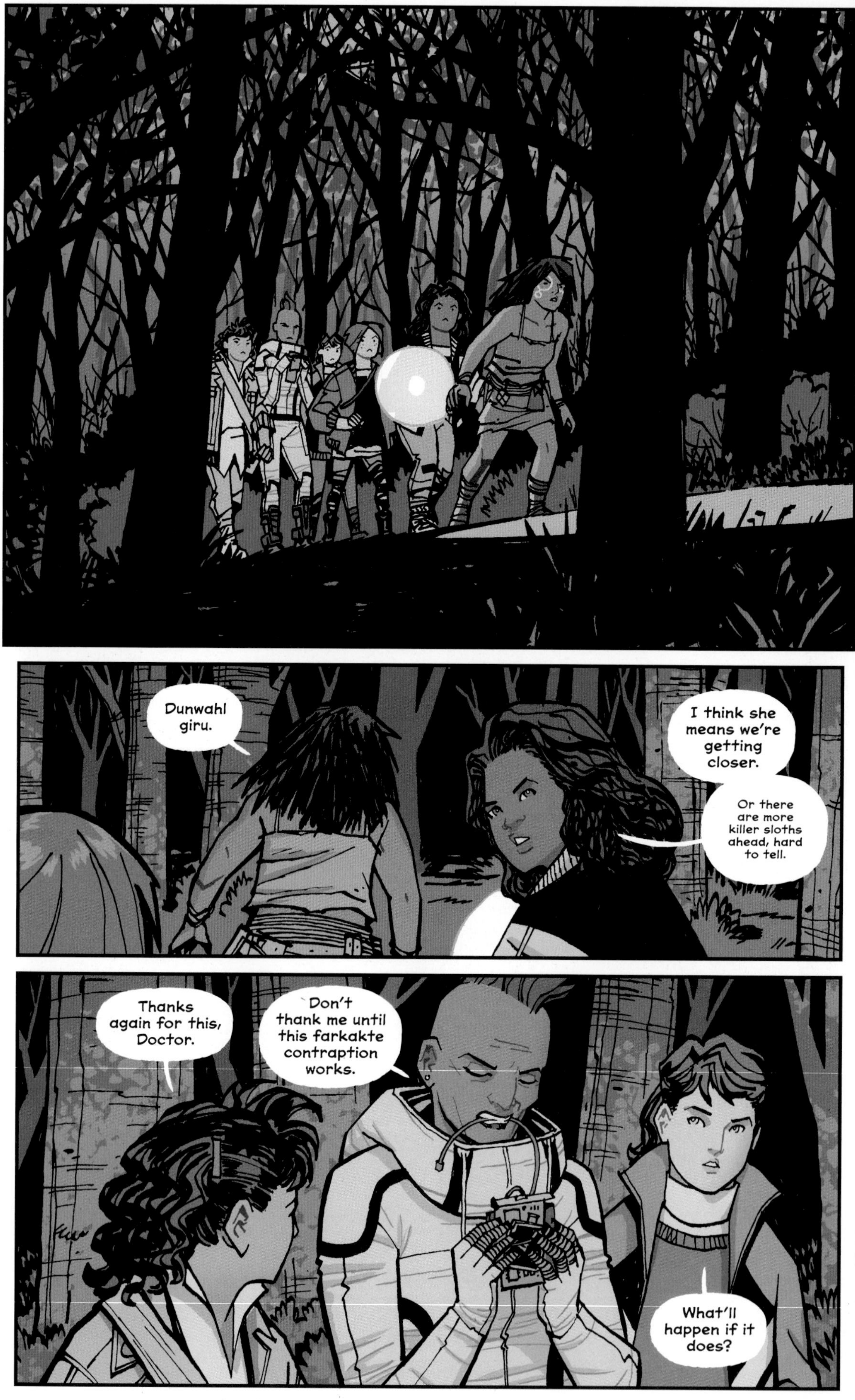
Dunwahl giru.
I think she means we're getting closer.
Or there are more killer sloths ahead, hard to tell.
Thanks again for this, Doctor.
Don't thank me until this farkakte contraption works.
What'll happen if it does?

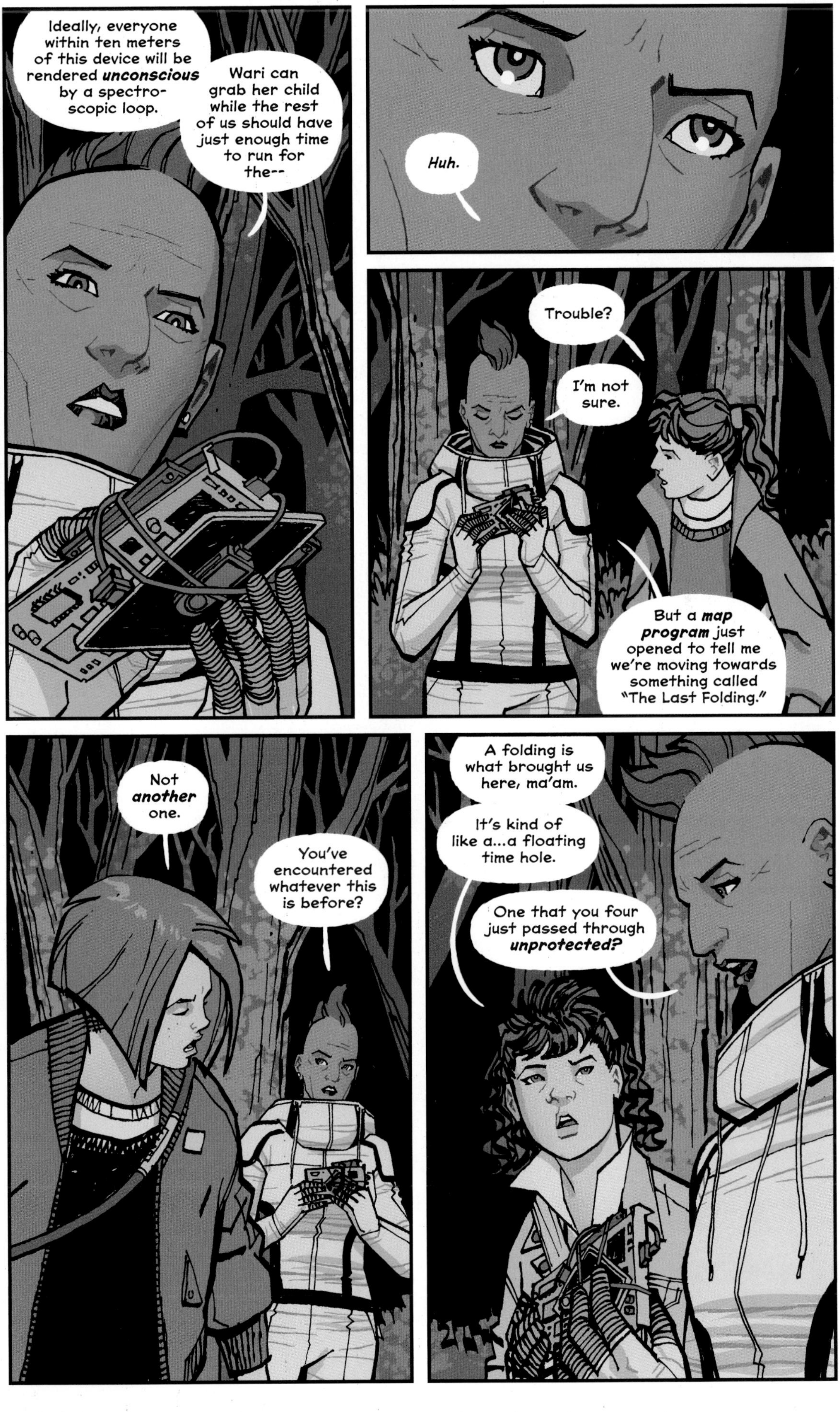
Ideally, everyone within ten meters of this device will be rendered ***unconscious*** by a spectro-scopic loop.
Wari can grab her child while the rest of us should have just enough time to run for the--
Huh.
Trouble?
I'm not sure.
But a ***map program*** just opened to tell me we're moving towards something called "The Last Folding."
Not ***another*** one.
You've encountered whatever this is before?
A folding is what brought us here, ma'am.
It's kind of like a...a floating time hole.
One that you four just passed through ***unprotected?***

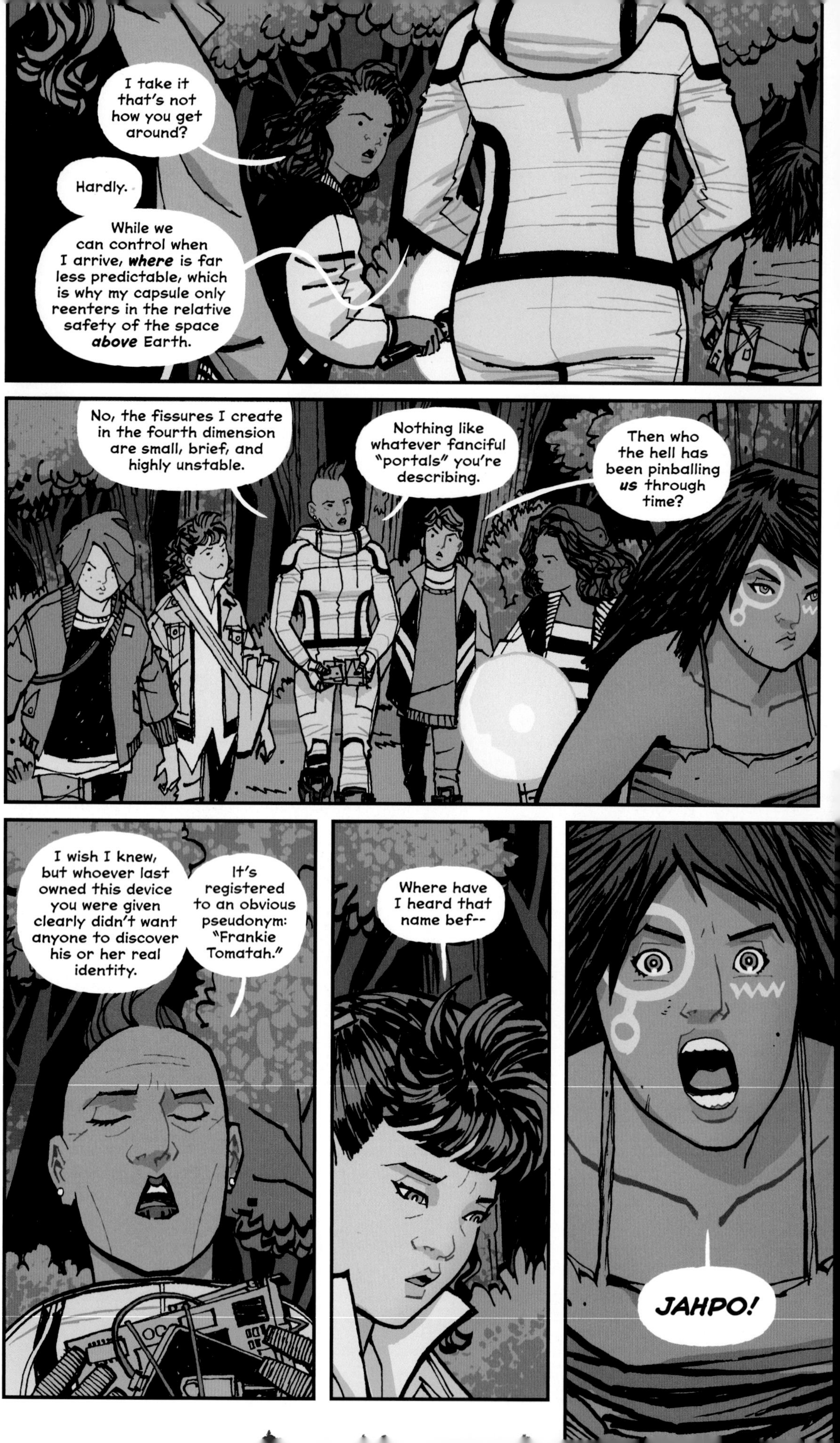
I take it that's not how you get around?
Hardly.
While we can control when I arrive, ***where*** is far less predictable, which is why my capsule only reenters in the relative safety of the space ***above*** Earth.
No, the fissures I create in the fourth dimension are small, brief, and highly unstable.
Nothing like whatever fanciful "portals" you're describing.
Then who the hell has been pinballing ***us*** through time?
I wish I knew, but whoever last owned this device you were given clearly didn't want anyone to discover his or her real identity.
It's registered to an obvious pseudonym: "Frankie Tomatah."
Where have I heard that name bef--
JAHPO!

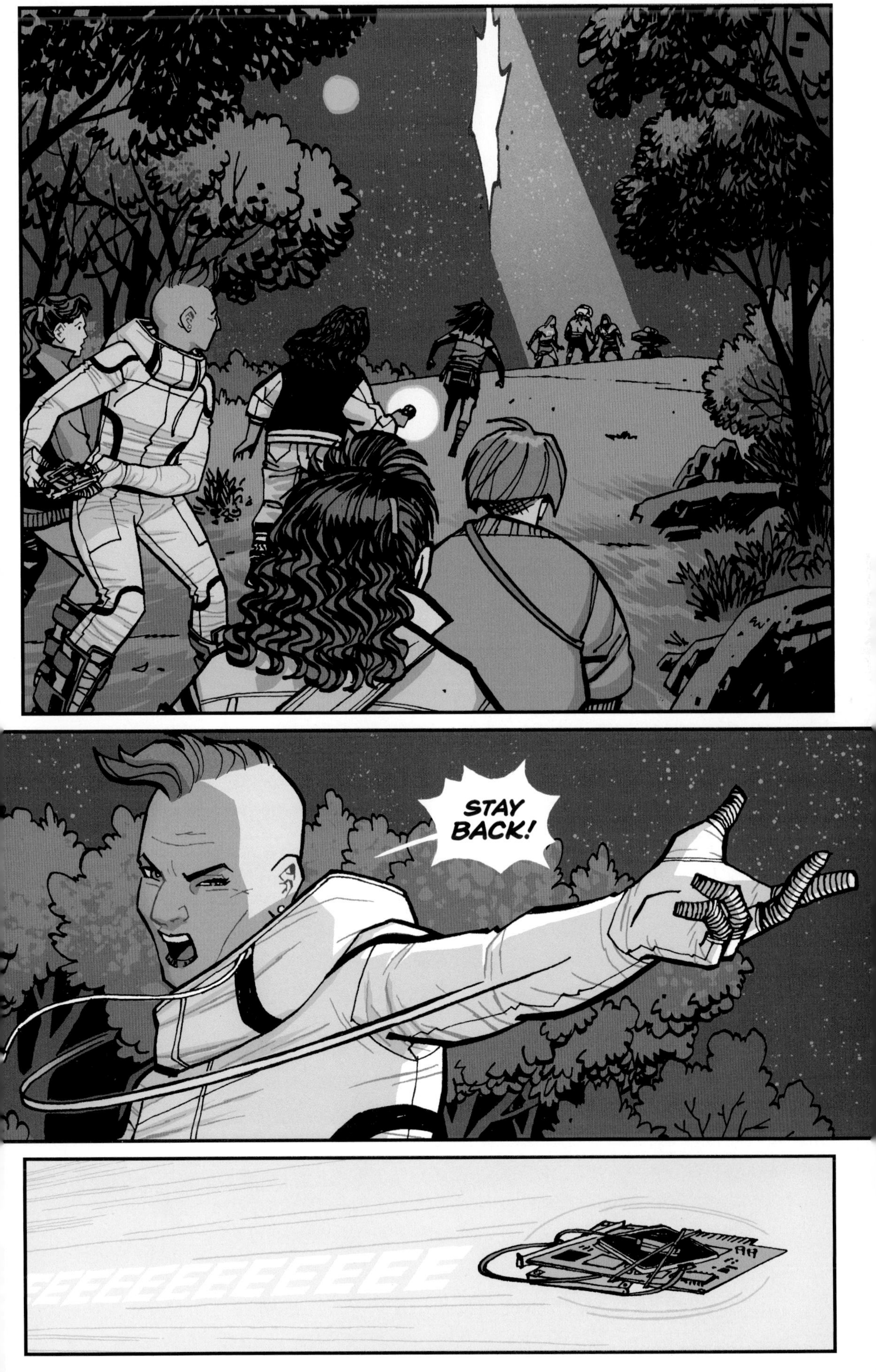
STAY BACK!
EEEEEEEEEEEEEE

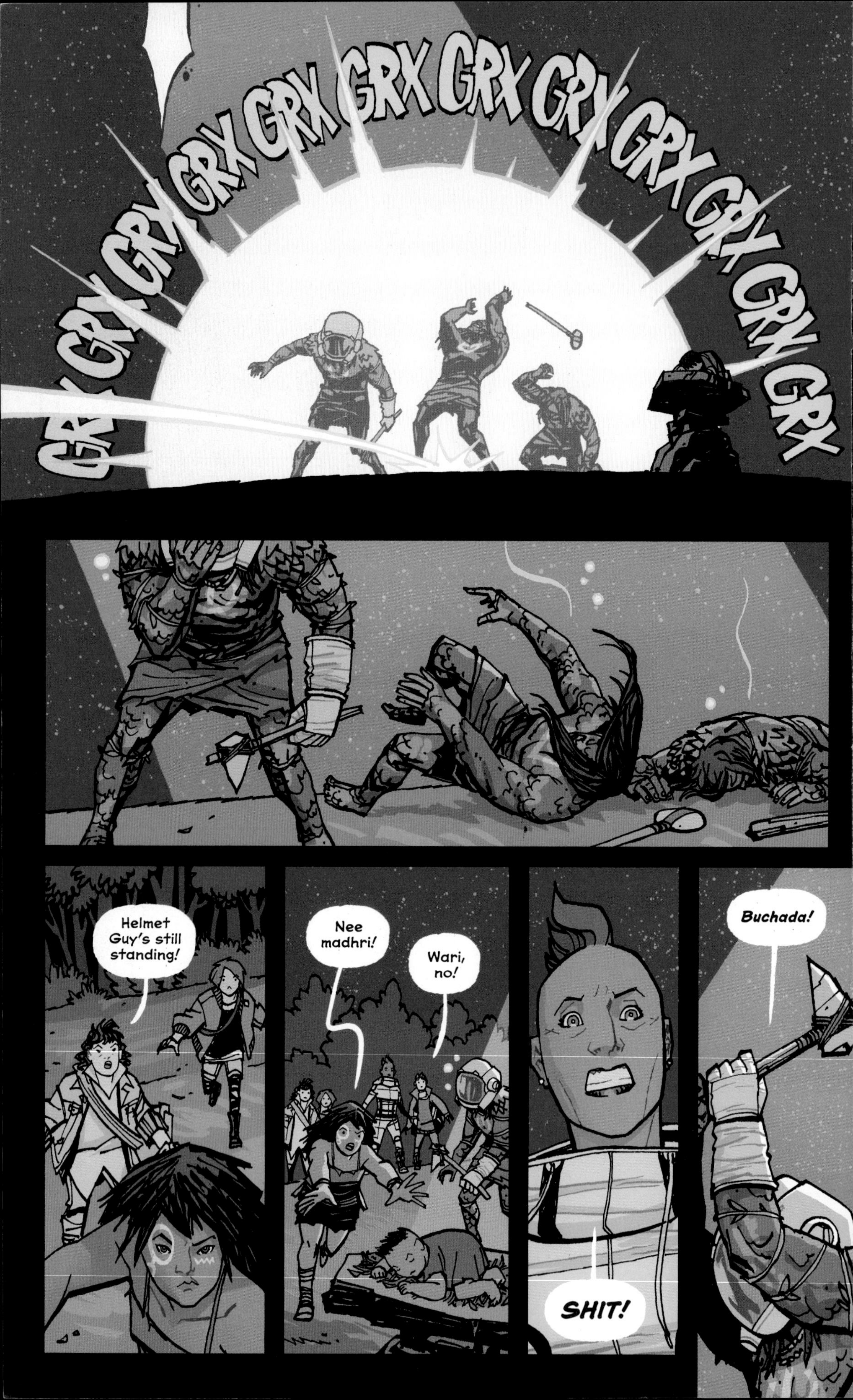
GRX GRX GRX GRX GRX GRX GRX GRX GRX GRX GRX GRX GRX GRX
Helmet Guy's still standing!
Nee madhri!
Wari, no!
SHIT!
Buchada!

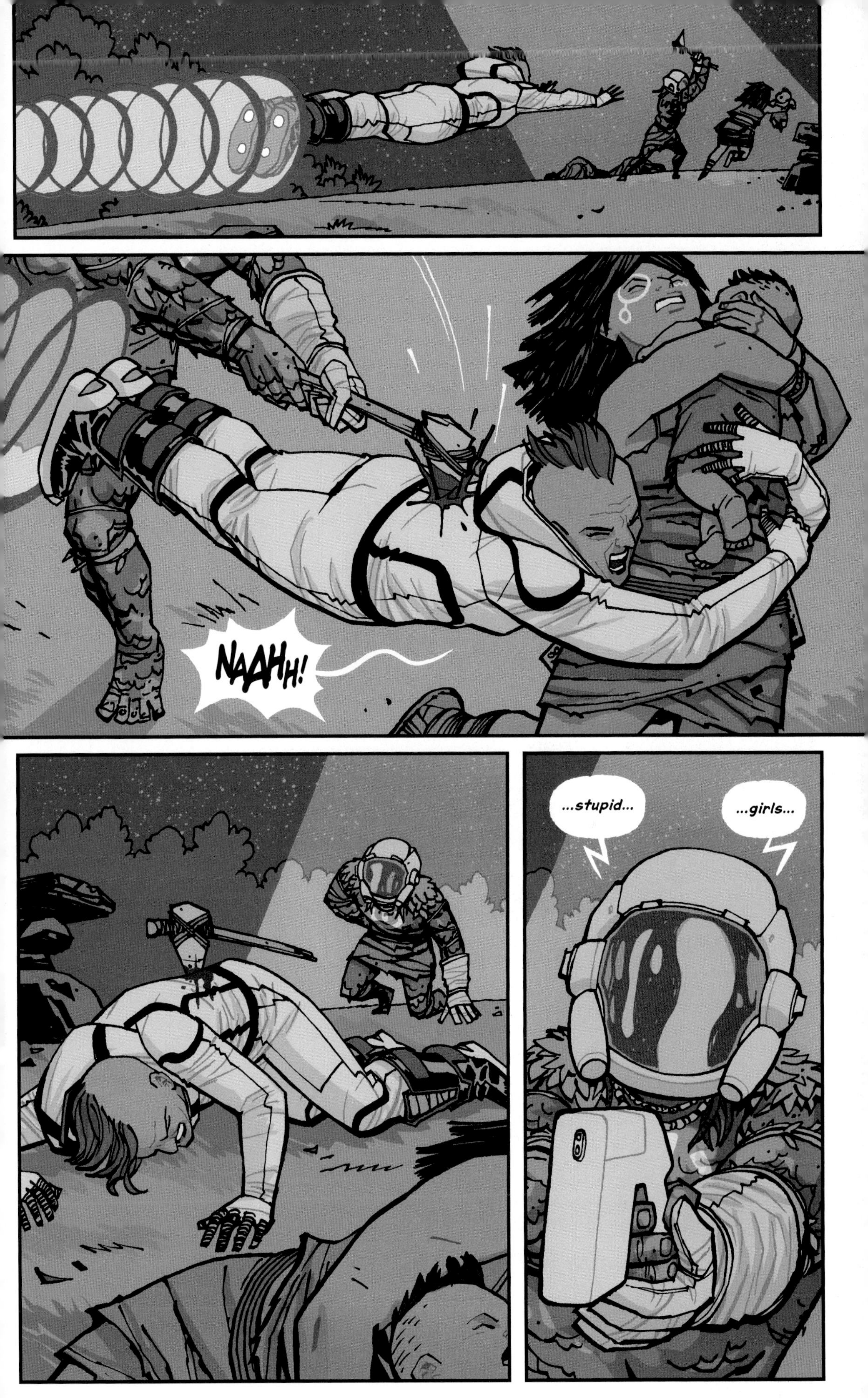
NAAHH!
...stupid...
...girls...

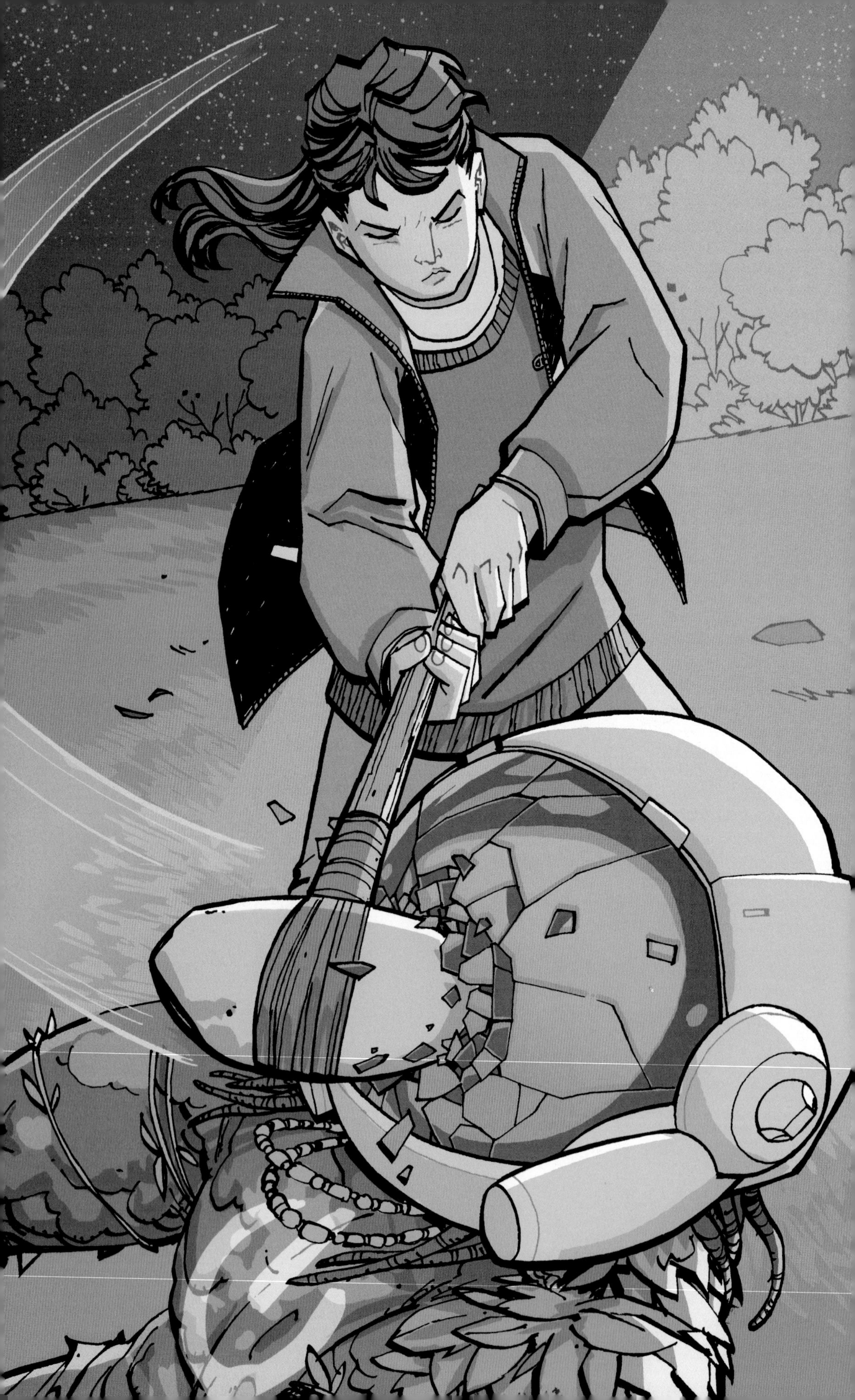

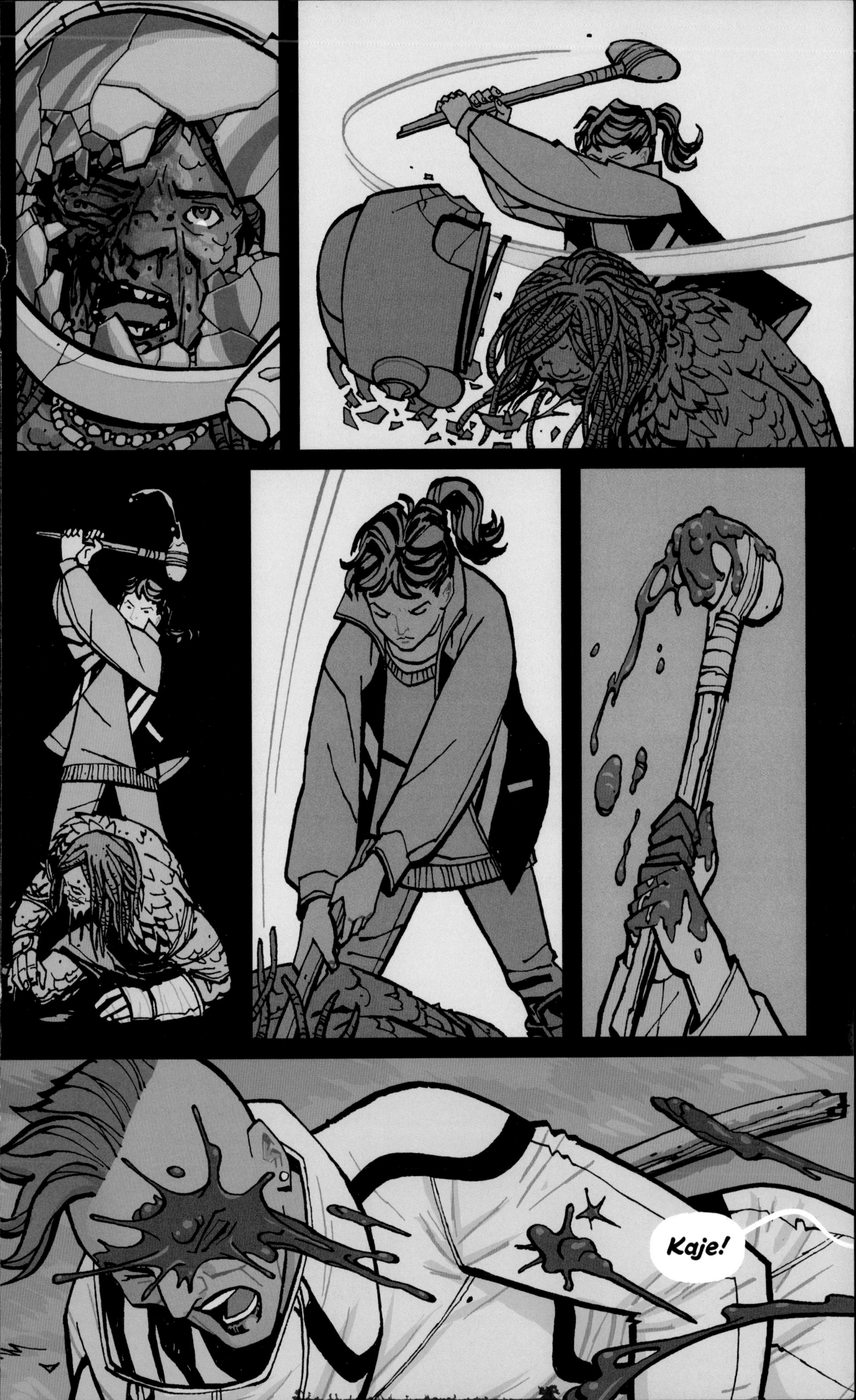
Kaje!

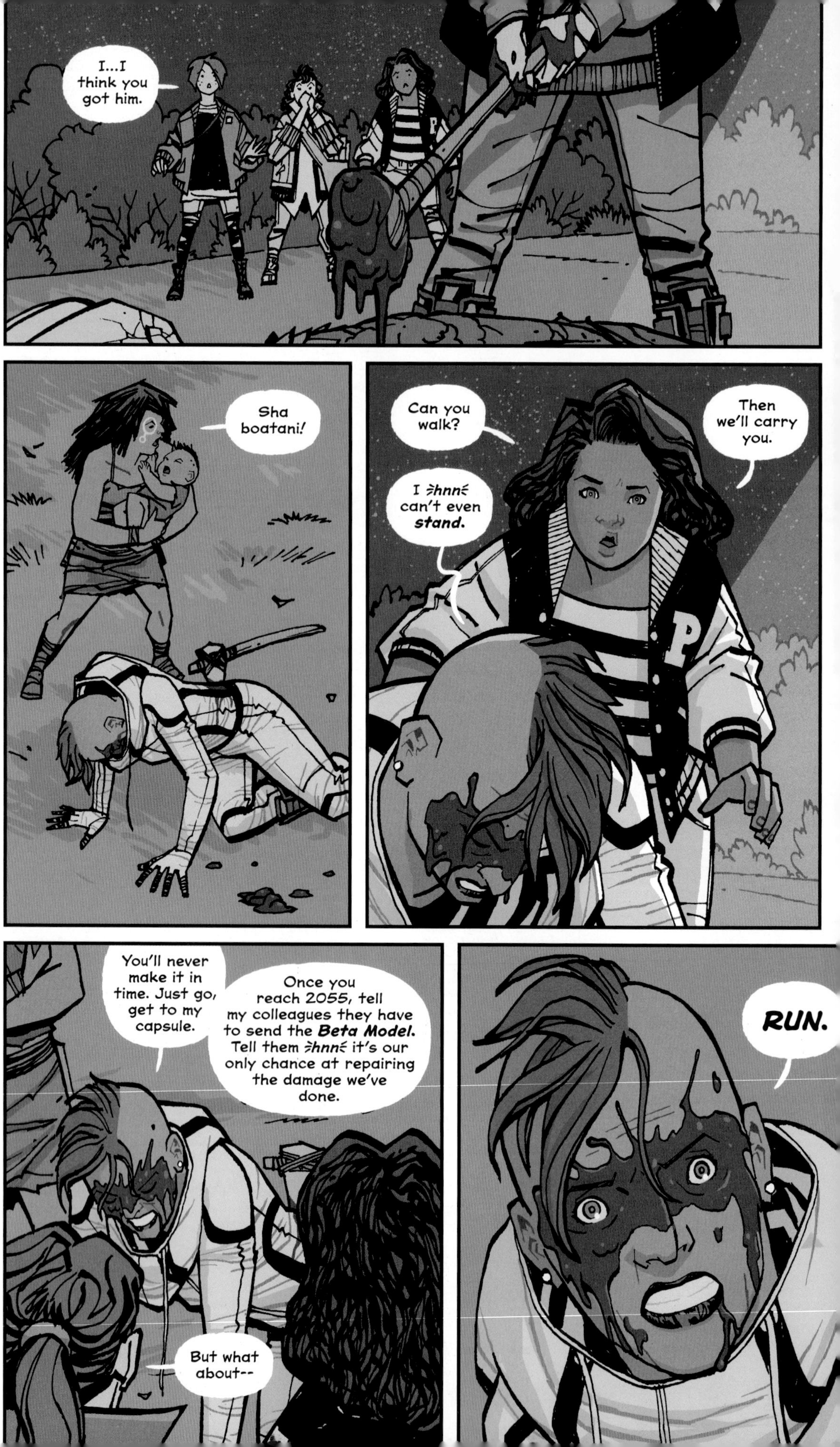
I...I think you got him.
Sha boatani!
Can you walk?
I ≑hnn≑ can't even **stand.**
Then we'll carry you.
You'll never make it in time. Just go, get to my capsule.
Once you reach 2055, tell my colleagues they have to send the **Beta Model.** Tell them ≑hnn≑ it's our only chance at repairing the damage we've done.
But what about--
RUN.